RUTHLESS COMMANDER

The Institute Series

A.K ROSE

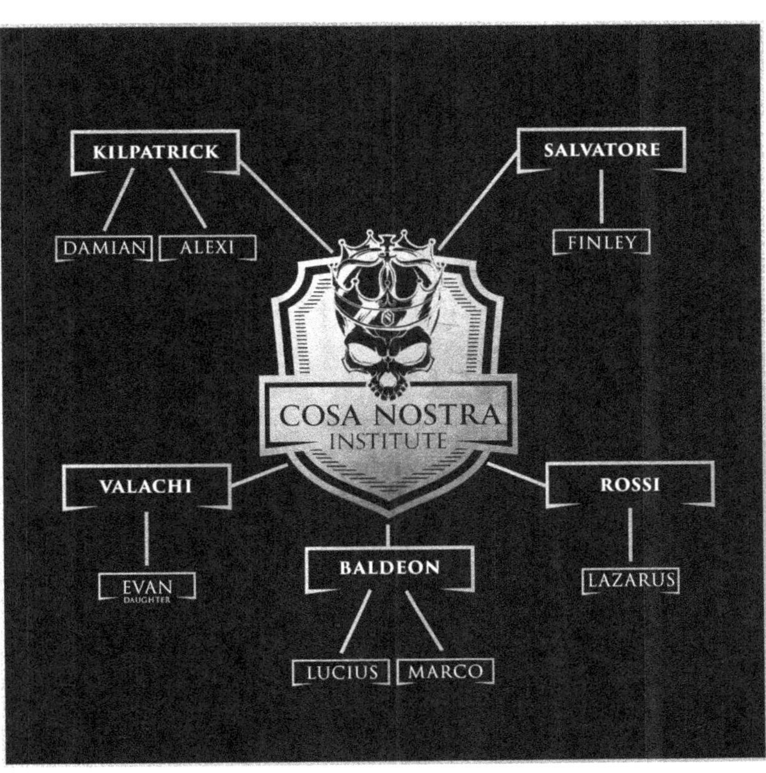

KILPATRICK
DAMIAN
ALEXI
SALVATORE
FINLEY
COSA NOSTRA
INSTITUTE
VALACHI
EVAN
DAUGHTER
ROSSI
LAZARUS
BALDEON
LUCIUS
MARCO

Mateo

Ten years old

THEY'D BE HOME SOON.

I sat in the bedroom and wrapped my arms around my knees, watching as the shadows grew along the floor, waiting for the front door to open and my parents to walk through.

They were going to come.

Because they had to.

I waited until night came and my little brother cried, tugging on my shirt beside me.

He was hungry, he was always hungry. When I couldn't wait anymore, I pushed up from the floor and made my way through the house and into the kitchen. I opened the cupboards, finding a few scraps of food, the last piece of bread wrapped in waxed paper. My belly howled, but it didn't matter, I only cared about him.

"Ma..." he whimpered. At four years old, that was what he called me.

I scraped what was left of the margarine against the stale piece of bread and cut it into small squares, placing them onto a plate that I slid in front of him as he sat at the small table. "Eat."

Big brown eyes looked up at me, waiting for me to nod. He didn't care the bread was more than a week old, dried and hard at the edges. All he saw was food as he grabbed a piece and stuffed it in his mouth, chewing hard. I patted his head, feeling the greasy hair, and looked around the house. Our place was empty, and cold. Too cold.

My parents had left for Vlahna before first light this morning and still they hadn't come home. They always came home, always before the sun went down, always carrying food for us to have that night.

I swallowed hard, patting my little brother's shoulder as he ate.

"Ma?" he murmured through his food.

"How many times do I have to tell you?" I snapped, turning toward him. "It's Ma-te-o. Mateo. *Say it.*"

But he didn't say my name, he just chewed the last piece of bread and swallowed it down before lifting his hands for a cup. I wanted to hate him, wanted nothing more than to walk away from his greedy little hands and his big brown eyes.

I wanted to be the one taken care of, instead of taking care of him. I wanted to be the one who felt sadness, the one who showed fear. I wanted to be the one who played and sang. But I wasn't. I was the one that took care of him. The one who watched out for him, the one who fed him when I was just as hungry. I was the one who put his needs in front of my own, just like now. I turned and walked into the kitchen, grabbed the plastic cup from the sink, and twisted the tap.

The water spluttered, running brown. I waited for the water to run clear, but it didn't. I pushed the cup underneath, filling it with the murky brown liquid, then walked back to the greedy little kid sitting at the table.

"Momma?" he asked, gulping the water down. He didn't care that it tasted bad. In this moment it sated his thirst, and that was all that mattered.

I shook my head. "Bed." He didn't move, giving me a shake of his head, until I crossed my arms and demanded, "Bed, Edon. *Now.*"

He did as he was told, but with a scowl. Shoving out his chair, he made his way to the filthy mattress shoved into the corner of our room and flopped down hard, curling his bare, dirty feet against his ass. I bent down, grabbed the end of the blanket, and pulled it over his body. "They'll be here when you wake up, okay?"

He just gave a nod, watching me with careful eyes. I hated myself in that moment, hated the way I was angry at him. He depended on me, and it wasn't just for food and water. I lifted my gaze, my attention drifting. It was dangerous here on our own. "Sleep now."

I turned and walked out as he started singing, small at first until his voice got used to the strain. He sang like an angel, like someone far too perfect to belong to us. I walked back into the front room, pushed the curtains aside, and looked out. It was dark out there, too dark for my parents to walk without a light. I grew worried, flinching as a howl came from outside. It wasn't a dog, but a wolf. I'd know that sound anywhere.

I shivered, dropped the curtains back, and stepped away, looking at the door. "Where are you?"

Cold moved in, whistling through the gaps in the walls to cut right through me. I shivered, wrapped my arms around my body, and stepped backwards until I hit the wall. I slid down until my ass met the floor and there I waited, staring at the door that never opened, not that night nor the next day, and when the next night came, I realized they were never coming back.

⊏━⊐

SIXTEEN YEARS *old*

"YOU GOING TO EAT THAT?"

I gave a shrug and pushed the sandwich toward him. "No, you eat it," I replied, watching my brother out of the corner of my eye.

My stomach tightened like a fist, one that battered my insides and screamed. But I was used to being hungry, I was used to going without, and Edon always came first. Even at ten years old, he was still skinny, but he was fast, snatching the sandwich from my hand and wolfing it down, guzzling the beer after it.

"Tell Mom or Dad that I gave you that and I'll beat you bloody," I muttered.

But he just gave a nod, knowing there was no truth to it. Mom and Dad weren't coming back. They'd left for work that day six years ago and never returned. It had been up to me all this time, up to me to make sure he never went hungry. I tried my best, but still there was never quite enough.

I shoved up from the chair and motioned him to come. He swallowed the last of the sandwich and followed. We walked along the empty street of our town, our bare feet slapping against the hard ground.

"Hey!" The hard bark came from behind us.

I turned, finding the one called Davol striding toward us with his gang. "Behind me, Edon."

"But—"

I whipped my head around and snarled, *"Now."*

Anger flared in his eyes, resentment lingered there, as well. But I didn't care about that in this moment, all I cared about was facing them and not backing down.

"So here he is, the great Mateo," Davol sniggered, glancing at my brother behind me. But he couldn't see him, he couldn't get to him, and he never would.

I said nothing as the five older guys stopped in front of us. I knew who they were, and the stories that others in the town told. Some called them thugs, others criminals in the making. They bullied, and they beat. They stole what they wanted, and when they couldn't steal it, they ruined it for everyone else.

"When are you going to join us, Mateo?" Davol took a step forward, crossed his arms over his chest, and stared down at me. He was four years older than me, taller and heavier. But he wasn't hungrier, he wasn't more dangerous, and we both knew it.

I gave a shake of my head and met his gaze. It was the same answer I'd given before, and it was the same answer I'd give again. I wasn't interested in fighting and hurting. All I cared about was surviving, not for me but for my brother.

"You'll join us one day." Davol glanced behind me. "Or else..."

That brutal fist inside my body clenched once more, but this time it wasn't because I was starving. It was out of fear.

"Edon, right?" he said, his attention on the scrawny kid at my back.

"Stay away from him," I warned, and took a step forward. "You don't go near him, you don't look at him. You don't even know he exists."

"Or else what?" Davol met my gaze. "Who are you going to run to? You have nowhere to go."

▭

EIGHTEEN YEARS *old*

"WHERE ARE YOU GOING?" I lifted my gaze as he strode out of the bedroom. My brother was different now, no longer as scrawny, no longer innocent and sweet. This kid who looked eerily familiar was almost a stranger to me now. I rose from the sofa and took a step toward him as he headed for the front door. "Edon."

He stopped, his shoulders hunched. "What?"

"They only use you, they'll only get you into trouble."

A sharp whistle came from outside, the sound piercing. I glanced toward the doorway, my lips curling. "Do not go out there."

"Yeah, well it's better than staying here and looking at these fucking walls."

"You'll get caught," I growled, taking a step toward him and grabbing his arm. "Is that what you want? You want to go away with these assholes, because I guarantee, that's what will happen. Whatever you got yourself caught up in, you need to get out of."

He wrenched his arm from my hold. "Get the fuck off me, Mateo. You're not my damn father, so stop acting like one."

The whistle came once more, summoning him like a goddamn dog.

Hate moved through me. "You walk out, and you'll regret it."

"I stay here and I'll regret it more. I'm not you, Mateo. I didn't fucking die the day Mom and Dad left us and didn't come home."

I flinched as though he'd slapped me. But he didn't see how his words hit, only shoved his hands into his pockets and I watched my twelve year old brother walk out, leaving me standing there, watching an empty doorway once more.

2

Mateo

Twenty-one years old

THE TOWERING gates of Ispeli prison rolled open with a squeal, leaving me to walk through on my own. Guards watched me from the towers, fingers poised over the triggers of their sniper rifles aimed my way. One wrong move, one wrong look, and I'd never make it to the door.

But I had to make it...

I had no choice.

I looked away from them, keeping my focus fixed on the barbed wire that ran the length of the fence beside me. Strands of hair waved in the wind from the sharpened ends. Razor wire stained with blood ran along the top. Not that they needed honed steel. The name of this place alone was enough to make even the beast in us cower in submission.

Ispeli.

This place...*this goddamn fucking place was notorious.*

My heart was heavy, weighing down my steps. But my rage made up for it, driving me toward that locked steel door on the other side of the fence. A guard waited at the entrance, standing sentry against the bleak goddamn backdrop of this place.

My brother was in there.

In there, with those fucking monsters.

In there, with the beatings and the betrayal.

In there, where pain was currency and they hungered for your blood.

I tried not to think about that, tried not to think about the events that had led him here. Instead, I lifted my ID to the officer at the gate and waited. He took my papers, glared at the photo, and shifted his gaze to me. He never spoke, never said a word, and for a second, I thought he was going to shake his head and deny me entrance.

I lifted my gaze to the moss-covered walls and the bleak towering building, trying to figure out how I was going to get inside. *Because leaving without him wasn't an option.*

But then the guard stepped forward, unlocked the gate, and swung it inwards. Howls came from inside those walls. I kept my gaze down and strode toward the door that opened in the distance. The stench of piss and blood hit me as I stepped through the doorway. I looked around in the gloom.

"Mateo." A man stepped out of the shadows and nodded toward me.

I narrowed in on him. His fresh suit, sparkling gold rings, and the big fat cigar between his fingers all whispered of the kind of man he was, but it wasn't until he met my gaze and I looked into his eyes that I truly knew the kind of monster that lived in a man's skin.

"Edon," I responded. "Is he..."

"Still alive," he answered. "Barely."

Barely...my heart raced at the word. A nod toward the guard and he turned, looking along the dark and dank hallway screams of men echoed in the distance. Screams filled with hate and rage bordering on something broken.

I turned and stopped at a gate across the hallway. Inside the gate, the guard watched us, glancing me up and down before leaning forward and hitting a button. The steel gate opened, leaving me to walk through. They didn't take me to his cell, instead they walked me through the massive recreation room and out the other side to a corridor. A shiver raced along my skin as we made it through the other side, stepping through another set of doors into another hallway.

Our boots echoed, resounding against the walls and slamming back at me until the guard stopped outside the doorway and motioned with his head, leaving me to enter on my own. *Infirmary* the sign printed on the doorway said, but this was no place of salvation. No, this place was another one where you came to die. I stepped in, scanning the gurneys where the dead lay covered in sheets, and turned away.

He wasn't dead...

He. Wasn't. Dead.

I lifted my gaze to the movement of a doctor as he came toward me, his green smock stained with blood.

"You are here for Edon Ristani?"

I gave a nod, glancing behind him to a partially uncovered cadaver. *Was that...was that...*my pulse boomed in my ears.

"He is in the next room," the doctor continued as he turned and headed for the doorway.

Orders were barked to the staff, and another man hurried through an open door. Each step was a deafening *boom...boom... boom* inside my head as I followed them through the door and into the prison ward. I scanned the beds, then stopped.

My brother's face was barely recognizable. Swollen, bloody... and blue. But I knew it was him, knew without needing to see the familiar eyes of our mother which haunted me every single day.

"You can take him," the doctor declared. "Here are his release papers."

"Just like that?" I jerked my gaze toward him.

One nod and that was all I needed. *You're coming home now, Edon...you're coming home.* I moved to the side of his bed, watching his closed eyes and steady breaths. "Edon."

A flicker, that's all I received. He opened his eyes for an instant, didn't even find me before they closed once more. Still, it was enough....it had to be. I glanced around for a way to wheel him out of there, but the bare, ugly ward gave me nothing.

So I stepped closer and dragged the sheet from his body, wincing at the blood that soaked his dressings and his shirt. "He's bleeding."

"They're all bleeding," he snapped. "You want me to patch him up with a dirty rag? 'Cause that's what I have to work with."

I looked around the room, finding the cabinets empty and the shelves bare. There was nothing there, nothing but bodies, nothing but despair. I gripped the bottom of my t-shirt and dragged it over my head, stepping close to slide the garment under his prison uniform and press it against the largest blood-stain. "I'm getting you out of here, brother. I'm getting you out."

He muttered something through pale, bloodless lips but I didn't wait long enough to find out what it was. I just lifted him under his knees with one arm, and slid the other under his shoulders, and carried my brother out of there.

The warden watched me from the open doorway, glancing at my limp brother in my arms as I carried him.

"We are done here, Komandant?" he muttered, those beady black eyes scanning the tattoo on my chest before they fixed on mine.

I didn't answer, didn't even give the bastard another second of my attention, just carried my brother through the door of that fucking hell and out toward the yard. The gate howled as it opened and that same guard watched me carefully, lowering the muzzle of his rifle as I neared.

One hand snapped upward, the blade of his palm almost touching his forehead. I gave a nod and carried Edon through the gate and across the yard. Soldiers watched me from above, only this time their fingers weren't itching against their triggers. It seemed word had spread I was here. It didn't matter, I wasn't here for them...*not yet.*

I wasn't focussed on the end...more on the beginning. I lowered my gaze as the double gates to the prison slid open, the cameras above following my every move as I carried my brother from the prison and out into the world once more.

My car sat alone in the carpark. I heaved my brother higher in my arms and reached for the door handle. The car was old and cheap, paid for with a small wad of cash and a savage stare. It was more than I'd wanted to spend here, after all, we weren't sticking around.

I laid my brother on the back seat before closing the door and rounding the car. I didn't need to look over my shoulder to know they were watching me as I climbed behind the wheel and started the engine.

Edon let out a groan as I backed out of the parking lot and left that hell behind. He was in pain, more than I could imagine...I lifted my gaze to the rear-view mirror, catching the sight of my own lifeless dark eyes. On second thought, I did imagine, in fact I did one better. I relived. "You're out now," I reassured, and drove my boot against the accelerator. "And you're never going back."

Home was the last place my brother expected to be, but it was the place where we were going, for a while at least. I drove along the quiet roads, making my way from Ispeli back to the familiar countryside of home.

By the time we reached the dirt streets, it was growing dark. I hit the lights, finding one headlight already blown, and cursed under my breath. But I knew these streets, I knew this town...*and I knew these people.*

Whispers had reached me, even in the dark pit where I was.

There was talk of what was going on back home...

Then there was talk of my brother.

It took me three months to leave. Three months of demands and threats. Three months of waiting for them to come and silence me forever. No one did what I did and saw what I saw only to walk away. But in the end, that's exactly what happened. I was discharged with a nice payout and sent on my way. It was either that or bloodshed...*theirs, not mine.*

Three months.

Still, it had been three months too long. I pulled into my family's driveway and killed the engine. Ten minutes later, I shoved the key into the lock and switched on the lights inside my home. Memories slammed into me and all the hate and rage came flooding back from those last few months before I'd left for the army.

Edon didn't want a brother anymore, not one he shared by blood, anyway.

His family had become the ones he'd chosen.

The ones he bled for.

And the ones who betrayed him in the end.

I strode back to the car, lifted him out of the back seat, carried him inside into the tiny room we'd shared as kids, and laid him down on the mattress. There were holes in the walls. Holes the size of a man's fist, and I didn't need an explanation to know whose they were.

I strode back out to the car, hauled my packs inside, and kicked the door closed behind me. The small amount of medical supplies I carried was more than the goddamn prison had had. I yanked my ration packs out, then carried my first aid kit into the bedroom and hit the lights.

The weak glow spilled across his body. Jesus, he looked even worse now than he did before. I bent beside him and lifted his shirt, then I froze. Hard breaths consumed me. He was a fucking mess. Crisscrossed knife wounds up his side...it looked like they took a whip to his back. I was betting it hadn't been just the inmates, either...no...it wasn't just them, not at first.

The moment the news of his arrest reached me, I'd sent word to the prison. But by then, it'd been too late, too late to stop my brother from talking. Some burn marks were still blistered, some already scarring in savage, angry welts. I lifted my gaze to his closed eyes and then eased his shirt from his body and set to work on the wounds.

The knife marks were the worst. One was deep...too deep. I winced, then cleaned what I could and prayed there was nothing internally severed, not that that doctor gave a shit. By the time I peeled free the filthy rags that covered his wounds and cleaned them all with peroxide, I eased down onto the floor.

My stomach howled with hunger, but the thought of eating made me sick...

Instead, I leaned against the bed, watching the slow and steady rise of little brother's chest. "Why the fuck didn't you listen to me, Edon? Why the fuck didn't you take my goddamn side?"

If he had, he wouldn't be here.

If he had, he wouldn't be so close to goddamn death.

I clenched my fists, my arms resting on my knees, and thought of them.

Laughing...

Joking...

Thinking they'd gotten away with it all.

But they hadn't. I slowly climbed to my feet and strode out of the room. My packs were open on the makeshift table. Metal gleamed from medals I'd never wear. I couldn't care less about the goddamn pretense. I cared about two things...*getting him out alive...then revenge.*

I stepped closer, reached inside the pack, and drew out my gun. Slipping it into the waistband at the small of my back, I pulled out a clean black t-shirt and slipped it on. A glance over my shoulder at the light that spilled through the doorway of my room, and I turned back.

Edon was safe...for now.

But I knew the men he called *brothers*.

I knew that one day, when my brother was least expecting it, they'd come.

After all, he was a liability. Loose lips and all that.

I turned back to the bedroom and flipped off the light, and when I left the house...I left it in darkness.

They'd come alright.

But not if I came for them first.

<hr>

3

Mateo

<hr>

The car started with a splutter, but this time I didn't reach for the lights. Instead, I backed out of my driveway and nosed the car toward town with only the soft spill of the moon to guide me. Davol and his posse had become famous, no longer the street kids who bullied and stole. They'd upgraded their reputations into guns for hire and drug runners that traveled across the country.

No one touched them.

Not while the Besnik Organization paid their bills. Those men controlled the money and the drugs and paid men like Davol handsomely. *Mafia*...that's basically what it was. I knew who they were and what reach they held. But it didn't matter, we'd be long gone before they figured out it was me.

I pulled the car down a darkened street and parked behind a set of dumpsters at the back of a row of houses. A nightjar let out a call as I climbed out of the car and quietly eased the door closed. A kid's wooden baseball bat and glove sat beside the dumpster. I grabbed the bat's handle, taking it with me as I walked, heading to where the *thud...thud...thud...*of music echoed from a house further down the street.

Mafia.

The word stayed with me as I crossed the dirt road and stepped behind parked cars. I knew what they were, knew what they'd do to someone like Edon. Still, he hadn't listened, he never did. Movement came from the corner of my eye. I slowed my steps as a wolf sniffed the rubbish bins at the entrance to the street, then stopped and lifted its head, the beast's gaze fixed on me.

I kept moving, keeping my steps light, and slowed only when lights from inside the house flickered through the window. The music was loud...too loud, making the wolf lower its ears and trot away. I gripped the bat and stepped closer, moving underneath a steel carport, and sank into the shadows.

Which were fine by me.

I relaxed my grip, then tightened it once more and headed to a screen door at the side of the building. The heavy thump of the music muffled the howl of the hinges as I slipped inside. The tiny kitchen stank and was filthy. But I wasn't there to critique the way they lived...only end it.

I moved quietly, slipping through a doorway into a hallway and headed further along the back of the house. Voices spilled out of a bedroom at the far end of the hall. Still, I stopped at the closed door to the first room, turned the handle, and slipped inside.

I blinked into the darkness, letting my eyes adjust to the gloom, to find the monstrous outline of a guy lying spread-eagled on top of the bed. *Balla,* it had to be. The man-mountain was more than their heavy, he also covered up the filth they left behind.

Young girls snatched from their families and used by Davol and his scum. It all ended here. I lifted the bat as a deep, thunderous snore came from the man. The closer I came, the more I realized he wasn't alone...

I glanced toward the corner of the room to where a young girl cowered. Her eyes were wide, the whites stark in the gloom. I lifted my hand and pressed a finger to my lips, gave a shake to my head, and motioned she turn away.

She did.

Smart girl.

I gripped the end of the bat with one hand and clenched the other around the handle, pulled the bat up as far as I could, then drove the end into the bastard's face. "This is for my brother."

The *crunch* was sickening.

Blood spurted in an instant, the warmth splashing over my hand. But I was ready, jumping on the bastard's flabby chest without a sound and driving the length of the bat against his throat. My muscles roared, straining as I crushed his fucking neck.

Still he fought, his eyes bulging as he kicked and bucked. I took his blows, I took his fear. I took it all, driving the length of that bat against his throat until his hands fell to the mattress and he stopped moving. My lips slid back against my teeth as I pulled away, listening to the hiss of escaping air, then slowly climbed off the piece of shit.

A whimper slipped through the room. I jerked my gaze toward the sound, having forgotten the girl was there, and in an instant, I saw myself in her terrified eyes. I wore the face of a monster, compete with empty, unflinching eyes. I opened my mouth to say something, to justify my rage, but one glance at the cuffs around her wrists told me I didn't need to.

I just reached out, patted down the bastard's pockets until I found the keys and threw them her way. "Don't leave until I'm done," I said, leaving her to scurry forward and nod.

That cold, unforgiving well of rage moved inside me as I left her behind and headed for the door once more. I turned the handle and peered through the crack before easing the door open and slipping out into the hallway. But something had changed. The *thud* of a drawer came from the kitchen. I back-tracked, moving quickly, and stepped up beside one of the others as he busied himself carving slabs of ham with a large carving knife, then moved toward the end of the counter.

He never made it.

I grabbed the knife and, with bits of ham still clinging to the blade, I buried it into his neck. He stumbled to the side, his hand going straight for the blade still embedded as blood spurted, arcing outwards to splash across the counter. I didn't know his name, didn't know his face. Nor did I care.

He fell, slipping against the counter to crumple onto the floor, and that's where he stayed. I left him behind, moving deeper into the house, finding one more of them sprawled out asleep on the sofa. I grabbed the gun from behind my back and reached for the cushion, pressing it over his face as I fired.

Boom.

The sound was swallowed by the thud of the music.

"Hey!"

I jerked my gaze at the sound as one of them shoved up from the floor and stumbled. His eyes widened as he took in the bloody mess behind me, then met my gaze. One second, that's all it took for him to make the wrong goddamn move.

He lunged, driving his lanky body through the air toward me, hitting me hard. The gun slipped from my hold, but it didn't matter. Reflexes kicked in, the rage consuming me as I attacked with savage ferocity. There weren't enough medals they could award me to make up for what I'd become. Only a name...only a title.

Komandant.

I gripped his throat with one hand and unleashed my fist with the other, driving us both backwards to the floor. A scream ripped from him. One shattering blow from my elbow, and the sound ended a second before I drove my thumb into the socket of his eye and reached into his skull.

His body twitched, his arms flopping violently before they flopped no more.

I lifted my head, climbed from his body, and retrieved my gun from the floor, then made my way back along the hallway to where the voices slipped from the room at the end of the hall. The room where I knew *he* would be.

My fingers slipped on the handle, slick with blood...and other things. I just clenched tighter, turned the handle, and entered.

"That's it," Davol urged, sitting at the end of his bed with his legs splayed, between them a woman, bent at the knees and swallowing his cock. She didn't have much choice.

I glanced at his fisted hand with a mass of her hair, his grip unyielding as he drove her head down on his shaft harder and harder. "Take it all, you fucking cunt."

She whimpered.

I shot.

The bullet narrowly missed her head as she filled her mouth with all of him. The bullet struck him in the shoulder. He jerked, letting her go as his eyes jerked to mine.

With a roar, he lunged, reaching for the bedside table.

Boom!

The bullet hit the edge of the bed, mere inches from his face. With a cry, he jumped up and scurried across the room toward a dresser.

"You had to know I'd come," I snarled, and crossed the room toward him.

The woman screamed and lunged for me, but I aimed the gun at her face and shook my head. "I *will* kill you."

There was madness in her eyes. Maybe a bullet to her brain would be compassionate. But I wasn't there for her. I was there for him, *Davol.*

"I warned you." I swung the muzzle his way again, watching as he cowered against the wall. "I told you to leave my brother alone. But you didn't listen."

With no gun and only one way out, he unleashed a roar and hurled himself toward me. The gun was too easy, too simple... too *fast*. I dropped the weapon and took the brunt of the impact as we fell to the floor.

"I'll fucking kill you!" he screamed.

I unleashed my fists, driving them into his stomach, hearing the *whoosh* of his breath. *Thump,* I drove my fists into his cheek, watching as his head snapped to the side. *Thump. Thump. Thump.*

Over and over. I was lost in the rhythm.

Lost to the sight of the blood and the broken teeth.

Lost to that spark in his eyes.

That spark I was chasing.

With an unmerciful scream, I hunted that glimmer, driving my fists into his body over and over until there was nothing but silence, nothing more than emptiness. Nothing more than dullness as the glint in his eyes flickered, then died.

The harsh roar of my breaths was the only reality...until I became aware of movement.

My gun, pointed at me.

The woman's hand trembled as she pointed it. I rose slowly, looking down at the mess, then lifted my gaze to her. There was nothing inside me. No flinch of fear, there wasn't even rage anymore. Just...*nothing*.

I slowly reached out and took my gun from her hand. She didn't fight me, didn't even say a word.

The thud of a door echoed out in the hall. Rapid footsteps followed, slipping away. "You're safe now. He can't hurt you ever again."

I left her there, stepping over the body of the man who'd come for my brother and found me instead. There was no sign of the wolf as I made my way out of that house and back into the night. There was only the moonlight, only the night...only the promise of a new beginning. One I'd killed for.

I climbed back into the car and started the engine, and this time I hit the headlights, making my way home by the muted glow. By the time I pulled back into the driveway, my stomach was trembling and clenching. The heady stench of blood was sickening, driving acid into the back of my throat as I lunged from the car.

Acid splashed on the ground as I braced my hand against the side of the car.

The burn stung my nose. Still, I stayed there, heaving and retching while my eyes watered and I gasped.

It wasn't the thought of the blood that made me weak, it wasn't knowing what I'd become.

It was the finality of our life here.

The cornering. The hunting.

The doing things that could not be undone.

Because as much as I'd brought death to Davol and his men tonight, I'd also brought death to me.

The Besnik Organization would come for me, and they'd come for Edon, too.

I shoved from the car and straightened, that thought slapping the disgust from me. They'd come...but by then we needed to be gone. I strode back inside the house, grabbing a change of clothes from my pack as I went. I checked on my brother before I headed for the bathroom and washed the blood of my enemy from my skin.

They'd come...

I knew it.

I felt it.

Because I'd do the same.

I scrubbed and rinsed, stepped out of the chipped tub, and wiped myself dry with my dirty shirt before pulling on clean jeans and a shirt.

"Mat..." The croak reached my ears as I stepped into the bedroom.

"It's me."

"Thought you were a dream." The hoarse words were barely a whisper.

"No," I answered coldly. "I'm real."

He closed his eyes once more. "Where are we?"

"In the past," I answered. "And the United States is our future."

"United States?"

"That's right." I lowered my gaze to him. "Just as soon as you can move."

4

Xael

Twelve months before Cosa Nostra

CHAMPAGNE FLOWED, fake smiles followed, and my family was thriving with it all at the bullshit gala dinner. I wasn't sure which one annoyed me more, their lack of spine or the crappy taste of the alcohol. Either way, I'd had enough, enough of my family and enough of this. I shoved up from my chair, drawing my brother's attention. He scowled, then motioned with his head for me to sit back down. As if I wanted to watch him finger the new bitch he'd brought to the gala under the table once more.

Did he think I was fucking stupid?

No thank you.

I grasped my dress and stepped away, leaving him to mutter something under his breath. Let him bitch, I was over it. My father's deep roar came across the tables. I glanced his way, to the table where he sat with my mother. But it wasn't my mother who captured his attention. No, she sat alone, her hands clasped on the table in front of her, empty seats on either side, while my father made a fucking fool of himself flirting with a thirty-something redhead.

The great Taran Davies.

Serial adulterer. Mob boss with bodies buried in our backyard...*literally.*

Christ, my family was a mess.

I left the party behind. It was getting late, or maybe early, who the fuck knew anymore. All I knew was, the celebrations and the toasts were well and truly over and I was bored. I clutched my dress as I climbed the stairs of the massive mansion and strode along the landing, peering down at the celebration.

But all I could see was my father pressing himself against the redhead a mere three steps from my mother's back and my brother's hand disappearing up the skirt of his date once more. I wished he'd get a goddamn room and a fucking life, and stop trying to control mine.

I turned away, glancing along the paintings that covered the walls up here. Whose fucking place was this, anyway? I moved closer, drawn by the dark, messy shades of charcoal on white and stared at the naked form of a woman's body. It was actually...stunning.

There were more of them around the corner. I followed one after another, until the charcoal turned into some ghastly bright yellow mess that looked like vomit. I winced and kept on walking, not wanting to turn around and go back to the party which was more like a fuckfest.

I found myself wandering, taking in the hallways of the massive place. It was expensive, that was evident. Cabinets filled with medieval weapons that looked like they belonged in a museum drew my gaze. I made my way over to them before catching sight of a door cracked open, darkness waiting inside...

Curiosity had captured me now. I needed to know whose place this was, what kind of man liked both the naked charcoal form of a woman's body and the bloody violence of blades honed by hand a century ago? I slipped inside and closed the door quietly behind me.

A delicious masculine scent hit me. I breathed deep, taking in the faint, seductive scent of cigar and sweat and...*Fuck, what was that?* Some kind of heady cologne. Heat moved through me as I drew it deeper inside me and glanced around the room, stopping on a wide wooden desk in the middle of the room.

I made my way to the desk and trailed my fingers along the surface, then dropped my palm, bent over, and laid my body along the top. My midnight blue dress sparkled, glinting like stars as I rose and moved to the cabinet against the wall. I liked invading, liked taking the tumbler from the cabinet and pouring what had to be top-shelf Scotch into the glass before taking a sip...

Until I stiffened, sensing a shift in the air of the room.

"You shouldn't be back here," a man murmured.

I jerked my gaze toward the low growl, stopping on the floor-length black curtains against the window. My heart stuttered, and the tumbler lowered. "I'm sorry..."

"No you're not."

Anger flared for a second as I narrowed in on that voice, but I didn't retreat, didn't go scurrying out of the room like a naughty little girl. "No, I'm not."

I took a step toward him, lifting the glass to my lips once more, then from the edge of the open curtain I caught the outline of him, tall...*fucking gorgeous.* The soft spill of moonlight caught one side of his face as he watched me with midnight eyes.

He was riveted by the movement as I took another mouthful of what had to be his very expensive alcohol and swallowed. That predatory gaze was fixed on the motion, but it wasn't the Scotch he cared about. It was my throat.

Electricity hummed in my veins as I moved closer, the hairs on my arms rising as I stepped. A voice inside me was screaming, howling at me to turn and run from the room, to run far away from this man...this man who, without me even knowing who he was, reeked of danger.

"Maybe I'm not sorry at all," I murmured, slipping around the edge of the curtain to stop in front of him. I took another swallow of the Scotch, feeling that heady burn move through my stomach, then licked my lips.

He reached out and grasped my jaw with a cruel grip. Then without saying a word, he gently caressed my lips with his thumb. My breaths deepened as my focus fixed on the sight of him as he took a slow step forward and leaned down.

His lips weren't soft. There was nothing soft about this man.

Not his touch. Not his kiss, but still, I heard myself moan.

He took the tumbler from my hand and pushed himself against me, forcing me against the edge of the window, then he bent down, placing it on the windowsill before straightening. Under the glow of the moonlight, he looked down, taking in every inch of me. I didn't know this man...didn't know his name, nor did I give him mine.

If he knew me, he'd stop.

If he knew me, he'd run.

They always did.

I said nothing as he reached out, spreading the thigh-high slit in my dress. My breath caught as he moved closer, sliding his hand along the inside of my thigh, slowly rubbing his finger along the crease of my pussy.

Jesus Christ...

I fought the need to close my eyes as I unleashed a low moan. This was the hottest fucking thing I'd ever had happen to me. So hot...lower and lower his hand went, pushing my thighs wider apart to run his finger along the edge of my G-string. I was transfixed by the sight of him, by the icy control in his eyes.

He never showed me even a flicker of desire. For all he cared, he could have been touching *anything*.

He didn't even care, and for some reason that made this even hotter.

He didn't care...and neither did I. I lifted my foot from the floor and he moved closer, capturing the back of my knee. Those dark, bottomless eyes gave nothing away as his finger rose along that fucking edge, sliding under for a second before it moved out.

I dropped my head backwards and moaned, "If you don't touch me, I'll goddamn do it myself."

A hint of a smile, that's all I got before he slipped his finger under the edge of my G-string and plunged it inside me. I couldn't stop myself from grabbing hold of him and winding my hand around the back of his neck as he fingered me.

Heat rushed to my face. I was no better than my brother in that moment.

Actually, I was worse.

I was letting a stranger fuck me with his fingers.

I'd let him fuck me with his cock, too, *and* his lips. Those firm lips. I dragged my teeth along my own, fixed on the image of him sinking to his knees and sucking my pussy. That fantasy mingled with the slow slide of his fingers as he pushed two inside, pulling a guttural moan free.

In an instant, he slammed his hand over my mouth, muffling the sound, the movement insistent and menacing. Those dark eyes glittered with something unholy as I suddenly became aware of another sound in the room.

The sound of the door closing.

"Hurry," a woman urged. "I'm going to come."

"You'll come when I tell you to."

Unfamiliar voices filtered in. With his hand over my mouth, the beautiful stranger gave a shake of his head. The movement was obvious as soon as he started the slow thrust of his hand once more. I stiffened, my hand clenching around him as hunger roared to the surface once more.

The sound of a zipper came from the couple in the study. I couldn't see them, closed off by the heavy curtain, which meant they couldn't see us, either. My stranger slowly dropped his hand from my mouth, his gaze fixed on me as he knelt.

It was like he could see inside my head, knew what turned me on...knew what I hungered for and, as a low moan came from the couple, he lifted my leg, sliding it over his shoulder as he pulled my G-string to the side and lowered his head.

My hand dropped to his thick, dark hair as I surged my hips forward, eager to feel his mouth. Fuck, he didn't disappoint, bending his head low to slide his tongue along my crease, then sucked. I bit the inside of my cheek to stop from moaning, and that exquisite torture was almost too much. My knees trembled as he introduced his fingers once again. I stared into the stranger's eyes and felt myself sinking, falling...*Christ, who the fuck was he?*

I didn't know...*didn't...Oh...* I gripped his head, bucked my hips forward, and came hard and fast. The slow slide of his fingers made me twitch and shudder. I grasped his wrist, holding onto him as he rose and moved against me, kissing me hard.

My pulse was booming, threatening to bring me undone.

He *was threatening to bring me undone.*

He broke the kiss as that head rush was echoed beyond the curtain. Hard breaths followed a second later, then the sound of a zipper, before the door was opened and closed.

"Ms. Davies," my stranger murmured in my ear before he pulled away.

He was gone in an instant, slipping outside the curtain, leaving my own name ringing in my ears.

He knew who I was...

He. Knew. Who. I. Was.

I surged forward, praying my knees didn't buckle and send me crashing to the floor. But the moment I swept the curtain aside, I felt it...the change in the room...*the emptiness.*

He was gone.

My beautiful stranger.

Like he'd never been there at all.

5

Xael

But he *was* there...he'd been in that room and in the twelve months that followed, in my dreams. It didn't matter who I fucked, didn't matter what toy I bought, nothing made me feel like that.

Nothing made me feel like him...

Mateo Ristani.

That was his name. I looked down at the black and white surveillance image of him in Mauritius on my phone. The photo had been taken a week ago by my own private investigator. One I'd paid very well indeed.

"Gotcha," I whispered, staring at the image once more. I didn't want to close it down, zooming the image of his face until it filled my screen. Those lips...those fucking lips I felt in my sleep.

I swiped my cell and pressed the unknown number, listening to it ring three times before it was answered. "I trust you received the file?"

"Yes. Is he still there?"

"Yes."

I swallowed hard, trying to keep the tremble out of my voice. "Good. I'll be sending you a bonus."

"Pleasure doing business with you, Ms. Davies," she said and hung up the call.

Ms. Davies...

Mateo's voice echoed in my head. I'd give anything to hear it once more. I rose from my desk, listening to the *bang* of a door come from somewhere in the house.

"Fucking bitch!" my brother screamed.

"Another one bites the dust," I murmured, and strode into my closet, pulling out my smaller suitcase. My brother was a controlling pain in the ass, almost as bad as my father. And right now, they both had their own problems. It sounded like my brother's latest girlfriend had just left his ass and there'd been something about an attack at one of the shipping yards my family owned, an attack that had kept my father busy.

I didn't really know about the attack...nor did I care.

I had my own project, getting to Mauritius and finding my not-so-secret lover once more.

I didn't care if he was married or a goddamn priest. I didn't care about whatever reason he'd had to run after our encounter in the first place. Short of him not wanting me, I was determined to take what was mine, and Mateo Ristani *was* mine. I wanted him. In a *very* bad way. The only thing stopping us was *him*...and my escape out of here.

The *bang* of a door came again and this time the sound of my brother's Ferrari followed. "Sounds like one down. Now to get past good 'ol cheating dad."

I opened my small suitcase and started packing, loading my best lingerie, then stopped. *What if he didn't want me?* What if I was flying halfway across the world to make a damn fool of myself? I froze, my heart booming, but I decided I didn't care.

I yanked the zipper closed on my suitcase, then hurried to pack my passport and made a move to call our family's jet, then stopped. My family'd know in an instant where I was heading. Maybe they wouldn't know why, but the last thing I needed was them knowing *anything*.

With a wince, I grabbed my cell and made a call, booking a first-class seat to Mauritius, leaving in four hours. Plenty of time to get out of here. I called a taxi, grabbed my things, then walked out the door.

And was met with silence.

I made my way along the corridor, stopping at the sound of muffled sobs coming from my parents' wing in the house. A pang of agony tore through me with the sound, then I forced myself to move, to leave this mess of a damn family behind, and headed out the door.

Thirty minutes later, I was ignoring stares as I nursed a glass of Scotch in the private lounge at the airport. My damn hand shook as I lifted the glass, hating how memories of that night slammed into me with the touch of the rim against my lips. The truth was, everything reminded me of that night.

Life was my own private torture chamber of *almost*. I unlocked my cell and found the PI's message and opened the attachment, looking at Mateo Ristani once more. *Ms. Davies...*

Christ, I hated how my heart fluttered when I stared into those dark, empty eyes, hated how a simple fucking hour had so much control over my life. I couldn't move on, couldn't have a relationship. I couldn't plan a goddamn future, not until he was out of my system. I closed my eyes. Out of it or part of it. Either way, I was fucked...

The call for my flight came over the speaker overhead. I rose, drained my glass and grabbed my bag. Ten hours, ten hours and a shower and I guess I was going to find out one way or the other.

━━

SO THIS WAS where Mateo Ristani lived when he wasn't hiding behind curtains waiting for unsuspecting women. I lifted my gaze to the expensive apartment building, my gaze lingering on the darkened penthouse windows. "You sure he's not here."

"Positive."

I glanced at the PI standing behind me, leaning against the brick wall. "And your man knows what to do?"

He just gave a nod. I hoped so...he was taking a nice chunk of my money for the damn effort.

"He knows," Liam answered. "You really want go through with this? You don't really know the guy."

"I know enough," I cut him off.

It wasn't the first time my investigator had tried to warn me away from Mateo, but I was fucking hoping it'd be the last. I took a step, giving him a nod. "I want this…"

"Your funeral," he muttered, and shoved off the wall, rounded the front of the Chrysler, and climbed in behind the wheel.

My funeral? What the hell was *that* supposed to mean? Annoyance flashed through me as I yanked open the passenger door and followed him inside.

My nerves were on fire as he started the car and pulled out into the street. Instead of driving right up to the foyer of the expensive building, we took the back streets, making our way to the rear and parked in darkness. My pulse raced as I climbed back out of the car, grabbed my purse, and waited.

Liam grabbed my suitcase and his cell, punching out a message as he headed for the rear entrance. The cameras above turned from green to red, and a few seconds later the lock gave a *clunk,* allowing my PI to open it. He held it for me, leaving me to follow close behind as we made our way to the penthouse suite of the apartment complex using the service elevator.

"I promised my man you wouldn't steal or damage anything," Damian muttered as I stepped out of the elevator.

I just turned and gave him a look.

"Yeah." He combed his hair back with thick fingers. "That was the look I was hoping to get. Just, be careful, Ms. Davies." He glanced at the corridor behind me. "Be careful with this guy. I might not have anything concrete on him, but my fucking gut is screaming when he's around."

"Noted," I answered.

He took a step forward, handed me a keycard with one hand, and wheeled my suitcase toward me with the other. "Just call me if you need anything."

A nod and he stepped backwards into the elevator once more, leaving me standing there with my damn future in my hands. So this guy was some rich billionaire with a reputation. One who liked his privacy as well as medieval weapons and charcoal illustrations of the female form. So what? I grabbed the handle of my suitcase and lifted my gaze to the doorway at the end of the hall.

Meant nothing really.

The CCTV cameras shifted my way as I took a step. I glanced at the beady glare and continued toward the door. My damn nerves were frayed and my pulse was skipping as I stepped up to the door and pressed the card to the scanner before letting myself inside.

The hallway was bright and stark. But once I stepped onto the foyer of the apartment, it was a different theme altogether. Dark and masculine, expansive. The blinds drawn open gave me an uninterrupted view of Mauritius at night. I was betting during the day it was even more spectacular.

Jesus...

I must be damn nervous if I was focused on the view. I wheeled my suitcase into his living room. "Don't steal anything," I repeated. "What did he think I was here for, to rob the guy blind?"

I moved through the space, pulling my suitcase behind me. Every inch screamed opulence, from the state-of-the-art kitchen to the damn Giio Vanii sculpture sitting as a showcase at the edge of the living room.

So what if he was a damn billionaire.

He still needed to fuck, right?

Christ, I got wet just walking through his place, invading his world—I reached out, dragging my finger along the marble kitchen island—touching his things. I pulled my suitcase with me as I made my way along the hallway, finding the master bedroom at the end of the hall.

In an instant, I was slammed by the scent of him, hungry, dangerous. I glanced at the suit jacket hanging over the back of a sex lounge and my gaze lingered on that hard dip. A perfect place for a woman to ride him.

I wondered how many had had the pleasure?

A tremor coursed through me as I lifted my suitcase and opened it on the bed before moving to the closet and flicking on the light. There were no dresses, no women's clothing at all hanging in the space. I moved to the bathroom and flicked on that light, then rifled through his drawers to find nothing but him.

So, he had no wife...

None he brought here, anyway.

I'd be his mistress if he'd let me.

I'd fly around the world just to have his cock inside me.

Hell...I just had, hadn't I?

I made my way back to my suitcase and pulled out black lacy lingerie before stowing my suitcase against the wall. I needed a shower, and I was betting that right about now Mr. Mateo Ristani was getting an alert of an intruder on his phone.

I smiled and made my way into the bathroom, undressing as I went. I took my time, using his washcloth under the hot spray, washing the tiredness from my body before I turned off the spray and stepped out. I used his towels, rubbing my body dry, and then dressed.

Flick.

Elastic slapped my hips as I slid my panties in place, looking at myself in the mirror before switching off the lights and stepping into the bedroom...and froze.

There was something different.

Something...

A shiver raced along my skin, making my pulse race as I stepped out of the bathroom and rounded the bed. Movement came from the doorway. He moved like a predator, striding from the shadows, and with a savage roar, he lunged.

I was gripped around the throat. Those dark eyes were wild as he roared, *"Who the fuck are you?"*

I tried to answer, tried to speak, tried to do anything other than tremble in the man's grasp. He drove me backward, his gaze boring into mine. I saw the flicker of recognition in the moment he shoved me toward the bedroom wall.

I readied myself for the impact, tensing a second before a breath rushed from his lips and he shoved his other hand out, taking the brunt of the impact. Still, I slammed hard against the wall, the back of my head hitting with a *thud.*

Pain followed, cleaving through my head as he sucked in hard breaths, then looked down at me. "Xael."

So, no Ms. Davies?

That was a start...

My chest rose and fell as I sucked in air.

He jerked his gaze to mine. "What the fuck are you doing in my apartment? And in *Mauritius,* for Christ's sake?"

I licked my lips as all the rehearsed lines I'd spent a year crafting went out of my head. "What does it look like?"

What does it look like? He lowered his gaze to my mouth, my lips, where his hand had clasped around my throat, then my breasts, shuddering as I still gasped for air. "What it looks like is a fucking mistake."

Fear speared through me.

But I couldn't speak, not as he stopped, his focus on my breasts, barely concealed by the lace cups. He didn't speak, didn't meet my gaze, just lifted his other hand and with a gentle caress, slipped the top edge of my bra lower.

My nipple popped out, tightening under his gaze. Still, he never moved his grip around my throat. "Are you a mistake, Ms. Davies?" He lifted his gaze to mine. I didn't answer. It didn't matter what I said.

Yes...

No...

Maybe, who the fuck cares?

He lowered his head and shifted his thumb, sliding it across until it lay along the middle of my throat. But his mouth found my nipple and warmth closed around it. Delicious. Fucking. Warmth. I unleashed a moan and he pressed his thumb harder against my throat.

As though he'd wanted that reaction.

As though he'd craved the sound.

This moment was all I'd hoped for...*and more.*

6

Mateo

Jesus...Xael Davies.

I opened my lips, taking her peak deeper into my mouth, and grew hard.

No.

You need to stop.

This is a mistake.

A bad fucking mistake.

One I'd tasted a year ago and had craved ever since, like a fucking drug. A haunting fucking drug. I'd spent a year trying to get her out of my damn system, burying myself in my work for the Commission until I didn't know which way was up.

I lowered my hand to between her legs and flicked her nipple with my tongue. This woman was my way up, but my way down, as well. Down to Hell. Fuck, if her father knew...

I slid my finger along her crease, knowing too well what waited for me there. Sweet. Tight. *Delicious.* My mouth watered, my thumb instinctively pressing harder against her throat. I wanted more of her, *fucking ached for more of her.*

More of her in my mouth, more under my hands.

More wrapped around my cock.

The image of another woman with her mouth filled with cock rose in my head, an image that was bloody and violent and a long fucking time ago. I shoved it from my mind. That shit didn't belong here. Not in this moment. Not with her.

I dragged my tongue along that tight peak and lifted my head. "What the fuck are you doing here, Xael?" I asked, my voice low and dangerous. Her long black hair spilled down over perfect, pale skin. She was just as fucking stunning as I remembered.

Christ, I had it bad.

"First you invade my study, then you fly halfway across the world to break into my apartment. What the fuck are you looking for?"

"You." Her answer was a moan as she settled those dark eyes on me. "I'm looking for you."

I never slowed my hand, curling my finger as I slid along her crease. "And what do you need from me?"

Her pussy trembled as she swallowed hard. I was playing cat and mouse here...only this little mouse had a lion at her back... actually, five of them.

Five families on the Commission, and *one* fucking rule.

No messing with their families.

That meant not fucking them, either. I fixed my gaze on her mouth. Her lips parted as I danced my finger around her clit. *Need to touch her...need to feel her.* I couldn't wait. I pulled away, watching as panic flared in her eyes for an instant before I gripped her, lifting her feet from the floor, and carried her to my bed.

I dove forward, cradling her as she hit the mattress, before pulling away and rising above her. "Well, you found me."

The words hung in the air as she lay underneath me, her feet hanging over the edge, one breast still peeking out of her bra. She looked desperate, *achingly desperate.* Poor little Mafia Princess, traveling halfway across the world hoping I'd fuck her.

My cock punched against my zipper and my pulse raced. It *never* raced. I gripped the other cup of her bra and yanked, watching as her other breast spilled free. "What the fuck do you want from me, Xael?"

She didn't answer, didn't say the words that howled in her eyes.

Begging eyes.

Pleading eyes.

I reached down and shoved against the inside of her knee, parting her thighs. My gaze shifted to the glimpse of pink behind her sheer panties. I licked my lips.

"Exactly what you want from me."

I jerked my gaze to hers as she finally answered, hating how she saw me. "And what makes you think I want *anything* from you?"

She reached down with trembling fingers, gripped the edge of her panties, and drew them aside. "Don't you, Mateo? Don't you want *something* from me?"

That was all it took.

My steely resolve cracked, shattering something that hadn't been shattered in a fucking lifetime, and I reached for my belt, yanking it with frenzied movements, tearing it free before I unbuttoned my pants and jerked my zipper down.

My cock sprang free as she widened her legs, leaving me to drive hard inside her. I closed my eyes, listening to her breath catch from the brutal impact. There was nothing kind about me. Nothing redeeming. Nothing worth saving.

I fucked her, driving my cock inside with unmerciful blows. I couldn't get enough, not enough of her heat. Not enough of her moans. She reached for me, lifting her legs to wrap around my waist. I leaned forward, bracing on my hands, and stared into her eyes.

A mistake...

She was a mistake.

"Xael," I moaned.

"Shut the fuck up, Mateo, and fuck me," she moaned right back.

I lowered my head, dragged my elbows down, and curled my hips, caging her in. Doing exactly what the woman wanted. I fucked her until her head dropped backwards and she let her panties go. I fucked her until I pulled free, watched her pussy clamp down from the absence of me, and tore her panties down before I flipped her over.

Her bare ass was exposed for me...her lips pink and blushed. I bent down and ran my tongue around that hard ring of muscle before I dipped lower. She dropped her chest to the mattress, letting me take what I wanted to take. I sank my thumb into her ass and drove my tongue into her core, feeling her clench around me.

She cried out as I fucked her, driving my thumb deeper, and circled her clit, lifting my head to watch her pussy weep and grow slick. I wanted every inch of this woman. Wanted to brand myself deep into her soul. I wanted to snatch away every fucking tremble and every quake...and brand them as mine.

Mine to fuck.

Mine to control.

Mine to play with.

"Mateo," she cried out, arching her spine and bucking against my fingers, then when she was done and her body was limp, I took my time, sliding my hands free and took what I wanted, nice and slow. I fucked her lying like that, with the scent of her cum heavy in the air, and when I spilled inside her, I roared.

We collapsed onto the bed, me on top of her.

I wanted to go again.

Wanted to not waste even a second getting out of these clothes. Wanted to not let her even catch her breath. But I had to. I rolled, leaving her to lie unmoving on the bed and even as I staggered, my breaths coming hard and fast, I pushed to stand.

I stumbled to the other side of the room, then turned, mesmer-ized as she stretched her legs out, her pussy shining with cum.

Mine. I looked away, but my head turned back to her. Fuck, I couldn't even control my own actions any longer.

She moaned, slowly kicked and reached out, dragging the sheet over her. That wouldn't do...not in the slightest. I rounded the bed, feeling far too removed from the man I was an hour ago, and eased the sheet from her body. I released the catch on her bra and slid the straps down low.

"Don't...don't make me leave. Not yet..." she murmured.

Leave...

The word hit me like a punch to my chest. "Sleep, Xael."

I pulled the comforter down and lifted her, sliding her underneath the sheet and pulled her bra free. She was asleep in an instant, her breath deepening and strangely comforting. I pulled my shirt free and kicked off my pants, leaving them in a pile on the floor, and that's when I saw it.

Her suitcase.

I jerked my gaze to her. The woman had come straight from the airport, she didn't even check into a damn hotel. A smile tugged at the corner of my mouth. Cocky, wasn't she? I glanced back at her, feeling that hunger move through me once more.

I stepped toward the bed, pulled down the covers, and slid under the sheets. I'd hauled ass to get here after receiving the alert someone had broken into my damn apartment. I thought for a while my past had returned. That finally the Commission had decided to turn their backs on me and that death had come.

But it wasn't death, was it?

I reached out and tugged the sheets lower, revealing her face in the gloom.

No, it was far from death.

I shifted closer, feeling the edge of her warmth. With a moan, she reached out and slid her hand against my chest.

"Mateo…" she whispered.

"Yeah?"

But no other word came from her lips. I realized then that she was gripped by the clutches of sleep, held down by the darkness. My name wasn't a conscious thought. No. Instead, it was dragged up from the darkness, unearthed from her deepest desires.

Ingrained in her…

My fucking name.

I closed my eyes as panic moved through me, but it didn't last long. Sleep came and, for the first time since I'd walked from that prison in Albania carrying my brother in my arms, my darkness wasn't plagued by nightmares. Instead, it was held for ransom by her.

I FUCKED her when she woke, taking far too much pleasure in the slow smile as I kissed her breasts and rolled her onto her back, crawling between her legs.

I fucked her in the shower after, with her legs wrapped around my waist and the hot water cascading from the showerhead to run into my eyes. I fucked her on the floor not more than three steps into the bedroom after tackling her to the floor and rolling in front of the Giio Vanii. And when I fed her strawberries from my fingers, I fucked her as she chewed, and licked the juice from her lips.

Three days I lost myself in her.

Three days of the kind of bliss a man like me didn't deserve. The kind that wasn't meant for a monster like me...and on the fourth day, the bubble burst.

I rolled over as my cell phone rang. The caller ID showed *Unknown,* yet I knew who it was. I pushed up from the bed, watching from the corner of my eye as she reached for me. My body hummed, aching and spent right down to my soul, but fuck me, I wanted more. I needed more. "Yeah?"

"They know."

I flinched, the happiness melting away in an instant. "How?"

"Does it matter?" The low growl came from the other end of the line, the trace of an accent indistinguishable. "I know, and if I do..."

"Then it's only a matter of time."

"Mateo," Xael called behind me. "You aren't done here."

My stomach clenched, and fear slipped in.

"You don't end this, and it'll be more than the Commission you need to worry about, brother."

"I know."

"Do you?"

I winced, hating how the past never left us the fuck alone. There was only one reason the beasts were kept at bay. Only one ring of power...the Commission. I swallowed hard, hating how we'd escaped one tyrannical power only to take refuge in another.

"Mateo?" Xael called behind me.

"It's not just your ass on the line here," Edon murmured. "They'll go after her. They'll hurt her and they'll use her to crush you."

I closed my eyes, hating how every fucking word he said was a stab to the heart. I shook my head.

"What's wrong?" Concern etched deep in her words.

"You want to put her in danger?" my brother growled. "Because that's what you're doing. You haven't spent longer than a fucking hour with a woman before and never with the same woman twice, yet here you are, holed up in your damn apartment for days with her. Days, Mateo."

"I know."

"Do you?"

I lowered my gaze and dropped my hand, pressing the button to end the call.

"What is it?" Xael inquired, shoving up from the bed.

For a second, I couldn't speak. *You don't love her. You don't...I* stopped cold. The words were fucking hollow...and a damn lie. I shoved up from the bed and went to the closet.

"You going somewhere?" she asked.

"Yeah," I answered. *They'll go after her...*Edon's words echoed, and he was right. I yanked on my clothes and grabbed my bag.

"Hey," she snapped shoving the covers back and standing up from the bed. "You want to talk to me here?"

Anger burned in her voice. Still, I didn't stop. "Something's come up."

She let out a bark of laugher. "Okay, sure. You're running, huh?"

I stopped, stunned at how my pulse was a roar in my ears. *Don't do it...don't do it...don't*—I met her gaze. "This was a mistake, Xael."

Her lips peeled back from her teeth in a snarl. "Fuck you, Mateo. Fuck you, you lying piece of shit." She glared at the cell in my hands. "Who the fuck called you?"

"Does it matter?"

Agony raged in her eyes. I saw it, the mortal blow...the stabbing, cruel puncture as any flicker of happiness we might have had was savagely snatched away. I had to get out of here. Had to get the fuck away from her before I—

Before I what?

I dropped my bag, sat on the bed, and shoved my feet into my boots. "Stay as long as you like, Ms. Davies." I forced the last words and pushed past her, driving my body forward in sheer desperation. I was out of the bedroom and across the living room before she unleashed a scream so guttural, I tasted blood.

"FUCK YOU! FUCK YOU, YOU...YOU...Y-YOU BASTARD!" Her voice broke, leaving shards behind.

You deserved this...

You deserved it all.

But she didn't.

The thud of my boots resounded in my chest. Hate grew inside me as I punched the button and stepped into the elevator. By the time I stepped out and headed for the garage, I was fucking savage. Hard breaths punctured the space as I climbed in behind the wheel of my Maserati. I reached for the engine button, and stopped.

YOU BASTARD!

Her pain resounded in my head. My fucking hands shook as I clawed the door handle and shoved out of the car. Agony ripped through my chest. I shoved my fist against the roar as the undercover garage blurred and I stumbled backwards until I hit something hard.

Red...

That's all I saw.

I wrenched the fire extinguisher from the wall. Rage *unleashed* and spilled free. I yanked the weapon above my head and drove it down with all I had.

BOOM!

I lifted and slammed it down once more.

CRUNCH!

Over and over, until the movement blurred and I lost myself in the sound of destruction. Yellow lights flashed from the once sleek sports car and the piercing siren blared. Others stumbled out of the stairwell door, watching me with wide eyes. I knew what they thought of me. Cold. Detached. Unapproachable.

I screamed my agony, until even the shrill alarm faded.

And when I was done, I left nothing but destruction behind.

For her...and me.

7

Xael

Three cars sat in the private parking lot of the exclusive jet terminal. *Nice, just what I needed, more people to stare.* I fought the twitch in the corner of my mouth and climbed out of the limousine. My escort, Rhys, was there, holding my door open, watching me carefully. Just like they all watched me now. I tugged my leather jacket closer around me, then turned and headed for the doors.

He hurried, grabbing my suitcases, and slammed the trunk closed. A cold wind picked up, slicing across the airfield to cut right through me. But I didn't feel it. I didn't feel much anymore. Instead, I strode toward the automatic doors, waiting for Rhys to leave the driver and car behind and surge forward to slam his card on the scanner and wait for the doors to open.

But I was caught in the movement as he pressed the card to the sensor, captured by that tiny blinking light turning from red to green before the locks released and the doors swung open. The sight of that reminded me of another time, when I'd invaded, hoping things would change for me.

They did...

They just got worse.

I jerked my gaze up, walking through the doors, instantly hearing voices. *Shit.*

"I'll get these stowed on the jet," Rhys said behind me as the muffled voices of others filled the space.

I just nodded, watching as our pilot strode across the tarmac and headed our way, dressed to perfection. Gold stripes at the cuffs of his dark jacket, the white shirt and black tie, glinting wings shining on his pocket. He wore the uniform like a second skin. Matching dark pants hugged his powerful thighs that flexed as he headed my way. Kilkivan wasn't just sexy, he was drop-dead gorgeous.

"Oh my," came a woman's quiet voice from the expensive lounge of the private terminal.

I didn't need to turn my head to know she stared through the glass windows at the man as he lifted his head, those dark eyes glinting as he found mine. Dark eyes...just like...*like his.*

My heart thundered, but it wasn't because of desire. Panic thrummed in my veins as I fixed on that stare, that hint of danger...hint of the *beast.* Until the pilot ruined it all...and smiled, his white teeth flashing in the night.

"What, mommy?" the little girl at the woman's side asked, tearing me from the reverie.

I flinched, recoiling inside as his smile grew wider. He didn't look like him anymore. Didn't remind me of another...didn't look like him at all. I turned my gaze from the pilot's grin as he reached the automatic doors and stepped inside, along with the howl of the wind.

The husband fussed, carrying over drinks from the bar toward the wife as she just stared, open-mouthed, at the man heading my way. Their suitcases were stacked beside the sofa as they waited for their chartered plane. Rich, but not quite rich enough.

"Xael?" Kilkivan called my name.

I flinched, catching the movement from the corner of my eye as the woman and her husband turned their heads toward me.

"Holy shit," the husband muttered as he stared.

I just reached for my iPods, slipped them into my ears, and pressed the button, listening to the raw, husky cries of Ramsey in my ears.

Are you ready to leave? Kilkivan mouthed the words.

I just nodded, striding forward, leaving the stares behind. Rhys strode ahead and disappeared through the double doors. If there was one thing I liked about him, it was that he melted into the background. The last thing I needed was someone taking notice of who I was. Next time I traveled by jet, I'd leave at midnight. Maybe then I'd avoid the whispers and the stares. Maybe then I'd be left the hell alone. I followed my pilot as he walked back out the automatic doors and into the cold wind as though he never felt it at all.

No one else's pilot escorted them across the tarmac, but then again, a million-dollar retainer afforded you five-star service. He strode toward the ten-million-dollar jet waiting with the doors open and the lights on, and stopped at the foot of the stairs.

I didn't wait, just climbed, tearing myself away from the wind as I sank into the opulence of the cream interior, finding Rhys seated toward the rear of the plane.

Ms. Davies. The stewardess mouthed the words.

I just gave a nod, not removing my iPods, and slipped into the plush seat. I didn't care about the scowl she gave me, or the shrug Kilkivan gave her with a slow shake of his head. I didn't care about any of them as I turned to stare out the windows at the night.

The doors were closed and the sound of the engine grew until it mingled with the seductive call in my ears. I closed my eyes as the jet began to roll, hating how I was even here at all. But there was something broken inside me...something *not quite right.*

A hunger for cruelty.

A need for stabbing pain.

A sick craving for the darkness. The kind of darkness I searched for in every set of brooding eyes. My pulse picked up as the jet surged forward, ripping us along the tarmac before we lifted...and left reality behind.

Because it wasn't reality where I was heading...it was an island. Off the coast of Mauritius, a place where a year ago I'd sworn I'd never go again.

If you'd told me then I'd be coming back, I would've probably ripped your tongue out and shoved those words down your throat. I would've screamed and beaten you to death with bloody fists. I would've emptied my bank account hiring a hitman to cut you up into pieces and bury your body in the four corners of the world.

I would've wiped your name from existence.

Still it wouldn't have been enough.

Not for the agony he'd left behind.

I was ruined.

More than ruined.

I was broken beyond repair, changed right down to my DNA. The stewardess headed toward me, carrying a drinks tray. Had we leveled out already? I drew back into my body, the one walking around without a heart, and took the glass she offered.

"Keep them coming," I muttered, and lifted the glass to my lips.

If I was doing this torture, if I was putting myself in *his* fucking path again...there was no way I was doing it sober.

But sober I was when we landed in the Mauritius private terminal. Sober and awake...and fucking terrified. I'd almost told them to turn around four times during the flight. Instead, I drank vodka, then tried to sleep it off in the bedroom in the rear of the plane...and when that failed, I resigned myself to my fate and drank coffee, staring out the window and watching the night turn to day and then afternoon.

The stewardess had only come near me carrying drinks and a tray laden with seared steak and vegetables. But here she came again, only this time her hands were empty. I reached up, pulled out my earpods, and lifted my gaze to her.

"We'll be arriving in the next twenty minutes, Ms. Davies."

I swallowed hard. "Okay."

"Is there anything else we can do for you?"

Short of therapy and maybe a heart transplant? "No," I answered, then added, "Thank you."

She gave me a warm smile and a nod, leaving me to a horror movie of my own making as the plane dipped lower in the sky and headed for land. Not just land...*Mauritius.* I tried not to remember that blur of time when Mateo Ristani walked out of the bedroom, carrying my fucking heart in his taloned hand.

The man was a monster...

No. Not a monster. I clenched my fists. The Devil. That's what he was. Only an infernal piece of shit could do what he'd done. Without any explanation, he'd told me it was over, just like that...after giving me a taste of happiness. More than a taste, he'd rammed happiness down my throat along with his cock. Like the greedy little whore I was, I'd swallowed it, hook, line and sinker. Only for him to wrench it out again, tearing me apart from the inside.

Stupid, that's what I was. Fucking stupid for wanting. For craving. *For loving...*

Loving him.

A man like Mateo didn't love. A man like him betrayed, making me think what we had was anything more than a one-time fucking deal. I was stupid for fantasizing about it being more. *Stupid. So fucking stupid.*

Buildings rose toward me. The city crowded the edge of perfect blue. I hadn't even seen the water the last time I'd been here. Hadn't seen anything but the inside of his bedroom...and the tangled mess of sheets. My body reacted instantly with the memory, tightening my core and at the same time, growing warm, humming with the kind of sickness there was no cure for.

Believe me...I'd tried to find one.

I reached my hand down, fingers sliding under the waistband of my pants, and closed my eyes. *The Devil.* Dark, piercing eyes. A cold, bloodless slash of a mouth, one that glistened as he licked me clean. I bit my lip and sank my fingers under the edge of my panties, not caring that others watched.

Fuck...I needed...I needed to exorcise him from my head.

What do you want from me, Xael?

His words resounded as I skimmed the edge of my clit and lifted my leg.

Ms. Davies.

No...no...not him, not this—I slipped two fingers inside, pumping my hand, my other hand clenched around the cream leather armrest.

This is a fucking mistake.

In and out...in and out.

This. Was. A. Mistake.

I let out a growl, savage and desperate, as I fucked the need for Mateo from my body...

My core clenched, my fingers pressing along each side of my clit as I drew out the orgasm. Shudders tore through me as I came down from the high, sliding my fingers from my pants. But I wasn't wet. I hadn't been wet in the last goddamn year.

The shrink said it was all in my head, that somehow that day had affected me physically. I was determined to fuck him wrong. Turned out he knew what he was saying, and I walked out of his office, never to go back. Fuck him...and fuck Mateo Ristani.

I jolted as we dipped lower and lower, the engine of the jet roaring until the wheels touched down. I grabbed my iPods and placed them into my ears once more. I grabbed my purse as the jet headed for the separate hanger, bypassing the commercial arrivals.

Rhys was there beside me as the jet came to a stop and the engine powered down to a dull roar. He gave a yawn, then stepped up. "I'll meet the driver and grab your bags."

I just gave a nod. My father had been insistent on a damn bodyguard, and as much as I was loath to draw attention, I gave in. I wasn't the only one who'd changed in the last year. My father's warehouses had been attacked, and even our house had been firebombed, making us leave the city and escape to our house in the country.

Things were bad. So bad, barely a word was spoken after I came back home carrying my shattered heart in my hands. Instead, my father only cared that I was alive...and home. He didn't even ask where I'd been or who I'd been with. No one cared, which hurt more.

If there had been yelling and screaming and threats and demands, I might've felt a little better.

At least I'd know the brutality of what I'd been going through was for a reason.

But it hadn't been.

It hadn't been for anything at all.

Only at his whim...

I winced and strode out of the jet as Kilkivan stepped through the cockpit's door. *Xael* he mouthed, and licked his lips, his gaze moving to my hand...my fingers, to be exact. I didn't need a confession to know he'd watched me finger myself. I hoped he'd enjoyed the show.

I left him behind and made my way down the stairs, my boots hitting the tarmac hard. Rhys waved me forward, toward the hangar. I followed him out, making for a small door in the private terminal.

Cool, airconditioned air hit me as I stepped through, leaving the tropical heat behind. Darkness descended as my eyes adjusted to the sudden change and before I could slow my steps, I smacked into something hard.

I stumbled sideways before strong hands grabbed me.

"Shit," the shadow behind those hands muttered.

I lifted my gaze to the man wearing black aviator sunglasses, in mid-stride and oblivious to those around him.

"Sorry." He glanced at his grip around my arm and released me, smoothing out my black leather jacket as he did so.

He was gorgeous, with full lips, kind brown eyes, and an awkward smile. Totally not my type. I lowered my gaze, taking in the hard, strong chest behind the tight black t-shirt he wore. "It's fine."

"No, I'm an idiot, fucking up my first goddamn command."

I smiled at that. "Unless the command is walk without barging into people, I'd say you just fi—" I started...and stopped.

Across the waiting room, he stood...*Mateo Ristani.*

"They'll be arriving any minute," he growled at two men dressed in the same black tees and tight black khakis, only those two were armed to the teeth. "Security is our main concern, do I make myself clear?"

"Hey," the stranger that'd smacked into me murmured. "You okay?"

I couldn't nod, couldn't move, dimly aware that I stood in the middle of the doorway of the arrivals with the door opening and closing behind me.

He was there...

My heart *boomed.*

He. Was. There.

And as Mateo turned, that raw, unmerciful agony ripped through my chest once more. The stranger glanced from me to Mateo, his eyes widening.

"Xael," Mateo groaned, flinching as though I'd hit him.

But it hadn't been *me* who'd done the hitting, had it?

It had been him.

And his aim was still on-fucking-point. That dark, unflinching stare ripped through me like the blast of a shotgun, taking out my heart like he had twelve months ago, leaving me hollow and empty...and bleeding all over the goddamn floor.

8

Mateo

Jesus Christ...

I couldn't move, couldn't speak, couldn't do a damn thing but stare at her like a fucking idiot. In a blinding second, all that rage came roaring back.

Rage I'd felt when I broke her heart.

Rage when I'd ripped my own from my fucking chest.

I lowered my gaze to where the new guy's hands touched her arms. In my head, all I could see was his fingers skimming her bare skin, reaching to drag her bra strap low, his mouth on those breasts...breasts I'd tasted. *Soft, supple.* Those peaks hardening as he licked and reached between her legs to her sweet fucking pussy. A pussy I'd had...*a pussy I wanted again,* like it was my next fucking breath and I was drowning.

"BLAKE!" I barked.

In an instant, I was the killer, the savage who strode into a house in my hometown and walked out wearing someone else's blood. *A lot of someone else's blood.* I forced my gaze from his hands on her arms, and Blake slowly stepped away. "Yeah, Commander?"

Komandant.

The name resounded, echoing from the past and slamming into my present. "Mind where you fucking step in future."

Still he touched her...he touched her. Did he know her? Did he...fuck...her?

"You just can't help but make a fool of me, can you, Mateo?" Xael strode toward me like wrath itself. Pain moved behind her eyes...cold and vengeful. *Fuck, she was beautiful.*

My body reacted, hardening as she closed the distance, as though it sensed what it craved. *Taste her...have her. Lose myself in her over and over again. Need her...need her so fucking bad.*

"Do you like to embarrass me?" she snapped, each word a lash of a whip.

"No," my voice was void of emotion, belying the hurricane in my head. "Ms. Davies."

"Ms. Davies?" Her lips curled with the formal use of her name before she shoved past me and stormed through the terminal.

Jesus...

Jesus...

"Commander, you okay?"

I wrenched my gaze from her as the new guard strode toward me.

"Totally my fault," he muttered, his gaze taking in every fucking flinch on my face as though he saw me.

But he didn't see me...no one did. *Except for her, right?* That voice rose inside me. *She saw you, saw the man and not the monster.* She wasn't afraid of me, not like everyone else. "It won't happen again."

"When we get to the island, you're to report to me in my office," I growled. *"Before you unpack."*

"Yes, sir," he answered carefully.

I turned away, fighting the urge to rip those fingers from his hands. Fingers that had touched what wasn't his to touch. *No messing with the families, right?* That was one of the goddamn rules. No touching, no licking, no fucking...no having what every cell in my body howled for.

I caught the shine of a jet in the sky as it descended. Within the next twenty-four hours, they'd come. The sons and now the daughters of those who sat on the Commission. Ready to learn how to take over the family's bloody businesses...*and fuck and play when daddy wasn't around.*

I turned away at the thought of that. I didn't give a fuck about any of the others. But the thought of her...of *Xael*, touching another man drove me to distraction. I had to focus, had to keep busy. I had to drive myself into the ground, exactly what I'd been doing since the moment I walked out of her life.

It was better this way...

Better to see her smiling and laughing. Better to see the seductive curl of her lips for someone else. Better to watch her fall in love with someone suited for her, someone young and powerful, someone who'd give her everything I couldn't. All I had to give was pain. All I had to give was terror. All I had to give her was a life watching our backs, always waiting for the past to rise up and take what it wanted. I strode through the doors and stepped out into the glare of the sun and watched the back of the sleek black Audi drive away, taking the other half of my soul with it.

I closed my eyes and stole a breath, feeling the cruel shiver pass through me. She was going to fuck someone else here, going to give herself to another, and there wasn't a damn thing I could do about it...

"Sir," came a voice behind me. "Another jet has just landed."

Another jet.

Another boat.

Another helicopter.

I just gave a nod. "Make sure they have protection all the way to the boat."

"Yes, sir," he answered before striding away.

I didn't turn from the glaring rays of the sun, didn't let the world invade. Instead, I stood in the agony of my own making. I could've been anyone...could've been *one of them* if I'd wanted. I could've had a seat on the Commission, taken one by force if I'd wanted to. But I didn't...I didn't because violence and death were all I knew. I didn't because I needed protection, and working for five powerful families was the kind of protection I needed.

The kind my brother needed.

I strode toward the sleek steel gray Mercedes and pressed the button in my pocket, unlocking the car before I climbed in. I had enough men on the mainland to ensure the safety of the heirs and the others who were now coming to the island. They didn't need me, so I turned my attention to the island, started the ignition, and headed for the marina.

A driver was waiting for me when I pulled up. I yanked the latch for the trunk and climbed out, leaving the door open, then rounded the rear of the car to pull my bag free. "I'll call if I require the vehicle."

"Yes, Commander."

I didn't look at him, didn't look at anything except the next fucking week. That's all I had to focus on. Seven days…seven days with her being on the island within reach. I lowered my gaze and clenched my grip around the handle of my bag, feeling savage.

The speedboat's engine started with a roar as I stepped onto the dock, then climbed across, stepped down, and took a seat in the cabin. I didn't even have to speak before the boat surged forward, taking me from the mainland and headed out into the endless blue.

It should be all I wanted.

It should be all I needed.

Rolex watches, expensive cars. The kind of champagne that my parents would have worked an entire year just to sip. But it meant nothing. I thought of them, the two strangers that had given me life. Nothing was ever found of them after that day, they'd just…disappeared. *Like they'd never existed at all.*

But they had. I saw my mother in the eyes of my brother and heard my father in my own cold tone.

I knew they had lived. But I still felt nothing. Not loss, not anger.

Just an endless ache that never went away.

I sat back and rested my feet on the console, closing my eyes. I'd worked eighteen hours straight to make sure everything was secure for their arrival...and I'd work many more to make sure everything was going to plan. I dozed, lulled by the hard rise and crash of the bow of the boat as I traveled toward the island. But I didn't rest, just slowed my mind, letting it drift to the only thing that gave me any sense of peace.

Her...

Her body. Her mind. Her mouth widening under the force of mine. Her legs wrapped around my waist as I buried myself deep inside her. Xael Davies was the only one who made me forget who I'd become. Those three days we'd spent together hadn't been happy, *they'd been peace.*

Her touch was a balm for my scarred soul.

Her lips lulled me to oblivion, letting me drift away.

Just like I drifted now.

Seven days. Seven days of watching her from a distance, watching her find happiness in anything she could. Maybe it wouldn't be so bad. Maybe seeing her laughing and smiling would finally sever this claim she had over me. Maybe a little more pain was exactly what I needed.

Move the fuck on.

That's what I needed to do.

9

Xael

This place was supposed to be fun. Supposed to be exciting. By the way my brother talked to his buddies about it, it was supposed to be full of sex and violence, dark and dangerous crammed with debauchery. Maybe I'd come to the wrong fucking island? *Figured.*

This island was none of that. Only filled with blue skies and chumps playing the part of wannabe gangsters. They were boys, really...boys messing around, and I wasn't interested in the least in any of that. The only one who had an ounce of potential was Finley Salvatore. I thought about fucking him... but then, he was a little too much like family, wasn't he? And that just turned me right off.

Besides, he seemed to have his eye on another, some brunette that arrived last night with some of the others, apparently in a hail of bullets. One of them had bitten Marcus Baldeon in the shoulder. He was alive, and screaming. But it was her arrival others were talking about, and it wasn't just the way she'd tripped, falling flat on her face. It was the way Finley Salvatore had reacted when some others had laughed. Apparently he'd gone savage, threatening to shatter his cool, calm, and controlled exterior. Not only had she fallen, but then she'd been humiliated. Poor bitch. Not a way you wanted to make a first impression.

Maybe I should reach out to her?

I pushed the door to Building Two open and strode out into the sunlight. God knows you needed friends in this fucking cesspool of male dominance and power. But it wouldn't be like that forever, would it? The corners of my lips twitched. The famous Evan Valachi was sharing my apartment, even if I hadn't seen her for longer than a damn second. The only female heir to someone who sat on the Commission. I knew that alone was huge.

Made me feel a little jealous.

Maybe if I was an heir, I would've been in control of my own destiny.

Could've fucked who I wanted. *Loved them, as well.*

I was tired of it being out of my control.

Pain flared across my chest as I headed for the towering building in the distance. The class was bullshit, a boring waste of my fucking time. Who gave a shit about interrogation techniques? To care about that meant you weren't planning shit right.

It didn't matter what I'd do...I didn't plan on getting caught.

A blur of movement came around the corner of the building. I glanced behind me to Rhys. "Wait for me in the foyer."

He just scowled, then glanced ahead to the glimpse of blue. "I'll just stand outside," he answered. "Call out if you need me."

"I'm sure I'll survive five goddamn minutes without being watched, Rhys."

He just gave a nod and headed for the automatic doors of the building, leaving me to step around the corner and walk toward the view of the water.

"Hi there."

I flinched at the words and wrenched my gaze to a guy standing behind my building staring out at the water.

"Jesus." I pressed my hand to my chest. "You scared the shit out of me."

"Sorry." He turned toward me. "Oh, it's you."

I scowled and fixed my gaze on him before recognition dawned. "The blind guy from the terminal."

He just grinned and lowered those aviator sunglasses. "Yeah, that's me." He held out his hand. "Damien...Damien Blake."

"Xael," I answered, tucking his name into my mind.

He just chuckled and shook his head. "I know who you are, Ms. Davies."

"Right." I dropped his hand, my stomach sinking. "Back to that."

"Unless you prefer Xael," he added. "Out of the Commander's hearing, of course."

Just the mention of his name made me recoil. "Fuck the Commander."

Damien stilled for a second before his smile widened. "Fuck the Commander, indeed." He took a step closer. "I like a woman who's not intimidated by someone like him."

"Intimidated?"

"You know, by what he does."

What he does...oh, this guy has no *idea* what Mateo Ristani does. But I did. I knew *very well indeed*.

"You're not like the others," he said, wrenching me out of the spell of Mateo and took another step closer. The slow bite of his lip was seductive. "You're not like the others at all."

Holy shit, this guy was coming on to me.

I just gave a throaty laugh. "You're about to lose your job, Damien."

"I won't tell if you don't." The husky murmur was full of need. He lowered his gaze, taking in the ripped-up black wifebeater and torn jeans under the heavy leather jacket. He was right, I wasn't like the others. I didn't wrap myself in Armani, didn't dip myself in Chanel No. 5.

No, I didn't like to flash my shit around all over the place. I liked luxury comfort, expensive cars and jets, and unlimited credit when I needed it. But most of the time, I was just a nobody. Outside the Commission, that was.

I took a step backwards as he crowded closer again. "How about it, Xael?" he asked as he lowered his gaze to my breasts.

"How about what?" I snapped, even as the thought excited me.

"You gotta fuck, right?" He lifted his hand and braced it on the wall beside me. "Unless you have someone else in mind?"

I flinched as Mateo filled my head. "What?"

He dipped his head and stepped closer, pressing that strong body against mine. "One of the other rich assholes on the island...like Lazarus, for instance."

"Lazarus Rossi?" I let out a chuckle.

But the guy wasn't laughing. No, he was all business, thrusting his hips until he gently pressed my spine against the wall. "Yeah, or Bernardi. He's got a rep, I bet he'd be all over someone like you in a heartbeat."

Anger flared for a second. "Someone like me?"

"Yeah," he scowled. "You're hot as fuck."

"Oh..." Excitement made me smile.

He leaned down. "You gotta know that, right?"

His mouth moved close to mine. One turn of my head and he'd kiss me. "No. I don't know that."

"You, Xael Davies, are the hottest woman on this damn island." His voice turned deep and husky. "Just one chance to fuck you good. I promise you won't be disappointed." He thrust his hips against me a little harder.

I could almost mistake this heady rush for desire.

Almost turn it into something else.

Maybe he was the one who'd get me wet?

I bit my lip and sucked in a hard breath. Mateo was mere meters away, sitting behind his desk, his stone-cold heart caged by loyalty...just not to me. "Why the fuck not," I murmured, drawing away from the thought of him.

"Your phone," Damien directed as he pulled back. "I'll give you my number, you can text me when you're free, and we can sneak around."

I drew my cell from my pocket and unlocked it. "You forget, we're on a damn island and watched by cameras." I lifted my gaze to the camera at the edge of the building's roof, one pointing away from us.

"Forget?" He took my phone and punched in his number before handing it back. "Who do you think watches you all damn day?"

A surge of excitement tore through me. "You?"

He just smiled and gave me a wink. "I'll be seeing you, Ms. Davies." He took a step backwards. "As much as I damn well can without getting busted."

Busted...*by Mateo.*

The thought of that hurt. Hurt for what could've been...and what will never be. He'd made sure of that. I gave a nod. "Looking forward to it."

He walked off with a smirk, throwing over his shoulder, "Not as much as I am."

I watched him disappear, hating how even sex with a stranger felt hollow and empty. I bet if I reached between my legs, I would be dry as the goddamn desert. "Fuck you, Mateo," I whispered and turned away, rounding the corner of the building and headed to the foyer.

"Relaxed now?" Rhys murmured, leaning against the wall outside the doors, waiting for me.

"Not even remotely," I replied, watching as he pressed his card to the scanner and waited for the doors to open.

10

Mateo

This was a goddamn mess. "Yes, I understand, Mr. Baldeon," I answered.

"You find the bastards who did this. I want them *fucking dead, Mateo. Do I make myself clear?*"

"Perfectly." I lifted my gaze to the door of my study as though I hadn't already tracked one of them down...and disposed of him. "I have my best men on it as we speak. As soon as we find them, you'll be the first to know."

"He'll have a goddamn scar," Baldeon snapped.

"We all have scars," I answered. "It'll make others think before they speak, especially when it comes to threatening him."

"I have Lucius for that. *He* is the one who makes people think before they threaten."

I exhaled nice and slow. I knew Lucius well...was he a force to be reckoned with? Absolutely. But did he instill fear? *No. No, he didn't.* "I understand."

"One more thing goes wrong, Mateo, and I want Marcus on the first boat out of there."

"Without question."

"Keep me informed."

I opened my mouth to speak, but the line went dead. It was the third goddamn call I'd taken since the attack on the boat. I doubted it'd be the last. I rose from behind my desk and walked around to the floor to ceiling window, staring out of the mirror tint to the world outside. It didn't matter how many calls I received or how pissed off I'd been after the attack...I couldn't help but be relieved.

Relieved Xael was already on the island and not on the cruiser that had come under attack.

We'd caught one of them, but even after an hour of just him and me in that cold, dark basement, he given me no information to go on. He'd just been a shooter, just a trigger-happy asshole that ended up on the receiving end of my goddamn silencer. He didn't know who pulled the strings.

That left my team of former special forces men. Men that'd hunt the shooter or shooters down. But had it been a random attack? I wasn't so sure, not after all the other seemingly random attacks the Commission had been under...and then there was the murder of Cian Salvatore.

I raked my fingers through my hair...*fuck.*

If I didn't know any better, I'd think—my phone vibrated. "What the fuck now?" *Caller ID Unknown.* I licked my lips and answered. "Brother."

"You didn't call."

I winced. "No, I didn't."

"Doesn't matter, I'm already on my way."

"I don't think..."

"You don't need to, brother. I'll do all the thinking for you...and all the killing."

"Edon." My pulse sped at the thought. Just like I'd done all the killing for him all those years ago.

"You think I'd sit this out if I thought there was even a hint of danger to you?" The tone deepened, bordering on something dangerous, and my brother feeling dangerous was a very bad thing indeed.

"No."

"Good. Then I'm coming. Do you still have the apartment on the mainland?"

My stomach tightened at the words. *No, not that one, not the one where she...* "Yes."

"Then I'll take the spare room. See you in twelve hours, brother."

"Where are you?"

"Out." *Out*...that's all the information he gave and I knew better than to ask for more. Dominic Salvatore had been keeping him busy after the death of his wife.

"Have you found them?"

"Parts." My brother answered. "Should I go into detail?"

That change in his tone told me all he needed to know. "No."

"Then I'll be seeing you brother."

"On the mainland, not here.," I ordered. But he was already gone, leaving the line empty. *Shit...he better not come to the island, not with all these rich kids...and her...Xael.*

The thought of my brother amongst those on the island fucking terrified me, but the thought of him meeting Xael almost brought me undone. A shiver tore through me. I lifted my cell, debating calling him back, but then realized it'd be pointless. You didn't call Edon. He called you.

I turned and left the window behind, yanked the door to my office open, and strode through. Edon wouldn't just casually stumble into her path. No, he'd place himself in her way with pinpoint accuracy. He'd be the man she didn't notice, not unless he wanted her to. *Would he want her to?* I closed my eyes as a moan tore free.

No. Please, unmerciful God, no.

"Let me the fuck out now!" The roar came from the infirmary.

I winced, and tried to breathe, reminding myself that killing the second son was a bad goddamn move, especially one who'd already been shot. I strode toward that whiny fucking demand and left my office wing behind. My boots thudded on the hard tiled floor as I turned and stepped into the hallway that looked faintly like a hospital. It should, since it had cost a fortune, equipped with a small emergency room and an X-ray suite. One that'd seen its fair share of trauma, just like it had now.

"You don't let me out and I'll—"

"Settle the fuck down, Marcus," I snapped, striding into his room and parting the curtain.

The pompous little asshole just scowled at the reprimand. I was betting he didn't get many of those at home. His lips curled and I was sure there was something riveting just itching to spill from his lips in return. But I glanced at the doctor with Marcus's chart still in his hand, then looked at the bandage wrapped around his shoulder. "Will he die if he's discharged?"

"No, but—" Doctor Neale Grey started.

"Then let him go. If he wants to cause permeant damage to his body, then there's nothing we can do to stop him."

"I don't think that's advisable. He's just had surgery..."

I glared at the kid sitting in the bed. The one who looked at me with a glimmer of satisfaction. He shouldn't look at me like that, not thinking he'd won. He didn't win a damn thing...just an opportunity to get himself right back in here. "Discharge him within the hour."

I turned with the command and left the room, listening to Grey splutter and bark behind me. He was riled up...welcome to the fucking club. My pulse sped as I left the infirmary wing behind, hating how my gaze went to the door of the command center. Maybe if I just kept an eye on her I wouldn't feel so fucking worked up all the damn time?

Maybe if I just saw her, just once watched her smile and laugh and have all the things I could never give her, I'd finally be able to drive her from my mind and burn her out from under my skin. I winced and reached up, adjusting my tie, because right now I couldn't feel anything other than her squirming boring holes through my heart.

I pressed my card against the scanner and stepped into the darkened hallway as my phone gave a *beep.*

Bruno Bernardi: I want access to CCTV and arrival information for Evan Valachi. Make it happen.

Shit. I pressed the button, listening to his phone ring once before it was answered. "You realize the situation you're putting me in here, right?" I kept walking, leaving the control room door to close behind me. "*You* know I can't give out access to other Commission members."

"*I'm* a Commission member...*and* an heir."

"So is *she,* Bruno," I snarled. "If *she* wanted to spy on *you,* would you allow it?"

There was a second where the rush of a slow, hard exhale filled my ear. The little punk had it bad for Evan Valachi, so bad he was about to step across a line...a line that'd been specifically dotted by the entire Commission.

They wanted their sons and daughters to exert their power, wanted them to explore what it meant to be the one controlling the shots. They wanted them to fight it out amongst each other. That's what the island was for, fighting, fucking, backstabbing, and betrayal all within a confined, safe environment. As I stepped around the corner, I lifted my gaze to the banks of monitors, ones that gave visual access to a good portion of the island...and its buildings. I was the one in control of that supposedly safe environment.

"Yeah," Bruno answered. "I would."

"*I* specifically can't allow your request," I answered, already searching the monitors for Xael's building. "But the control room is open to *all* serving Commission members, and as an heir, you have full access to gather the information for yourself."

I could almost *see* the grin on his face as he spoke. "Then I guess I'll be visiting the control room."

"Enjoy your stay, Mr. Bernardi," I muttered and ended the call, lifting my gaze to the communications officer behind the desk, and stopped...it was him, the one who'd walked into Xael.

He lifted his gaze to me and adjusted his posture. Those dark eyes fixed on me as I stepped around the desk and raised my gaze to the monitors.

"Commander," the new guy murmured an acknowledgement.

"Blake." I searched the monitors, tracking each one until I narrowed in on her building and leaned forward, punching in the details for her building.

"Is there anything I can help you with, sir?"

There she was, standing in the middle of her living room and staring out the window at the water. It was already getting darker, almost night. I wanted her there, in the building further back from the others. The building closer to...I winced, watching as she turned, grabbed her shirt, and pulled it over her head.

Long, shaggy midnight strands came crashing down across her pale skin. She was an enigma, one born for the night. She wasn't like the others, not so controlled. Xael Davies was a little wildcat, earning a reputation as someone who didn't exactly like to play by the rules. I liked that, liked that she was ruthless and undeniable. I liked that she went after what she wanted and as she'd come onto my radar, I'd watched her blossom into a woman from afar, never once making my presence known...*until that night.*

A night fate had decided otherwise.

Now I was dealing with the repercussions, trying to unravel something wound so tight it had embedded itself into me. "I want a dedicated feed set up on my cell," I directed as I unlocked my phone.

"Any building in particular, sir?"

I motioned my head toward Xael's apartment, unable to say the words. "That one."

"Only that one?"

"Yes." I swung my gaze to him. This guy...this guy was starting to piss me off. "Do you have a problem with that?"

He just took my phone. "Not at all."

"Good. I'll wait."

He scowled, met my gaze, and gave a nod, then took my cell and got to work. When I walked out of the command center, I was staring at the feed to her apartment, including her bedroom. Evan Valachi shared the space, but I didn't care about her...

No.

All I wanted to see was the nightmare I craved. I strode back to my apartment, my steps quickening, turning into long, consuming strides. My hands worked on their own, their movement a blur as I pressed the card to the scanner outside the door to my private wing in the building and stepped inside.

Darkness consumed me.

Darkness and the black and white image of her in my hands. She stepped out of the bathroom dressed in nothing more than a towel wrapped around her body.

"Jesus." I tore the phone away, placing it down as I braced my hands on the table and dropped my head.

I didn't know why I did this to myself, didn't know why I kept coming back to this torture...I licked my lips, straightened, and lifted the phone once more. She turned and unwound the towel, lifting it to slowly run the fabric down the strands of her midnight black hair.

I was lost in the sweet curve of her ass and her fucking milky smooth skin, and found myself dragging my thumb across the screen right as the damn cell rang. The vision was snatched away, the screen replaced with the caller ID.

Neale Grey.

"What the fuck, now?" I groaned, lifted it, and answered. "Yes?"

"He's discharged." The doctor sounded pissy. "You do know he's going to a party tonight?"

"Without a doubt."

"And there'll be alcohol, less than twenty-four hours after I pulled a bullet from his shoulder."

I gave a sigh. "Listen, doc..."

"Surgeon," he corrected.

"What?"

"I'm a *surgeon.* That's why you hired me, remember?"

Remember his goddamn credentials? Fuck, I was going flat out just remembering what fucking day it was. "Get to the point, Neale."

There was silence, then his tone, low and, yeah, most definitely pissy. "I want them checked on."

"What?"

"I want them checked on, Mateo," he was insistent.

"What, like they're fucking five?" I snapped.

"I don't care. You wanted him discharged, so I'm holding you fully responsible."

Anger cut through me, chilling me to the bone. "Or what?"

"Or I walk," he said. The goddamn bastard was holding me to this, like any of this was *my* fucking fault? "And good luck finding someone with my credentials prepared to work in this fucking war zone."

I clenched my grip around the phone, anger burning inside me. "Fine. You want me to crash their goddamn party, then I will...*will that satisfy you?*"

"Yes."

"Good." I forced the word through clenched teeth. "Is there anything *else* I can do for you, *doctor?*"

"Goodnight, Mateo." He just finished. "Call me if there are any complications."

"Oh," I clenched my fist, my tone bordering on murderous. "I will, rest assured of that."

He hung up the line, leaving me fucking fuming. By the time I'd paced the floor and calmed down, I remembered the live video feed of Xael's apartment. I snatched my cell from the table and pulled up the feed, but she'd already gone, leaving nothing but a messy bed and the wet towel dropped on the floor of her bedroom behind.

11

Xael

Baldeon's getting out. Party at his place.

I read the text once more and straightened my dress. "Sure," I murmured, looking at myself in the bathroom mirror. "Why the hell not."

The beige free-flowing dress draped from my body, coming in tighter below my knees. Gaping armholes left the sides of my sheer black bra unavoidably visible. I skimmed my hands down my body, taking in the black, strappy lace-up stilettos that mirrored the shock of my messy hair. Not bad...not bad at all.

A noise came from the room next to mine, drawing my focus to my roommate. I sighed, stared at the wall, and debated just sneaking out and leaving her behind. But that was a shitty thing to do, and right now it looked like Evan Valachi could do with a friend.

I walked out of my bedroom and made my way to her closed door, knocking gently. "Hey, Evan, it's me. I'm heading out to a party at Zakharov's, you want to come?"

Silence came from behind the door. Maybe she had her iPods in and didn't hear me? I lifted my hand and knocked once more, louder. "Evan, can you hear me?"

Something shifted behind the door and goosebumps raced along my arms, making me shiver. I scowled at the door and took a step backwards. A shadow moved across the gap on the floor. She was there, standing right in front of me. *That's fucking weird.*

I stepped backwards, all of a sudden wanting to put distance between us. *"Okay."* I made my way out of the apartment and headed to the elevator, pressed the button, and stepped inside.

Valachi was starting to weird me the fuck out.

But then again, we were all a little weird.

Me included.

I'd gone off the rails when Mateo had broken my fucking heart. I'd tried to attend college, tried women too, anything to get the taste of Mateo Ristani out of my goddamn mouth. That turned out disastrous.

"Ms. Davies." Rhys lifted his gaze from his laptop as I stepped off the elevator into the foyer.

"You don't need to come," I muttered. "I'll literally be in an apartment surrounded by security."

"How about I walk you to the building then?" He rose from the seat, leaving his laptop behind.

"That's not a request, is it?"

He smiled and gave me a wink.

"Fine," I sighed, and turned for the door.

The moment the doors opened, a brutal gust of wind smacked into me, knocking me backwards. Rhys was there, grabbing my arm and steadying me. "Easy," he murmured.

I righted my stance, leaned forward, and stepped back out into the wind. There was a change coming. Don't ask me how I knew, I just felt it in my bones. My mother called me 'intuitive'. Dad just called me foolish. But I knew...I knew a change was coming in the gusts that tore through the gaps in my dress to slide across my body.

I brushed my hair to the side, draping it over my shoulder, strode past the thick green foliage that filled the garden outside the entrance to the building, and stepped out of its protection.

Lights drew my gaze to a building nearby. *"See!"* I yelled over my shoulder, fighting the wind. *"Right over there!"*

But Rhys never moved from my side, his hand hovering discreetly an inch from my arm, never once giving me an impression he thought of me as anything other than his job. Which was just fine with me. I sure as hell didn't need any more complications. Not after the last one...that was enough to turn me off love forever.

I lowered my head, squinting as my hair lashed my eyes. Tears came quickly as I slammed my card against the reader to Zakharov's building and the foyer doors opened instantly.

I focused on watching Rhys, making sure he stayed true to his word, hanging back outside the building, before I turned away. The last thing I needed was the buzzkill of him watching over my shoulder, knowing that every little fucking thing would be relayed back to good 'ol dad.

I didn't swipe away the blur in my eyes, just lifted my gaze as the elevator doors started to close. *"Hey! Hold the door!"* I hurried, heels clattering, fighting the deafening roar still lingering in my ears from the wind.

I made it just in time, shoving out my hand and stumbling inside...then I lifted my head, meeting Mateo's sullen glare as the doors closed with a *thud*.

"Oh." The word slipped free before I slammed up the walls around my heart.

He just stared as I dragged my wind-blown hair over my shoulder, his eyes captured by the movement, taking in the gaping armholes of my dress as I moved. I knew my bra was showing, the edge of my breast spilling free. But I didn't care. I liked him watching, liked that tortured wince in his eyes.

"You sure you should be wearing that?" he said carefully.

"Wearing what? Oh, you mean this?" I murmured, skimming my hands down my body, sliding the fabric over the swell, revealing the sheer bra.

He looked away, the muscles flaring in his jaw. "Yes, *that*."

How fucking dare he look away...like he didn't enjoy this body...maybe that was it? Maybe I hadn't fucked him right... maybe I wasn't *enough*. I arched my spine, jutted my hips forward and fisted my dress at my hips, dragging the hemline higher until it barely skimmed my thighs. "Twelve months ago, you would've liked me in it. Liked me out of it, as well."

With a blinding surge, he closed the distance, slamming his hand against the button, stopping the elevator mid-floor. Those infernal dark eyes bored into mine as he lifted his hand, bracing it against the wall beside my head. "You fucking push me, Xael."

"Push you?" I asked carefully. Mateo Ristani might terrify everyone else on this island, but he didn't scare me. "I seem to remember you were the one doing all the pushing, Mateo."

He lowered his gaze, staring at my partially exposed breast, the sheer black fabric against my skin. I deepened my breaths, riveted by the agony in his eyes. He still wanted me...

I felt it, saw it...I tasted it...just like I'd once tasted him.

One swallow of Mateo and I was hooked. I'd drunk him down like a ravenous whore, craving him then...just like I craved him now.

"You don't like me in this, then I'm sure I can find someone who will."

He jerked his gaze to mine, and something savage moved in the darkness. His lips curled in a sneer, revealing his teeth. Excitement surged, making me breathless.

"What if I called Bernardi?" I taunted carefully. It was like dancing with death, teasing fate.

That's what Mateo was to me...*fate*.

"Go ahead," he snarled, his tone cruel. But that flare of his jaw came once more. What did you know...the mighty Commander was jealous.

"I bet he'd come right over," I continued, my voice growing husky. "I bet he'd come all over me too."

The sound of his breaths was like the savage wind outside.

His fingers curled into a fist.

Was he thinking about that?

"I bet he fucks real good, too." A flicker of pain tore through me as I said the words. Sadness mingled with regret. "And in the morning, I bet he wouldn't tell me it was a mistake."

Mateo flinched as though I'd slapped him.

He pushed off the wall, taking a step backwards, and hit the button, sending the elevator rising once more. I wanted to hate him, wanted to see him squirm. But the agony that shone in his eyes right now...stole everything away. And in an instant, I couldn't breathe.

I didn't look away as we came shuddering to a stop, just stared at the man standing on the other side of the elevator, pushing his spine flat against the wall as though he was desperate to get away from me. But I couldn't bear to see him walk away from me once more.

Even as agony howled inside me, clawing at my heart, I forced myself to move. It was me who left Mateo behind that time. Me who gave him my back...me who staggered through the entrance and stumbled into the blur of faces.

"Hey, Xael..." someone called.

But I didn't care. *I couldn't care.* I was bleeding on the inside, screaming inside my head. I needed a drink. I swung my gaze toward the kitchen counter that right now was an open bar and scanned the bottles, desperate for something that was going to get me drunk *fast*.

I poured, splashing vodka into the glass, and lifted it to my lips.

"Hey, the Commander's here!"

I slammed my eyes closed and swallowed. Cold burned like fire, sliding down my throat. I tried to tune out the words...his name, to be exact. But I couldn't. I was fucking sick, so fucking sick. Because there was no other way to explain why I glanced toward the entrance to meet Mateo's gaze. He lowered his to the glass in my hand as I swallowed and echoes of the past rose. The pang of desire hit me as I lifted the glass to my mouth again. Someone from the party tried to talk to him. But the mighty Commander wasn't listening. He wasn't even giving them a second of his focus...because it was all on me. Was he remembering our past...to a time where he took another glass from my hand and filled his own hand with the heat of my pussy?

The memory rose inside me, cruel and deadly. One push of his hand and he'd widened my thighs, commanding and demanding. A beast of a man who took what he wanted. I licked my lips, jutting my breasts forward, daring him now just as I'd dared him then. *Do something!*

He did. He wrenched his gaze from mine, then turned and walked away, leaving the party behind. Gutless piece of shit! I drank again, taking in four more gulps before that cold ice warmed in my belly.

And after a while, I could finally breathe. I poured another, scowling at the way the bottle was emptying way too fast, then turned around, finally able to face the party. I couldn't stop myself from looking for him, couldn't help searching the crowd. Needing him...even with the pain.

Tears came at the corners of my eyes as someone waved at me.

I forced a smile, flicked away the tears before they slid free, and drank.

Fuck you, Mateo.

Fuck you very fucking much.

I took a step, then cut through the crowd as I caught sight of Kat VanHalen. "Hey, sexy." I leaned forward, giving her a kiss on the cheek.

"Hey," she answered, smiled, then scanned the room as though she was searching for someone.

I sank into small talk, hating how I couldn't stand to be here. Kat stiffened, her gaze hooked on some tall, blonde rich asshole. I was sure I knew his name. "Who the fuck is that?"

"No one," she answered. "Excuse me, Xael. It was nice seeing you, we need to catch up soon, okay?"

"Sure," I muttered as she rose from the sofa and rounded the edge of the living room before disappearing. "Nice."

"OMG...*NO!*" a woman's scream ripped through the space.

I flinched, searching, and found her. Tears streamed down her cheeks as she dropped the cell phone from her ear. *"Baldeon is dead...someone just killed him."*

12

Mateo

"FUCK!" I roared, staring at the body of a man I'd seen alive and breathing only two fucking hours ago.

"They're still here." Lazarus Rossi sucked in hard breaths and lifted a shell-shocked gaze to me. "I saw them...*if* it was them."

I turned away, lifted the two-way from my pocket, and barked into the radio. "I want the entire island searched *now!*"

"Heading to the east side now," squawked the reply.

My men were hunting, every fucking man...every goddamn soldier. "Who found him?"

"I did." Rossi turned his gaze to mine.

"Did you see anything else?"

"Two men...or two people, I couldn't get a good look, running from this building toward the beach. I heard the faint sound of a motor."

"And they didn't come after you?" I narrowed my gaze on the Stidda son.

He just shook his head. "No, they didn't come after me."

"Thank Christ for that," his bodyguard grunted.

I nodded and took a step away, lifting the two-way once more. "I want every building searched, leave nothing untouched. Do I make myself clear?"

"On it, Commander," came the bark from the other end.

Jesus...Jesus, this was going to be bad.

"Rossi." I glanced toward Lazarus, taking in his shell-shocked gaze. I wondered if he'd ever seen a body...not one like this, I bet. "I'm going to need a statement."

He gave a slow nod and I could almost see the kid slowly unraveling. Did he see himself lying there in the pool of blood? See his fucking future? In a blink, I saw Edon lying in front of me on that stainless steel gurney meant for the dead. Had my brother felt the icy hand of death reaching for him as they beat and stabbed and unleashed their rage on him? Had he seen his end as clearly as Lazarus Rossi was seeing his own right now?

"Freddy," Lazarus whispered.

"I got you." His bodyguard was right there, grabbing him by the shoulder and turning them. "Move," he snapped at my men standing in the basement hallway of the building assigned to Marcus Baldeon. Then they were gone in a heartbeat under the soft *thud* of the elevator doors.

I was alone...staring at my failure.

Something dangerous moved through me. Something that hadn't stirred since that night. I'd killed before, beaten and stabbed. I'd strangled with my own hands as I stared into panicked eyes...but this...*this felt different.*

This felt like war...

Luckily, war was what I did best.

I turned away. "Get the body to the refrigerator," I demanded, and turned my gaze to the man standing in the shadows. "Get him ready to ship back home. His father will want to see the body."

"I'll do my best," Doctor Grey murmured, his eyes riveted on mine.

There were no demands from him in that moment, lucky for him. I might just have rammed them down his fucking throat. A nod, and I turned away, leaving him to deal with the body. "Two of you stay with the doctor in case they come back, the others are with me."

"Yes, Commander," they answered in unison.

I strode for the elevator, then out into the night. The calls would come...and when they did, there'd be no more hiding, no more appeasing the dangerous men I worked for...they'd want blood, one way another. If not the men who'd done this...then they'd be after mine.

13

Xael

I couldn't believe it. No one could. Baldeon was dead and the island was in chaos. The kind of chaos that made me terrified. The moment the news broke out, the party was invaded by a swarm of bodyguards, Rhys being one of them. He gripped me by the arm, his gun in his other hand, and ushered me down the stairs and out of the building.

I'd been locked in the apartment ever since. I looked over at him, sitting on the sofa, his head resting on the back, his eyes closed. But I knew as soon as there was even a hint of a door opening or the elevator stopping, he'd be on his feet in an instant, the gun aimed at whoever was coming through that entrance.

He wouldn't let anyone get to us. I scowled and glanced along the hallway to my quiet roommate's room. For all the power she held, Evan Valachi had come to the island without even a body-guard to keep watch over her. I wanted to ask her if everything was okay, but she was...weird, to put it nicely. The few interactions we'd had had left me confused as hell.

She was weird...weirder than weird. Maybe the Valachis were like that, how the hell did I know? Even Kat VanHalen had texted me saying the exact same thing after bringing her room-mate, Anna, the perfectly delightful klutz from the boat, to meet her.

Now, Anna was the kind of roomie you wanted. She was shy, cute as hell, and goddamn scrumptious as she avoided every probing question about Finley Salvatore. I'd told Kat I wanted us to hang out more, desperate for at least *some* fucking interaction in this place. But that was before...

Before everything changed.

Before one of us was murdered.

The stories that circulated about what had happened to Marcus were terrifying. But they were only rumors. I had no way to find out the real story. If Rhys knew what happened, he wasn't telling me. No one was telling me jack shit. Now we were guarded twenty-four/seven.

The one person I wanted to ask, I also wanted to stab in the fucking eye with my stiletto. *Because I knew he didn't have a heart.*

"You need to stop pacing," Rhys muttered, his eyes still closed. "You're making me jumpy."

"I need..." *to get out of here.* The words lingered on the tip of my tongue. One mention of leaving and I'd be packed up and hauled off in the next second. I knew that, I'd ready fielded half a dozen calls from my father demanding just that.

But I wasn't leaving, and I sure as hell wasn't running with my tail between my legs. If I did, then I'd be always seen as the female who couldn't handle her shit. Forever the Davies that fled when things got a little rough.

"You're making me nervous, Xael."

I dragged my hand through my hair. "I need to get out of here, I feel like I'm going stir-crazy."

Without even a sigh, he opened his eyes and pushed up from the sofa. His eyes were red, his shoulders slumped.

"No, Rhys." I shook my head. "You haven't slept for two fucking days."

"I'm not letting you go out on your own, Xael," he insisted.

"Then I'll just get another escort." I lifted my hand. "Look, I know one of the Commander's men. I'll just ask him."

He scowled, his gaze growing darker.

"It's not like that," I muttered. "He's the one who walked into me when we got off the plane, okay? He's just a friend." *A fuck buddy, more like it. Well, he wanted to be.*

"Who the fuck is the guy?" he demanded.

I jerked my gaze along the hall toward the bedroom where Evan was permanently inside. "Lower your damn voice, Rhys. He's..."

"Jesus, Xael," he groaned, and shook his head.

Heat rose to my cheeks, and anger lashed deep. I wasn't doing anything fucking wrong here. And even if I was, what was it to him or my damn family? I'd only hooked up with him once since getting his number. Even that turned out disastrous, being sprung by Alexi Kilpatrick of all assholes. "So it's okay for my brother to nail anything that moves, but if I even try to have some resemblance of a relationship, all of a sudden I'm labeled a whore?"

He flinched. "I didn't say that."

"You didn't have to."

I was so sick of that double-standard bullshit. Why didn't they see that was why I fucking acted out? Why I'd taken off to the university and tried to pretend I was someone else. Someone who wasn't criticized, someone who wasn't looked at the way Rhys was looking at me now.

"You know what? Never mind," I snarled, then turned and strode back along the hallway and into my room, slamming the door behind me.

"Xael," Rhys called from behind the door. "Come on."

"Don't," I demanded.

But he didn't leave. Instead, he leaned closer to the door. "I just messaged one of the guys downstairs to take you to your class, okay? You're right, you can't stay in this apartment forever."

I jerked my gaze toward the door, took a step, and yanked it open. "Really?"

"Really." He gave a nod. "Whoever attacked Marcus Baldeon is long gone by now."

I noticed that he didn't say I was safe. Because Rhys was a man of his word, and there's no way he'd say something he didn't think was true. That meant...

"Want to give me your gun, Rhys?" I asked.

The sly smile was quick, even if he was exhausted. "You with a gun? Now, that's a scary prospect."

I gave a shrug. "You never know. I might surprise you."

"Terrify is more like it."

I gave a smile as he continued. "Go, get ready. Go to your class while I get a damn shower and some proper sleep."

"Thank fuck," I muttered. "I wasn't going to say anything, but..."

"Why you little." He feigned a lunge toward me.

I gave a chuckle that seemed awful and awkward given the circumstances as the sound of the elevator doors echoed from out in the entrance. I straightened, as did Rhys. We couldn't have anyone seeing the real person behind the stony mask, now could we?

"Ms. Davies," the guard called from the living room.

I straightened my shirt, tucked back my hair, slid my phone into my pocket, and stepped past Rhys, muttering, "Get some sleep, Rhys."

"Will do. Stay safe out there, kid. Don't leave his side, okay?"

"Got it, dad."

He gave a smile, but I knew he wasn't joking. Because none of this was even remotely funny. We were just trying to figure out a way to navigate what had happened. I strode toward the guard, watching him turn for the elevator. Not once did he speak as we rode down to the foyer and out of the building, heading for the classrooms.

But as soon as I was outside, I grabbed my cell and sent a text. *Are we really safe here?*

A second later, my phone vibrated. *Damien: Can't talk over the phone. Want to meet?*

Want to meet...

I lowered my cell and glanced at the building as the guard walked at my side. There wasn't anyone else outside. It was like they'd all left and even though I knew they hadn't, it still felt lonely as hell. I punched out a reply: *Okay.*

Damien: I finish my shift in an hour, wait for me where we met before?

I licked my lips as the guard stepped up to the building door and opened it, leaving me to walk through.

Okay, see you then.

In an hour it was going to be much darker. Gray skies already threatened the island and in the last few hours the wind had picked up, turning the idyllic good time into a moody, bloody affair. Maybe I should just go home.

I lifted my gaze to movement heading toward me and caught sight of Mateo, striding as he stared into his phone, flanked by guards on either side. My heart lunged, slamming against my chest as he lifted his gaze to me. And all of a sudden, the world around me faded into nothing.

We were back there in that elevator...

Back in that apartment.

Back in that bubble where only we existed.

But then in an instant, he was gone, leaving me behind with long strides. I heard the grating metal howl of the door before it thudded closed once more. He was dangerous in that moment.

Cold. Savage. Not the man I knew, but the man I knew of. I glanced over my shoulder, watching him stride away without a backward glance.

That hurt...more than it should.

I went to class and thought about him. If I thought I'd had it bad being locked in the apartment, I couldn't imagine what it must feel like to be in his shoes right now. Not only was Baldeon shot before he got here, he was also tortured and murdered right under Mateo's nose.

The Commission would be baying for blood.

I knew that for a fact.

Hardly anyone was in the class, and no one was really listening to the instructor, some former FBI guy. Still, he kept speaking, kept trying to engage those he could. This was a total waste of my time. By the time it was over, we were already walking toward the door. I looked around, catching Finley glancing my way. He gave a nod and a weak smile. Christ, he looked bad. Then again, he was there not long after they'd found Marcus. I took a step toward him, but saw him shake his head.

No, that's right. We can't be seen as weak.

Then he turned and left. By the time I stepped out and met my guard's gaze, everyone else who'd come to class was already gone.

"I got this, Ty."

I jerked my gaze to the hallway, watching as Damien strode toward us. Panic filled me for a second as I glanced back to the first guard.

"Blake," he muttered.

"I think the Commander is looking for more guys to search the far side of the island."

The protective guard just scowled. "I didn't hear anything. I can't really leave my post..."

Blake gave a shrug. "That's why I'm here. Got nothing else to do. I'm sure Ms. Davies won't mind, will you?"

He swung that glinting stare my way. "No, of course not," I answered. "Gotta do what the Commander says."

The guard scowled, then gave a slow nod. "If you're sure."

I just gave him a smile and waited awkwardly.

He left in a hurry, his thick thighs flexing as he lengthened his stride, then he was gone...leaving us alone.

Damien swung that careful glance my way. "Well, that was easier than I expected."

"Aren't you worried about being seen?" I muttered and nodded toward the camera.

He just smiled and I didn't know if it was meant to be seductive or creepy. I wanted it to be seductive, I really did. He motioned me forward and I took a slow step, keeping my voice low. "Well, are we safe?"

"It depends on what you call safe."

My pulse quickened as we walked along the corridor, even from here I could hear the howl of the wind outside. Damien slowed at the last classroom, reached out and tested the lock, opened the door when it gave way, and ushered me inside.

Darkness swallowed me in an instant and the panicked thunder of my heart followed. I licked my lips, glanced toward the door as he closed it, and caught the shine of my own reflection in the panel of glass.

"You know about the attack, obviously," he continued, wrenching my gaze from the door.

I didn't want to be in here, not with him. Not really. What the fuck was I doing with him, anyway?

"The Commander," he started, drawing my attention to him. He watched me, fixed on my reaction. "Has men combing every inch of the island."

"I got that already," I answered, and glanced toward the closed door behind him.

"But he won't find anything."

"Oh, yeah?" A flare of anger met with my concern. "Why do you say that?"

He took a step closer, shrugging his shoulders. "Just a feeling I have. Those who attacked Marcus Baldeon would be long gone by now."

He slid his hand around my neck and pulled me gently toward him. A flicker of fear raced through me as the memory of his hands on my body rose from the other night. I wanted to come. *I was desperate to come.* I wanted to be fucked and licked and hungered for. I wanted it all...and this...warm body promised.

I closed my eyes as his mouth met mine and yet all I could see was Mateo, his hard mouth, his careful touch. He was nothing like this fumbling idiot as he cupped my breast, kneading it slowly in his desperate paw.

I broke the kiss and pulled back, staring into his eyes. "You were saying?"

There was a flicker of annoyance behind his eyes and something else, something that sent a shudder through me. Something that made me swallow hard and take a step away. "So, do you think I should leave?"

"No," he snapped, then adjusted his tone. "The safest place right now is the island. There's more security."

"And more opportunity, wouldn't you say?"

"I say if you stay here, I can watch over you," he said carefully and closed the distance between us once more. This guy couldn't take a damn hint as he pulled me closer, pressing his body against mine. "Out there, I can't find you."

He kissed me, and this time I didn't stop him. In my head, all I saw was Mateo. In my head, I felt him, too.

Those hard hands replaced this fumbling baboon's. Mateo's urgency replaced Damien's mauling desperation as he pulled me against him and kissed the side of my neck.

In the reflection of the glass panel, I saw myself, saw those unflinching eyes filled with nothing but boredom...and pain.

"Fuck, you feel good, Xael."

I licked my lips and closed my eyes...wishing for the agony of this to be over.

But it'd never be over, would it?

Not while I still breathed...and Mateo Ristani lived.

Because while our hearts still beat, I'd always hope...

14

Mateo

There was no word after the attack. Not a bombing. Not a fucking fire. Not even a goddamn shot was aimed at any of the warehouses or homes owned by the Commission. There was just silence. The kind of silence that made me feel jumpy and trigger-happy.

I'd already had enough Commission meetings to choke the fucking life out of me. But no matter how many times I'd recounted the events leading up to the brutal murder, it wasn't enough. Threats were made. Savage, end-my-fucking-life threats...as if I gave a flying rodent's fuck about that. It was fucking empty anyway...*because of them.*

I'd given up everything for this, *even my one chance of actually happiness.*

For. This.

I turned from the window in my office, strode through the study, and headed out the door. There was no word from those who'd attacked, or my men hunting them...*and I didn't like it.*

I grabbed my phone and punched in the code to hit the one number I didn't want to. The one number I hadn't called in over five years and the number I never wanted to call again. I listened to it ring on the other end of the line and for a second, I thought he wasn't going to answer and I'd truly left that part of my life behind. Maybe Ion was dead...maybe the Sergeant finally—

"Komandant?"

"Thought you were dead there for a second," I answered, hating how I winced at the thick accent of my home.

"They can't kill what's already dead."

A smile tugged at the corners of my mouth at the growl. "Then it's a good thing I still have you in my corner. You are in my corner, right, Kurti?"

Sheets rustled in the background. "Do you even have to ask that, Mateo?"

A flare of shame rose inside me. "No...no, I don't."

"Then tell me what you need, old friend."

"Besnik, what do you have on them?"

"Wow, that's a name from the past. Not much, they're more underground than fucking hell, if you know what I mean."

I swallowed hard, my mind racing. "That's what I was worried about."

"Is there a problem? They reach out to you?"

Reach out...that's one way to explain what'd happened here. The only problem was, I didn't know for sure that it was them. "No, maybe...I don't know."

"Which is the reason for the phone call," Kurti clarified. "You've come to the right guy, Komandant. I'll make some calls and get back to you."

"I appreciate that."

"How is your...Edon. How is Edon, Komandant?"

I flinched at the question. "Fine. Alive, if that's what you're asking."

He just gave a chuckle. "And the rest of us shall live in fear."

I stopped walking, stopping in the middle of the hallway as his words hit home. "Do you have a reason to be afraid of him, Kurti?"

"Sir, the entire world needs to be afraid while a man like that is alive," he replied, his words careful. "A trained killer who hasn't wiped out every man who ever harmed him is a scary concept indeed."

Not as scary as the brother who'd killed to save him...

And would kill again.

"Get back to me with whatever you find out," I murmured.

"Of course. It's good to hear from you, Mateo," he finished, and hung up.

I didn't say it back. I never did...because the truth was, I wanted to forget that time of my life. I wanted to forget what happened in that arid land where I was born. I wanted to forget the crimes I'd committed for my country...and the things I'd seen.

I turned away, lifting my gaze to the darkening skies outside the building. Gray skies, whipping winds. The weather report indicated a cyclone headed our way, as if a murder wasn't enough, mother nature decided to demand some attention. Why the fuck not.

Beep.

I glanced at my phone, finding a message from *Caller ID Unknown.* I didn't need to be a genius to know who it was. But it wasn't just a message...it was a photo. I opened up the attachment and stared at two bodies lying flat on the floor. Clothed, bloody...an assassination.

My phone vibrated barely a second later. I answered with, "Who exactly am I looking at, brother?"

"By the information I found in the apartment, it looks like the two responsible for your kid's murder."

I flinched, my heart hammering as I pulled the phone away and brought up the image once more. I looked more closely, narrowing in on the clothes they wore and anything else I could find around them before lifting the phone to my ear once more. "You didn't think to keep them alive for us to question?"

"Oh, this wasn't me, brother. This was what I found."

"Where are you?"

"I'll send you coordinates," he replied. "And Mateo...you might want to lock the place down. This wasn't retribution, this was silence."

I froze, my mind racing as I took in his words. "They were the damn scapegoats." In an instant, the asshole from Marcus's shooting came to mind. We'd captured one...one that had screamed of this exact thing. We didn't get any information him, and now we wouldn't get any from the men who'd killed Marcus Baldeon. "I'm on my way."

"See you soon then," he answered, and hung up.

I made a call. Getting the chopper to the mainland would be quicker, but I couldn't risk it with the damn cyclone heading our way. So the boat would have to do. I headed for my office, stepped inside, and strode to the false wall. One push and the catch released before I pressed my thumb to the scanner.

The plexiglass wall popped open and slid back, revealing enough weapons to arm a small army. Memories of another war came echoing back as I grabbed two Sigs and a sniper's rifle. I was the kind of man they sent in first, the one that was dispensable...and who always came home, no matter what.

I grabbed my weapons and filled a backpack with loaded magazines and ammunition before hauling it over my shoulder and walking out. Barely fifteen minutes later and we were racing across the water, heading for the mainland. I had men waiting for me, men who'd take me not just to the place an hour away where the two bodies of the hitmen were found, but also to my brother.

FOUR HOURS LATER, I stood in the doorway of a dingy cabin in a seedy part of the city. Ruined buildings and lean-tos made up the landscape, reminding me far too much of the life I'd worked so hard to leave behind. But as I stepped into the doorway, it was like I was back there again.

Edon stood in the shadows, his arms crossed, watching me as I stepped forward and looked at the two bodies lying face-down in the middle of the space. "Has anything been touched?"

"Not a thing," he answered coldly, as though I should know better than to ask.

And I should. Sometimes I forgot who I spoke to.

Edon wasn't just a hitman. He was a trained specialist in covert operations, born not from the life our mother gave him...but from the death I'd saved him from. He and death danced the most terrifying dance. It hunted him....and he hunted it, bringing it out of the shadows and into the light. I glanced from my brother to the two men lying face-down and took a step closer.

They were evil dressed in black, the same clothing I'd seen on the monitors from the CCTV footage taken as they left the building and raced to the waiting boat on the shoreline. I turned them over and took pictures of their faces.

"I already ran them," Edon murmured. "Their fingerprints, too."

"And?" I lifted my gaze.

He just gave a shrug. "Ex-military, special ops. Nothing spectacular."

Spectacular enough to hire them to kill an unarmed man. Still, I stared into the milky hue of their wide eyes and took another picture, this time sending it to the members of the Commission. The men who'd killed Marcus Baldeon were dead. I didn't know if they'd organized the hit or someone else had, and I doubted I'd get any answers. Right now, honesty was the least common trait amongst the men who made up one of the most powerful rings on US soil. But at least now, with the men who'd completed the hit dead, it might appease them...for a moment, at least.

Just until I could get ahead of this.

I lifted my gaze to Edon. Maybe having my brother here wasn't a bad thing, after all...who better to hunt these bastards down? "Are you on the trail?"

He pushed off the wall and took a step toward me. "Do you want me on the trail?"

I thought about it for a second. Didn't really have a choice, did I? "Yeah. Yeah, I do."

He turned then, striding toward the door. "Then consider me employed."

I gave a nod to the two men standing outside, then watched as they bagged the bodies and hauled them out to the truck to dispose of them later. Right now, I needed to get back to the island and the cyclone bearing down on them.

15

Xael

"He's not here," Finley muttered, drawing my gaze.

"What?" I flinched, wrenching my focus to those commanding brown eyes as the smug bastard just smirked.

"Your new...*fuck buddy*. He's not here, right?" Fin leaned forward, that stare pinning me to the spot.

The music crowded in, drawing me back to the party. I licked my lips and shifted from one foot to the other, lifting my glass to my lips. "I have no idea what you're talking about, Salvatore."

"Sure you don't," he agreed slyly, and turned that glare toward the rest of the room, narrowing in on the host himself.

Bruno Bernardi laughed and cast another handful of chips across the table, then lifted his gaze to mine and winked. He was a cocky bastard, flashy with his money, especially when it came to his current opponent, Vad Kardinov. They had some kind of hate/love bromance, one I didn't understand...I doubted anyone did.

"Shit, don't tell me it's Kardinov," Fin growled. "That guy is a—"

"No, it's not Kardinov," I snapped, my gaze moving to the guy sitting across from Bernardi, dressed in fucking Armani and reeking of sanctimonious self-importance. The guy was a prick of the highest caliber. And...*unhinged.*

I'd heard some of the stories about him and Helene Kilpatrick, heard how she not only had to take out a restraining order on the asshole, but she'd paid a couple of men to pay him a visit and warn him away from her. I also heard how they'd found those men beaten within an inch of their lives and they'd had to spend two weeks in the hospital. It didn't stop him from going after her...that man was obsessive when it came to her.

So Helene went underground, and didn't surface...not until Fin's mom's funeral.

As if he'd read my thoughts, Vad glanced my way. I didn't look away, just held that glare with my own until his lips curled in a chilling smile.

"Thank fuck," Finley sighed. "That guy's an asshole."

"That he is," I agreed, still holding his stare as he laid his hand of cards onto the table, then reached for the pile of chips stacked to the side.

I looked away, giving Salvatore my full attention. "Anyway, you can't expect me to just stand here waiting for the day you finally notice me, Finley Salvatore, and bang my brains out."

He was taking a swallow of his Scotch, and choked and spluttered, almost dying before he jerked that watery stare my way. "You've got to be fucking kidding, Davies."

"Of course I'm fucking kidding," I laughed, amused by the horrified look on his face. "It'd be like banging my goddamn brother, and just the thought of that turns my stomach."

"Thank God for that." He swiped the back of his hand across his mouth as movement from the doorway caught my eye.

"Speaking of banging," I murmured, watching shy Anna Shaw scan the room and fix her gaze on Finley.

The electricity between them was undeniable. Finley, the poor sap, was badly smitten, holding her in his broody damn gaze. One that made me feel jealous as hell.

"Go after her, you idiot." I took a step and gently shoved him forward with my shoulder. "Go."

He took a step forward, not even giving me a glance. That's how it should be, right? Total infatuation. I lifted my glass and drained the contents. Yeah...that's how it should be.

In a blinding second, the excitement lost its shine.

I drank, and the more I drank, the less I felt.

That's what I really wanted...to not feel.

Rhys blurred, standing in the corner of the room. I waved him off, but my words slurred when they came. "Go...go, I don't need you."

"How about we get you back to the apartment," he offered, suddenly at my side.

"No." I shook my head and reached for the glass again.

"Xael," my bodyguard protested, and grabbed my arm as I stumbled.

"He's dead." The words slipped free as I lifted my gaze. "Marcus is dead."

Rhys flinched, then stilled, searching my gaze. "I know."

I shook my head. "No, I don't think you do." I pushed away from him and stumbled toward the entrance of the apartment. "Just leave me be, Rhys."

Agony roared through me as I made my way to the elevator, staggering in as a group of others stepped out. Tears filled my eyes as I smashed my fist against the button for the door. *"Close, goddammit!"*

Rhys was there, stepping forward just as the doors closed with a *thud,* and for a second, I was alone...the kind of alone that hit me soul deep. Marcus's death had hurt me...but it wasn't just that. It was seeing them happy. Fin, Anna...Hell, even Lazarus Rossi was after Kat and Bruno had made his interest well and truly known when it came to the weird one, Evan Valachi. That left me...alone...like I was destined to be forever.

That ache in my chest grew claws as the elevator came to a stop and the doors slowly opened. I stumbled out, blinded by the tears that spilled free and the alcohol that slammed into me. I had to get out of here, get back to the lonely fucking apartment, hole myself up in my room and wait for the ache to pass. It'd pass...*it had to.*

"Ma'am." One of the bodyguards came toward me as I stumbled out.

"No." I swung my hand through the air. "Leave me alone."

The door...that's what I focused on, and the darkness that waited outside, darkness where I could disappear. I charged through as the automatic doors opened and was hit by a gust of wind so brutal it shoved me sideways. I tripped, fell, and was caught by strong, steady hands before I hit the ground.

"Xael?"

*No...no...*I wrenched my gaze up and stared at the one man I couldn't handle...not now. Not when my emotions were so close to the surface. But there I was, drowning, with his grip my only tether. "Don't touch me...*don't you dare.*"

Pain carved through his gaze. "Xael, *please...*"

"No." I yanked my arm from his hold. *"You fucking bastard!"* I screamed, then unleashed a wounded sound. One that ripped free from that roaring agony in my chest. I closed my eyes and pressed my fist against that hole he'd left behind, then opened my eyes once more and stumbled backwards.

Wounded.

We were both so fucking wounded. I dropped my gaze to his hand still hovering in the air. "I can't get you out of my head." I'd never said the words before, not out loud. But here I was, finding that flinch in his eyes. "Doesn't matter what I do. Doesn't matter who I fuck. My body...my body doesn't respond. Not like it did with you. I'm broken, Mateo. But I guess none of that matters, does it? Not as much as your fucking job...*YOUR FUCKING JOB!*"

Tears came, streaming down my cheeks. I could've died tonight...in fact, I wished I was dying because this...this was goddamn torture. I spun and lunged away.

"Xael!" he roared behind me.

But I wasn't stopping, wasn't slowing, wasn't looking into his eyes a second longer. I drove my boots into the ground and plunged into the darkness. But I didn't get far. The shadows had barely swallowed me before I was grabbed and lifted back.

"Let me go!" I kicked and howled.

But he was still there, pulling me against his strong, warm chest and I was so cold...so fucking cold.

"Easy...easy now, Xael," he murmured in my ear in that cool, dangerous tone, one that nearly brought me undone. "I'm not going to hurt you."

I barked a cruel laugh and punched out, driving my fist against that chest I'd once rested my head against. "You don't get it, do you? *You do hurt me, Mateo.*"

He froze, those dark, unflinching eyes fixed on my pain. He saw me more clearly than anyone had ever seen me before.

"I can't do this..." I shook my head. "I thought I could. But I can't. *I...can't.*" I shoved away. "I feel like I'm dying. This is death...this is my fucking death."

I turned away, but there was no running this time...there was only me leaving.

Only that agony I carried with me as I made my way toward my building. As I walked in the dark, I felt another presence, this one familiar. I glanced behind me, finding Rhys a few steps away, walking with me as we stepped around the back of our building.

He never said a word, just pressed his card to the scanner until the doors opened, leaving me to step into the glaring lights. "I want to leave," I announced, wiping away my tears. "I want to leave this goddamn island. I want to get the *fuck* out of here...tonight."

"Okay," he answered. "I'll make the arrangements."

I nodded as the elevator doors opened and I stepped inside. I was getting out of here. Far away from Mateo and far away from these assholes...*I couldn't fucking wait.* I rose higher, my body shaking and twitching as the doors opened and I strode toward my bedroom.

Ten minutes was all it took. The cold and the agony sobered me fast enough. I stared down at my packed bags and lifted my gaze, taking in the empty room. It'd be like I was never here...

I grabbed my suitcase and hauled it from the bed, letting the wheels hit the floor before I yanked it forward. I thought of stopping for a second, thought of saying goodbye to my weird roommate, but then I turned away, not wanting to spend a second longer in this place than I had to.

I was already gone as I stepped into the elevator.

Already in the air and far away from here.

All I needed was to get there.

Mateo

Go after her... the howl rose in my head as she strode away. *Fuck them... Fuck them all. Let Besnik come. Let them all come. I'd kill them. I'd wipe them from the face of this earth just to be free of them...to be free of this.* I clenched my fists as that darkness inside me grew.

The price was too great. But it wasn't just my price, was it?

It was hers.

Xael Davies, the one perfect fucking thing in my goddamn life.

Her hurt hit me a thousandfold and all of a sudden, I was back there in that apartment, staring at her while I tore her life apart.

"Sir." The call came from behind me.

I didn't want to turn. I didn't want to be the man they demanded me to be anymore. I wanted to be the man *she* needed me to be. The one who put her before everyone else, including my brother. I'd leave him behind if it came to her. I'd walk away and never look back.

Because my heart beat outside my chest...and right now it was running away, hating me all over again.

I can't get you out of my head, she cried inside mine.

I couldn't get her out of mine either. Or my dreams. Or my veins.

I'd tried...I really had, and if she hadn't turned up in that airport looking just as fucking wild and stunning as she always had, I might've been able to continue living this shadowed existence...for a little while longer, at least.

"The party, sir," the guard called, drawing me away from her.

I turned and took two steps, then glanced over my shoulder, finding her as she disappeared into the night. But as I turned back, I found her own bodyguard striding toward me.

"You piece of shit," he growled as he passed. "Just stay the fuck away from her."

But that was it, wasn't it? It didn't matter where I was, or where she was.

Something had changed inside me, intrinsically changed, all the way down to my DNA. I wanted to burn this all to the ground just to be with her. I lifted my gaze to the party that'd spilled out into the foyer of Bernardi's building and knew I couldn't stay away from her. Not a second longer.

That wounded sound that had torn from her lips filled my head. All I could see was that pain in her eyes and the way she'd pressed her fist to the agony in her chest. The agony that consumed her, just as it consumed me.

Get this over. I strode toward the building. Then I was done. I was done with the lying to her and myself, and I was done with staying away from her.

The wind howled, thrashing the palms outside the building as I stepped through the automatic doors and into the foyer.

"Commander?" one of the rich assholes called as they laughed and stumbled, slamming into the bodyguards who were there to protect them, but instead were fucking babysitters.

I stepped into the elevator and waited for the doors to close. *After this job, I'm done.* I folded my arms in front of my body. I'd leave this island...and take Xael Davies with me.

17

Xael

The howling gusts of wind slammed into the walls of the hangar, making them boom, shudder, and shake. I jerked my gaze toward the sound, my heart racing before turning back to my bodyguard.

Rhys stood in the distance, talking to the pilot. But there was a lot of head shaking and pointing toward the jet. I didn't need to hear what they were saying to understand what that meant. There was no way I was flying off this island tonight.

Rhys turned and headed toward me, his long, commanding strides closing the distance rapidly. "No go on the jet, the wind is too strong. There's no way they could get us in the air safely. "

I just stared at him, feeling mixture of sadness and desperation. The roar of the wind gusts made me feel even more panicked and desperate.

"Don't worry," he said as he pulled out his phone. "I'll make a call to the captain and get us on the boat out of here, okay?"

I just nodded, standing in front of our suitcases. But even as he lifted his phone and pressed the button to summon the caption of the boat, I knew it was hopeless. There was no way we were getting out of here. Not tonight...and by the way the winds were picking up, probably not even tomorrow. My phone rang and I looked down, expecting my father, but it was Finley Salvatore...and he never called. I answered it instantly. "Fin?"

"Where are you?" he asked, his voice hard and strange.

Screams echoed in the background, savage male screams, roaring of rage and retribution. I caught the sound of Lazarus Rossi...and someone else...someone I didn't know. "I'm at the hangar," I answered unhesitatingly. "What's going on?"

"I need...I need you to get here, can you do that, X?"

Panic spiked at the desperation in his voice. I was already moving, already leaving Rhys and our suitcases behind. "What's happened?"

"Kat and Anna have been attacked."

*Attacked? No...*I lunged to the door, bore down on the handle, and shoved. But the door didn't budge, locked in place by the force of the wind. I almost dropped my phone as I gripped the handle with both hands, fighting the gusts as I dropped my shoulder and drove my body forward, slamming into the metal door with all I had, and stumbled out.

No...not like Baldeon...not like him.

The door flew backwards, slamming against the side of the building with a *boom!* But the sound was quickly swallowed by the screaming wind. I dropped my head down and hurried, fighting my way forward, pressing the phone to my ear. "Are they alive?"

"What?" His words were muffled.

"Are they ALIVE!" I screamed.

"Yes," he answered carefully, as though he didn't understand what he was saying.

Fin was never *like this.*

"I need you to get here," he pleaded. "Can you do that?"

"Where are you?" I stumbled toward the buildings in the dark.

That unknown male voice howled in the background of the call, muffling Fin as he answered.

"Shut the fuck up!" Lazarus Rossi roared. *"I'm going to fucking KILL YOU!"*

"Fin!" I shouted. *"Where the fuck are you?"*

"I'm at Kat and Anna's. I didn't know what to do, X. I don't know..."

"I'm on my way, okay?" I lifted my gaze to Kat and Anna's building in the distance and drove myself forward.

"Xael!" My name was yelled behind me.

But I couldn't slow for Rhys now. I couldn't do anything but thrust my phone into my pocket and charge forward, praying to hell I wasn't too late.

My boots hit the ground hard, but my heart beat even harder as I charged around the rear of their building, my breaths burning like fire in my lungs. I shoved my hand into my pocket and wrenched out the card before slamming it against the scanner.

There were no bodyguards in the foyer. No men protecting the building at all that I could see.

This was bad...

Really...really bad.

The doors opened, letting me charge through.

"Xael, for fuck's sake!" my bodyguard roared as the building doors closed behind me. I lunged toward the elevator, slamming my fist on the button as Rhys pounded on the glass door. *"Xael! What the fuck is happening?"*

I shook my head, desperation still roaring in my ears like the wind. I didn't have time to answer as the doors opened behind me, leaving me to stumble in.

My legs were on fire, my breaths nothing more than harsh gasps. I gripped the railing as the elevator doors closed, listening to the foyer's doors open. But Rhys wasn't calling me anymore, or if he was...I couldn't hear him.

I rose, holding on for my life, until I came to a shuddering stop. The moment the door opened I could hear them. I staggered out, hearing the deep male moans. As I got closer and my vision cleared, I caught the faint splatter of blood across the tiled floor in the entrance, then saw Damon Zakharov lying on the floor, barely conscious.

The air was charged with danger...making the hairs on my arms rise as I stepped forward. Mateo wrenched his gaze to mine and in an instant, his eyes widened. "Xael?" He murmured and scowled, licking his lips and taking a step toward me. "What are you doing here?"

For a second, it sounded like he thought I was there for him. But I wasn't...I scanned the mess in the apartment, broken glass glinted on the floor, the sofa was shoved aside...the sofa where two women huddled.

"I called her," Fin explained, drawing my gaze.

I stepped around Mateo even as he spoke. "She shouldn't be here."

"I'm *exactly* where I need to be," I snapped. "You're lucky I'm here. I was trying to get off this damn island."

"You were what?" Mateo growled.

But I didn't answer. I didn't owe him a goddamn thing, least of all explanations of my future...instead, I nodded to Fin and hurried to where Anna and Kat sat hugging each other.

"Fucking bitch!" Zakharov roared.

"Get him the hell out of here!" the Commander snarled, sounding even more pissed off than he was a second ago.

"Hey there," I murmured, sitting beside Kat.

She just stared straight ahead, her gaze unmoving in that detached stare I'd seen so many times. *Too many times.* I licked my lips. "Kat." I glanced at Anna, who stared back at me looking like she'd just gone a couple of rounds with a boxer.

I didn't need a blow-by-blow explanation to know that whatever had gone down had been between Zakharov and Kat... with Anna coming to her friend's defense.

Anna's hair was a mess and there was a red handprint on her face, one left behind from a slap. I jerked my gaze to Zakharov as Mateo's men hauled him out of the apartment, dragging more than carrying him. "Just perfect!" I directed my anger at Mateo, fixing him with a savage stare. "So this is what happens here?"

"It wasn't the Commander," Kat answered, her tone cold and unfeeling as she lifted that shell-shocked stare to me. "It wasn't him."

"Do you want to tell me what happened?" I asked gently.

"The doctor is on the way," Mateo said calmly behind me. I closed my eyes at the careful tone, hating how I almost knew he wanted to say more.

I pulled away from that agony and instead directed myself to Kat. "How about I get you a drink of water?"

She gave a slight nod, causing me to rise and place my hand on Anna's shoulder as I passed. Whatever happened here had been bad, but it could've been much worse...especially if Anna hadn't been here.

I made my way into the kitchen and pulled the refrigerator door open, grabbing three bottles from inside before turning back. I hated how my gaze instantly went to him.

Mateo watched me like he was fucking wired...like he hadn't just ripped my heart out all over again tonight. I forced my gaze away and stepped around Fin and Lazarus as they paced the floor, looking like they wanted to finish what they'd started. I glanced at Fin's clean hands, then at Lazarus's bloody ones.

So, the Stidda Prince had become the knight in bloody armor...

I felt a tremble of happiness about that as I made my way back to Kat and sat back down, cracking the lid on the bottle and handing it to her, then one to Anna.

"I'll leave you to it, then." Sullen words came from Mateo.

Ones I didn't acknowledge before he turned and left.

"I'll leave you, too," Lazarus said as he dragged his bloody hand through his hair.

Kat lifted a panicked gaze his way...and I just knew...this was it for them. This was their moment...it'd either work out...or it'd die a slow, painful, horrible death.

"Anna," Fin called, drawing her gaze upwards. "Will I see you later?"

There was that look...*again*. Heat raced to my cheeks as I saw it in his eyes, reflected back at him in Anna's. I looked away, suddenly feeling so very fucking alone.

"Yes," she answered as I unscrewed the lid from my own water and took a long, slow swallow.

My cheeks were still burning as Rhys stepped into the entrance of the apartment, his gaze moving rapidly across the blood splatter until he met my gaze. Hard breaths made his chest rise as he looked from me, to Kat next to me, then to Anna.

The elevator door opened and he was already turning, his fists clenched, ready to protect. But he didn't need to...the island's doctor stepped forward, nodding to Rhys as he passed, directing his gaze to the three of us sitting on the sofa.

"We'll just leave, then," Fin muttered, and stepped away, pulling Lazarus with him.

And in an instant, we were alone. I rose from the sofa. "I'll let you have some time with the doctor."

I met Rhys' gaze and stepped closer.

"What the *hell* happened?" he growled.

"Fin called me...he was panicked and desperate."

"You should've said something, X." he grumbled, searching my eyes, then licked his lips and looked away.

"Our bags," I said, suddenly remembering them.

"Don't worry," he answered. "I had them taken care of. We won't be going anywhere, not in a hurry, at least. It looks like we have a damn cyclone headed our way. So no one is going anywhere for a while."

"Of course, we have," I muttered, unable to believe my luck.

But it didn't matter, not right now. I glanced over my shoulder at Kat and Anna as they spoke with the doctor. They needed me...so there was no way I could leave, not right now. All I had to do was stay the hell away from Mateo Ristani.

18

Mateo

I followed the men hauling that piece of shit out of the apartment, taking the elevator down and out of the building and making my way toward my own once more. My thoughts were frantic. Part of me wanted to take that scumbag Zakharov and put him in a cold, dark place where no one would ever find him after what he'd done, and another part of me was still reeling from Xael's words.

So she wanted to leave? Not that I could blame her.

Still, her words stung like a bitch. But no more than knowing I was the cause of her wanting to run in the first place. I focused on the screams that battled the wind as I strode through the foyer doors and out into the night.

"Get the fuck off me!" Zakharov yelled as he fought against my bodyguards as they dragged him to the infirmary.

But unlike his earlier targets, they weren't taking any of his shit.

"Walk...*or we'll fucking drag you,*" Score ordered, glaring him down.

And what do you know...the bastard stumbled forward, like a good little fucking rapist.

Assholes like Zakharov liked to hunt those who weren't meant to be hunted. He didn't go after men, nor did he expose his fucking intentions for the rest of us to see. No, lowlifes like Zakharov liked to target those who didn't stand a chance against them...and when he encountered one...like Katerina VanHalen, the sorry excuse for a human being drugged her.

He'd fucking drugged her.

No matter how hard I tried to keep her out of it, Xael's face slipped in. What if it'd been her Zakharov wanted? She was at the same party, could've easily caught his attention. *Christ.* I raked my fingers through my hair, my strides lengthening to catch up to the piece of shit as my men shoved him toward the front doors of my building.

If he'd gone after Xael, there was no way I'd stop.

I'd kill him.

Fast...slow...*fuck, I didn't give a shit.*

If he so much as looked at her fucking wrong, I'd take the sniveling worm out without hesitation. My pulse raced as those images filled my head. It was only because of Fin that Lazarus had stopped unleashing his rage on Zakharov.

He would've killed him...

And in any other situation, I'd've fucking let him.

As a man, I wanted beasts like him taken out. No questions. No debate.

Once a predator, Is a predator.

But as the overseer of the island and its fucking privileged occupants, I couldn't.

I had to be the one who kept them from killing each other. It was a fucking rule...

I stepped through the doors and listened to Zakharov start up again.

"Get your fucking hands off me!" he shouted, wrenching his arm from Score's grip. "You fucking touch me again and I'll have you goddamn killed."

"Oh, yeah?" Score settled that steely gaze on him, his lips curling in a sinister smile. "I'd like to see that happen."

Damon Zakharov had no idea who he was dealing with. Score wasn't just any goddamn former special forces soldier. He was a sniper of the highest fucking calibre. You didn't just threaten a man like that, you made a promise...a promise for him to end your fucking life.

Score shoved him once more, sending Zakharov stumbling into the infirmary entrance. The soft thud of boots hitting carpet became slaps against the hard tiled floor of the medical wing. I followed them as Score drove him into one of the rooms.

"Sit." Score pointed to a chair in the corner.

I stepped into the room and focused my gaze on the scumbag. Under the harsh lights, he looked even worse. Bright blood covered his face. One eye was already closed and the other one was closing. By morning, he wouldn't even be able to see. But it was his mouth that had taken most of the damage.

His bloody lips were split all to hell. Two front teeth were cracked. He looked at me wild and frantic as he sat on the seat...I had to hold myself back from smiling.

"So, you like to hurt women?" I stepped toward him as Score towered over him.

He flinched, his busted lips trying to curl. "Fuck you."

"Fuck me?" The desire to fucking end him hit me hard.

I licked my lips, envisioning someone like Damon Zakharov in all the many dark, foul places I'd seen over the years. All the squalors I'd encountered as a soldier where people like him hid. And all the houses where animals still held women hostage, beating and raping them. All because he couldn't have it any other way.

"You have to prove it," he continued. "It's my word against hers, and she's a goddamn slut." His eyes sparkled with rage.

I closed the distance with a lunge, grabbed him around the neck, and hauled him from the seat. "Let me ask this again...*do you like to drug and rape women?*"

Say no and I'll fucking end you.

Responsibility or not. Xael pushed inside my head. Her pain. Her rage. That tortured moan she'd made still fucking lived there. I didn't flinch, didn't look away, just stared into the vile fucking piece of shit's eyes and envisioned me finishing the job Lazarus had started.

"I only gave her what she wanted."

I drove him backwards until he slammed into the wall. His head rebounded with a *crack*. His mouth dropped open, exposing those cracked fucking teeth. My fingers clenched harder, driving into the flesh of his throat. All I wanted to do was to rip it out.

"Commander," Score cautioned.

Hard breaths consumed me. All I saw was Katerina's dazed expression, one I'd seen before in the eyes of a girl cowering in the corner of a filthy room. *Do it...it'd be easy. I could even make it look like a suicide, say he hung himself, say he was full of fucking regret.*

But there lay the problem.

Animals like Damon Zakharov were *never* full of regret. Just hunger. Just unquenchable desire to inflict as much pain and terror as they possibly could. No one would believe it...no one who truly knew him, that was.

I could see it all, see the blood, see the life draining out of him, and in that moment, I wanted it I wanted so bad that it scared me. But if I took his life, if I dug the pit just a little bit deeper, then there was never any getting out of this, was there? They'd never let me escape this fucking hell.

And right now, that's what I wanted.

I wanted out of this hell...and I wanted to take Xael Davies with me. I released my hold, and took a step backwards.

He coughed and spluttered, gasping, and grasped his throat. "What the fuck was that?"

"*That*, Zakharov, was me allowing you to live," I answered as his face turned from a shade of red to washed-out gray. "You'll stay in this room until the doctor sees you. And when he's finished, Score, here, will take you to a nice little room with a locked door until I can figure out what the fuck to do with you."

"You can't do that!" The savage spark flared back into his eyes as he took a step forward. "You can't keep me locked up here!"

I turned and strode to the door. "It's not just about *me* locking *you* in, Mr. Zakharov. You just made yourself two very powerful enemies tonight...good luck surviving until mornig."

Silence filled the room as I strode past Score. "Keep alert tonight. Call me if Mr. Salvatore or Mr. Rossi decide to pay Mr. Zakharov a visit."

"Will do, Commander," he answered with a nod.

I had no doubt in my mind they wouldn't think twice about not letting a piece of shit like Damon live. If they didn't come for him tonight, it'd be a miracle. Either way...Zakharov's days were numbered. I left them behind and headed back along the hallway before stopping outside the control room door.

I pressed my card against the scanner and stepped in, closing the door quietly behind me.

"I want to see you." The words drifted to me as I walked along the darkened hallway. "What do you mean, you want to leave? No...*what I meant was,* let me at least try to change your mind."

I slowed my steps as my mind put a face to the voice. Blake. That's who it was...a chill swept along my spine as I stepped out of the gloom and into the brighter glow of the monitors.

Blake jerked his gaze my way and for a second, I saw a flicker of fear in his eyes. *Fear...now that was interesting.*

"I gotta go," he muttered into his phone, meeting my gaze. "I'll talk to you when my shift's over. Just don't leave without seeing me, okay?"

I waited patiently as he finished, then glanced at the cell phone in his hand as he placed it on the desk. "Taking personal calls at work?"

"It was an emergency."

"I see..." I didn't look away. "I'm heading in for the night. I'd like the latest full weather report on my desk by morning. Of course, if anything worsens, by all means, call."

He just gave a nod, his jaw flexing as I turned, then stopped. "And Blake, don't let it happen again."

I left the control room feeling the heat of his gaze on the back of my neck and for the life of me, I couldn't remember how he'd come into my employ. He'd been vetted, that's all I remembered. I made a mental note to investigate tomorrow when the chaos died down as I stepped through the door and left that part of the building behind, heading for my own private quarters.

I pressed my card against the scanner and waited for the lock to disengage before I shoved the door open and made my way inside. I unbuttoned my jacket and shrugged out of it as I made my way into the apartment. This was home, as close as I had to anything stable...and a helluva lot nicer than anything I'd had growing up. I dropped my jacket over the back of the leather sofa and pulled off my holster before laying the gun on the kitchen counter.

Dinner was a glass of Scotch, not top label, but it'd do. I didn't have that kind of luxuries...not here, at least. I kept those for my place in the States...the one where I'd met Xael Davies. I poured and lifted the glass to my lips, my thoughts returning to her once more.

I'd *hated* leaving her behind tonight...hated the entire fucking incident from the moment she'd stumbled into me after leaving the party. I grabbed my phone from my pocket and pulled up the camera feeds of her apartment as I drank. The elevator doors opened as I flicked through the images. I swallowed and lowered my glass, watching her as she stepped out and made her way into her apartment...alone.

I scowled, pressed the button on the feed of her building, and caught her bodyguard wrestling with the suitcases. So she was serious about leaving. Without Fin's call, she might've already gone. I clenched my jaw at the thought of that.

I closed down the feed and found her number in my contacts. *Don't leave...the* words lingered on my lips. *Don't go anywhere, not without me.*

My fingers shook as I clenched the phone, desperate to say the words...but I couldn't. I dropped my head, feeling my shoulders sag under the weight. I couldn't call her, couldn't say the words. Not yet.

Beep.

I raised my head, finding a message from an Unknown number: *Got some interesting news about an Evan Valachi.*

I scowled as my phone rang a second later. "Yeah?" I answered.

"So, I tracked a Ms. Valachi down tonight," he started.

"Are you on the island?"

"No," he answered. "Which is why I'm calling you now. She's here on the mainland...in fact, she's about to get on a boat to come to you."

"That can't be right." I shook my head. "She's here on the island right now."

"You sure of that, brother?"

"What? Yes." I answered, as the urge to pull up the cameras wore at me.

But Edon didn't call for no reason and he wasn't one to play games. "If Evan Valachi is getting on a boat to come to the island, then who the hell is here?"

My phone gave a *beep*. I pulled it away and glanced at the number of the caller. What do you know...*Michele Valachi*...

"Edon, Michele Valachi's calling me."

"Careful, brother, a storm is coming...it's dark and savage...and it's calling your name."

I scowled at his words as the same chill I'd felt moments ago walking into the command center returned. "Will do," I answered and hung up the call.

"Mr. Valachi," I answered the next call.

"You have a goddamn imposter on the island, Mateo," he growled. "And the bitch tried to kill my goddamn daughter."

19

Xael

When I woke up the next day, I felt like hell. Something had hit me with the force of a truck during the night. My thoughts were slow as my eyes opened. I blinked, then moaned as I moved, rolling to reach and grab my phone from the nightstand to peer, bleary-eyed, at the time. "You gotta be shitting me," I mumbled out loud.

It was already early afternoon when I pushed myself up, dragged my gaze from the phone, and glanced out into the darkened, savage storm outside my window.

Those dark clouds from yesterday swirled around us. It looked like the cyclone that'd threatened the island was making its presence known. Great. I shoved the sheets aside and crawled out of bed before stumbling to the bathroom. The harsh light inside made me wince. I tugged my t-shirt free and slid my panties down before stepping into the shower and hitting the spray, waiting for the water to heat before I stepped under it.

The moment the water hit my skin, memories of the events of last night came rushing back, Kat, Anna, then Mateo, and my desperate attempt to get away from here.

I closed my eyes as the haunting image of Kat's empty stare came roaring back to me. *Jesus...*

I washed my hair as rage returned. I wanted to kill that fucker Zakharov, wanted to beat him more than Lazarus had...it was lucky Rossi had left him alive at all. If it hadn't been for Fin and Anna being there, I guarantee he wouldn't have.

No. The Rossis were a special breed, savage, dangerous, and fiercely loyal. A shiver of jealousy rose inside me as I poured conditioner on my hair, then rinsed, taking my time until I felt somewhat human. I knew Anna and Fin would be together, had known from that first night when the boat docked. I'd never seen him so obsessed before, never seen him so *consumed*. Christ, I wanted that.

I wanted a man who didn't give a fuck about anyone or anything else.

I wanted a man who wanted me above everything. Someone who was prepared to not just make his feelings known, but gave zero fucks about anyone else when he rammed it down everyone else's throat. Fin wanted Anna, and after how she'd acted around him last night, she wanted him, as well. But Lazarus and Kat had taken me by surprise.

And for a second there, I was scared for her.

Lazarus Rossi wasn't the kind of man you played with...neither was he one who you betrayed. I'd heard the rumors about the shooting and I'd seen him at Fin's mom's funeral. I'd also seen when they'd carried out that poor bastard he'd beaten almost to death, as well.

No, with a man like Lazarus, you stayed the hell away from him...unless you felt the same way.

Did she? Did Kat have feelings for the Stidda Prince? She went to his apartment, right? She wasn't the kind of woman who did that. I turned, hit the taps, and ended the spray. No, Kat wasn't a player, and she sure as hell didn't sleep around, no matter what shit Zakharov spewed. She wasn't...*like me?*

I flinched as I grabbed a towel and ran it over my body. God, I was tired of all this. Tired of hurting...tired of wanting, tired of searching for a way to stop myself from feeling that emptiness. Damien was a mistake. I knew that now, maybe I'd known it all along.

When I'd tried to get off the island, it wasn't just Mateo I was running away from. I was running from the desperate need in his eyes and the way he wanted me.

Doesn't matter what I do. Doesn't matter who I fuck. My body... my body doesn't respond. Not like it did with you. I'm broken, Mateo. But I guess none of that matters, does it? My own words came back to me in a rush as I dropped my towel to the floor.

Heat rushed to my cheeks. I shouldn't have told him that, shouldn't have let myself get so fucking vulnerable around him. I shouldn't have let myself feel...not about him. I strode into my bedroom, grabbed my phone from the bed, and sent a message to Damien.

We need to talk. Meet me in our classroom in Building Two?"

I didn't even shake when I sent the message, just strode to the closet and grabbed my jeans. My suitcase was lying open, the last few things inside, as though part of me was still desperate to run. That frantic hum resounded inside me and part of it was this...I glanced down to my phone. This terrible need to open old wounds...and the longer I stayed here around Mateo, the stronger that need became.

If I didn't stop this, and soon, I'd tear myself apart.

I shrugged on a t-shirt, then slid into my jacket before reaching for my boots.

Beep.

My phone drew my gaze.

Damien: I'm on my way.

I swallowed and made my way over to the bed to sit on the edge and pull my boots on. Damien thought he could change my mind about leaving, but the truth was, even if I was stuck here for only another damn day, I didn't want what he thought we had anymore. I stood up and pulled down my jacket before making my way out of my room.

Murmurs came from the room next to mine, low, monotone, like she was talking to someone on the phone. A chill coursed along my spine at the sound. Evan Valachi wasn't anything like I'd expected...she was unraveled and unhinged ... a total recluse who was fixated on Bruno Bernardi.

But it wasn't anything like Kat or Anna. There wasn't desire in her eyes when his name was mentioned, just a dangerous glint that made me wary. But he seemed to be obsessed with her, urging me to lie and promise to get the two of them together.

Arranged marriage or not, I didn't like them together, not one bit.

There was something about her that rubbed me the wrong way...something that made me fearful of her and Bruno ever getting together. Something that made me want to warn him away from her. But I had nothing concrete, nothing more than a feeling in my gut and the low murmurs that came from her bedroom.

I left the sound behind and made my way through the apartment, heading to the elevator. By the time I reached the foyer, I was buzzing with desperation.

Rhys lifted his gaze the moment I stepped out of the elevator. He was reclining on the sofa, his feet crossed at the ankles, and the TV remote in his hand as he flicked through the channels. "We going somewhere?" He shoved up from the seat.

"You don't need to come, I'm just heading to Building Two for a few minutes."

"You know the drill, X." He lifted the remote and switched off the TV. "There're only reports on the damn cyclone anyway. Enough to scare the pants off me if I'm honest, so this is a welcome distraction."

"You mean heading out into that cyclone?"

"Nah. This," he declared as he glanced out the large windows of the foyer, "this is just some heavy gusts. The real thing is a lot worse."

"Great," I muttered as he rose, grabbed his jacket, and slipped it on over his holster.

The truth was, I was glad for the company, and it wasn't just because of the wind.

"Ready when you are," he said as he motioned toward the door.

I tugged my jacket tight around me as I headed for the door. The wind knocked me backwards as I stepped out. Rhys grabbed my arm, steadying me, and with the touch, memories of last night came flooding back, bringing Mateo with them.

"I'm okay!" I yelled, fighting the roaring wind.

I lowered my head and drove my body forward, cutting around the side of the building and into the shelter of the nearest row of buildings. The gusts died down a little, leaving me to right myself as I hurried along the sidewalk and headed to the next row of buildings.

Halfway there, I caught movement in the corner of my eye. Mateo was headed across the grounds, coming from the main building. He lifted his head, and that brooding, pissed-off glare met mine before his eyes widened. *"Xael?"* my name was on his lips even though I couldn't hear the sound.

He glanced behind me to Rhys, and scowled.

Fuck him...

Fuck you! That's what I wanted to mouth back, but I couldn't find the rage, not in that moment. Instead, I tore my gaze away, focused on the building in from of me, and quickened my strides.

By the time I slammed my card against the scanner of the door and pushed in, my ears were ringing from the wind. "Jesus," I gasped as Rhys charged in behind me.

"That was a helluva lot stronger than I expected," he muttered.

I jerked a look over my shoulder. "You think?"

He shivered, adjusted his jacket, and looked around. "There's no one here, X."

"I'm just going to one of the classrooms." I pointed to the hall-way. "Down there, so you can wait out here."

"X..." he warned.

"There's one way in and one way out, Rhys," I snapped. "A little space, yeah?"

The need for space was choking, like a noose around my throat. It was bad enough I needed a damn babysitter, but to watch me every second of the day...it was humiliating.

"Okay, X," he muttered, stepping closer to touch my arm. "I'll be right here if you need me."

My cheeks burned, but it wasn't just from the wind. It was because of this...*all of this*. Desperation filled me as I stepped toward the hallway, making my way to the classroom where we'd found ourselves before. I lifted my gaze as I turned the corner, finding the door cracked open and the lights still off inside.

Damien thought this was more than it was.

But it wasn't...

"There she is," Damien murmured, leaning against a desk in the front row.

He pushed off, striding toward me before I held up my hand. "Damien, wait."

"Wait?" He grabbed, pulling me close. "Wait for what?"

I lifted my gaze to his. He was a nice-looking guy, but excitable, like a love-sick puppy.

And that was just it.

"Stop." I pulled away when he tried to kiss me. "I didn't come here for that."

He scowled and dropped his hands. "Then what the fuck *did* you come here for?"

I swallowed hard, my heart racing. "I came here to tell you this...whatever this was, is over."

There was a flicker of something in his eyes. I looked away, desperate to hold onto the strength. "This is just a bad idea."

"No..." he urged, his voice low and careful. "No, it isn't."

"Yes." I jerked my gaze to his. "Yes, it is and I'm sorry, but it's over. Look," I licked my lips, searching for a way to make this easier. "It's not you, it's me."

He let out a hard bark. "I hear that a lot."

"This time it's true." I took a step and reached out to touch his arm, but he was stiff, unflinching.

"It's him, isn't it?" he said slowly. "The Commander."

I swallowed hard, the thunder of my pulse booming in my head. "No," I lied, and shook my head.

"Liar." The word was a hiss.

That same chill found me again, snaking its way along my spine. "It doesn't matter—"

"You'll regret it."

I scowled, anger rising to the surface. "What's that supposed to mean?"

"If you're so fucking smart, then you figure it out," he spat, striding past me.

He punched out his fist, driving it against the door. It slammed open with a *bang!* Then he was gone.

Jesus. A shudder tore through me...but behind it came that weightless feeling of relief. I waited for a moment before I turned and made my way back to the foyer where Rhys waited. By the time I got there, I was shaking.

20

Mateo

"So let me get this straight." Adrian Bernardi leaned forward on his desk and stared straight into the camera. "You can't track down the bastards who murdered one of our own, nor can you put the damn island on lockdown?"

I licked my lips and tried to remember to breathe. "At this time, no. Until our personnel levels are replenished, we just don't have enough guards."

"Then *get them*," Bernardi growled.

Four goddamn hours I'd wasted in these bullshit meetings. Four hours of explaining myself, the lack of enough security, and mother nature, and now I had a fucking crazed psycho impersonating one of the heirs. How the hell could I control anything?

"Adrian." Michele Valachi murmured, drawing my gaze. "I understand you're furious, but let's hear what Mateo is proposing."

Rage sparkled in the old man's eyes as he turned back to me. I was still reeling after his damn phone call, the one where he told me what had happened to his daughter, *his real daughter.* The one who'd been stabbed and left for dead in an underground bunker so the bitch who did it could take her place. Christ, this was *such* a goddamn mess.

I glanced at the camera. "We condense the security and have three buildings with each floor occupied. The remaining guards will be divided evenly, utilizing the private security for the heirs of the Commission, of course."

There was a twitch of Adrian Bernardi's lips. "So, your idea is a backpacker-hostel type scenario?"

I shifted in my seat. "Until we get reinforcements, yes."

"And when will that be?" Michele cut in.

"Three days, four at the most," I answered. "I've sent a request for a team of mercenaries."

"Three days, and until then, we have no protection."

"You have me and the island's security force." My voice deepened as I glared into the camera.

"There's no sense in bitching about what *should be done,*" Lazarus Rossi muttered, leaning against the desk in the same conference room.

"Hear, hear," I muttered.

"What I mean to say is, we're not fucking useless here. Bruno and I," Lazarus continued, shoving away from the desk and striding forward until he stood directly in front of the camera, "Evan, Alexi, and Ms. Ivanov are trained to protect ourselves. So we're better utilized combining forces. It's why we're here after all, isn't it? Make alliances…be an ally. What better time to do that than right now?"

There was silence.

Uncomfortable silence.

"We're under attack here." He leaned forward, glaring into the camera. "And we *need* to attack back. The best way to do that is to protect ourselves, gather our forces, and plan our attack. The Commander here is the best man for the job."

A twitch came at the corner of my mouth…*well, what do you know. The Stidda Prince had some balls.*

"You're right," Adrian muttered with a nod. Was there a hint of pride in his eyes? Fuck. He leaned backwards. "Get it done, Commander. I expect a full briefing as soon as your men arrive in Mauritius."

"Will do," I answered, and reached for the camera. "Gentleman." I ended the call before turning to Lazarus. "Thanks for having my back there."

"I didn't," he said as he turned to me. "It was the only logical step. But be warned, Commander, one more fuckup…one more attack, and I'll come for your fucking job."

The smile died on my lips. *Fucking punk…*

He left, closing the door with a *bang* behind him. I leaned forward, gripping the edge of the desk. He had no fucking idea. I clenched my jaw and closed my eyes as desperation rose inside me. Not three fucking rooms away was a woman with a goddamn stab wound to the stomach, desperate for revenge on the bitch who'd stabbed her.

But the question was, why...why try to kill Evan Valachi the day before she was due to arrive on the island...and why the hell did the imposter want to be here? I wanted to question her, wanted to tear the truth from her fucking throat, but my goddamn hands were tied...even more than they had been before.

I opened my eyes, shoved away from the desk, and strode toward the door. That coiled viper in my gut hissed and writhed. It was more than the psycho bitch and Baldeon's murder fueling this dread inside me. And it was more than the damn weather.

A storm is coming, brother...my brother's words returned as I stepped out of the conference room and headed for the front door of the building. I wanted to check on each team of guards, wanted to see for myself that the place wasn't going to fucking Hell.

Because that's how it felt.

Control was slipping through my fingers and that storm my brother had spoken of felt like it was bearing down on me. The brutal gusts hit me the moment I stepped out. Two of my men followed behind me as I lowered my head and strode across the grounds, until that viper inside lifted its head and its slitted black eyes blinked at me.

I jerked my gaze up, finding Xael hurrying along the sidewalk, heading toward the building. *What the fuck was she doing out in this?* I glanced behind her to her bodyguard, who just looked at me with that savage glare that said *back the fuck off*.

Then she was gone, disappearing through the door of Building Two. *I didn't like her out here...*

I fought the need to follow her. Instead, I made my way toward the back of the island to her own building. The fake Evan hadn't come with her own bodyguards and at first that had seemed strange. Now it all made perfect sense.

She was a fucking murderous liar.

That chill snaked its way along my spine, sending goosebumps across my skin. I glanced over my shoulder, found the door had swung shut after Xael, and pushed down the need to follow her again. She was fine, safe...her bodyguard was watching over her and for all intents and purposes, she didn't fucking want me.

Not after what I'd done.

I shoved aside the hunger and strode toward her building, catching sight of one of the new guards assigned to keep watch over them. He lifted his gaze as I pressed my card to the scanner and stepped through the doors.

"Commander." He stepped forward, scowling. "Everything okay?"

They didn't know about our little psycho situation. No one did, apart from myself, Michele Valachi, and the real Evan, who was at this moment holed up in an apartment not far from my own. Not even Bruno Bernardi knew of the psycho breathing down his neck.

The real Evan wanted it that way, until she was able to make contact. I lifted my gaze to the bodyguard and shook my head. "Yes. Any problems?"

"No, sir. Ms. Davies and her personal detail just left. Ms. Valachi is upstairs."

"Good. Call if there're any issues."

My phone vibrated. I looked down and found Laz's body-guard's name splashed across the screen. What now?

I answered the call. "Logan?"

"Katerina VanHalen's missing."

My gut clenched and that eerie feeling came rushing back, only this time with a vengeance. "What do you mean, missing?"

"I mean there are two guards here telling us they're assigned to Kat and they sure as hell aren't the ones she left with."

There's a storm coming, brother.

Edon's words rose in my mind. "I'm on my way."

I ended the call and pulled up the cameras on the island, left Xael's building behind, and hurried out. One scroll of the counter and I rewound the CCTV footage of her foyer, watching as Katerina VanHalen left with two men who weren't mine. The longer I watched, the more anxious I became.

She was jumpy...watching them.

They weren't my guys...*they weren't my guys*...that warning in my gut grew louder as I lengthened my stride. By the time I plunged headlong into the powerful gusts of wind, I was running.

I slammed my boots into the ground, and as I ran, something else roared to the surface.

Xael...

What if they had her, too?

I yanked up my phone, punching Xael's number as I drove myself toward Kat's building. It rang and rang and rang...

"Hey, you've reached Xael—"

"Fuck!" I roared and ended it, then called it again. "Answer...*answer, goddammit!"*

She'd been out there...striding across the grounds. She'd seemed all alone. My mind went to her bodyguard. If he'd hurt her, I'd fucking kill him. I'd rip out his fucking eyes, I'd mutilate his goddamn body, I'd do what they'd done to my brother.

"Commander!" my guards bellowed behind me.

But I couldn't answer as Laz tore out of his building.

"Laz?" I barked, seeing Freddy and Logan on his heels.

"Where the fuck is she?" Lazarus roared.

I snagged his arm as Logan rushed in behind, grabbing him as he swung his fist at me.

"Hey...*hey!"* I shook the punk. "I'm trying to help here."

Hard breaths consumed the out-of-control heir as he glared at me. I lifted the phone, showing him the screen paused on the two guards. "Those men...they're not mine."

"What the fuck do you mean, they weren't your men?" Lazarus barked.

I just stared at the men on the screen. "They aren't mine," I repeated, and lifted my gaze to his. "I know every man in my employ and those men...they're not mine."

Panic howled like a madman inside me as I turned to my second. *"Get the island shut down! I want every camera checked and every building searched. Find her...find Katerina VanHalen!"*

I turned from them, unable to stop the terror from unleashing a second longer.

Xael…Xael was out there…Xael…and her one fucking bodyguard.

If we were under attack…

"MATEO!" Lazarus screamed behind me. *"Where the fuck are you going?"*

I couldn't stay…not knowing she was out there. I needed my gun…*I needed her!*

I yanked my phone up and stabbed her number again as I hauled ass toward Building Two. *"Answer, for fuck's sake!"* I yelled at the phone as the call rang.

But it rang, and rang, and rang.

But there was no answer.

As I ran, that unmerciful howling in my head only grew louder until I slammed my card against the scanner and punched through the door of Building Two. *"Xael!"* I screamed and her name rebounded. *"XAEL!"*

I charged along the hallway, the thunder of my pulse booming in my head. I didn't unravel like this…*not for anyone.*

But Xael wasn't just anyone, was she? The door to a classroom was open, but the lights were off. Instinct drove me through the door, only to find the room empty. She wasn't here…*she wasn't here.*

In my head, it wasn't Baldeon's face who stared blankly up at me.

It was hers.

Hers because I'd failed her. Hers because when they came for me, they wouldn't just come to kill.

They'd come to destroy.

I left the classroom behind and raced along the hallway once more, unable to control the chaos swirling inside me. I had to find her...and when I did...all bets were off. She was mine...

21

Xael

It was a mistake. The thought resounded as I stood at the edge of the water and lifted my gaze to the swirling dark gray clouds above me. *So why the fuck do I keep doing this?* Hate circled me, just like the storm above.

"You okay?" Rhys asked behind me.

I just nodded as my phone went *beep*. I didn't want to look down...I knew exactly who it was...*it was him...Mateo.* "I wish I'd never come here," I muttered as I turned and strode past Rhys. "Biggest mistake of my goddamn life."

"I agree." He added, turning to walk behind me, "You need to stay away from him, X."

"Tell me something I don't know." I exhaled hard and slow. "It's over anyway. I told him today."

"I'm not talking about the control room guard."

I stopped walking, and turned. "What?"

Panic raced inside me. There was no way Rhys knew about Mateo. No one diI.

He scowled, then took a step closer. "You know who I'm talking about, X. A man like Mateo Ristani is dangerous."

"I..." I started as he shook his head...and my phone vibrated once more. He looked down, at *Mateo* splashed across the screen, and all the panicked thoughts rushed to burn my cheeks. "It's over...a long time ago."

"Nothing is over when it comes to Mateo, not until he decides it is...and by the looks of that, he hasn't decided it is."

I hit the button on my phone, sending the call to voicemail. Anger replaced embarrassment. I didn't know why I was so fucking upset. It wasn't like he could rip my heart out all over again. I stared into Rhys' eyes, and it hit me.

To be broken in front of Mateo was one thing...

But for everyone else to know about it was Ir.

"How long have you known?"

He gave a shrug. "About the same time your father did, I guess."

I flinched at the words and stumbled backwards with another savage gust. My hair lashed my face as I shook my head, and my phone vibrated. I was ready to hurl it into the ocean. Ready to hurl myself there, as well, and paddle my ass back to Mauritius if it came to that; cyclone and sharks be damned.

There was something broken inside me, some sick need to torture myself at every opportunity. I knew that as I glanced at the screen, expecting to see Mateo's name...but it wasn't...it was Fin's.

"Jesus Christ, not again. I answered the call. "Don't tell me Lazarus has actually killed the moth—"

"*Kat...*" Fin roared. "*Have you seen Kat?*"

"What? No...what's going on?" A terrible sinking feeling swept through me as Rhys looked down at his phone.

I'd never seen him pale before, never seen him so visibly shaken as he was now. He pulled out his gun and strode forward. "X, we're moving...*now!*"

"We think she's been taken," Fin's voice shook as he answered my question.

"Taken?" I hurried, letting Rhys practically drag me toward our building. "What do you mean *taken*, Fin?"

"She was seen leaving with two bodyguards, but they weren't the Commander's."

A cold shiver tore through me as I stumbled, racing up the sandy embankment to the grassy area and along behind the buildings to mine.

"We have to find her," I cried as I strode forward. "We have to find her, Fin!"

"The Commander is making a plan now," Fin answered as my phone *beeped* with another incoming call. I pulled it away, finding Mateo's number on the screen once more.

"I gotta go, call me if you find out more," I directed.

"Will do." He hung up, leaving me to answer the one call I didn't want to.

"Mateo—"

"Where the FUCK are you, Xael?" he roared through the line, sounding like a man possessed.

I flinched at the outburst. "Heading toward my building."

"Thank fucking Christ," he moaned as though he was in pain. "Thank Christ. Get to your building. I have another man on his way now. Get there, and don't fucking move from there...you understand me, Xael? Don't. Fucking. Move."

He sounded like a man obsessed.

A man unhinged.

Why the fuck would he care?

I ran with Rhys as he slammed his card against the scanner and shoved me inside the instant the doors opened. "Elevator!" he shouted, lifting his gun to scan the space, lingering on the stairwell door.

Stunned, I did as he told me, hitting the button and waiting while my heart thundered. Rhys spun, aiming his gun on movement as another guard ran toward us, gun in one hand and his ID in the other.

"Mateo sent him!" I barked as the elevator doors opened behind me.

But Rhys wasn't lowering his gun as the guard strode through the doors.

"Easy." The Commander's man lifted his hand. "I'm here to help."

"Rhys," I called, watching as my bodyguard scanned him, then slowly lowered his piece.

"What the fuck is going on?" Rhys snapped as they headed my way, following me into the elevator.

"No one knows. We're scanning footage of the island, but no one can find Ms. VanHalen."

"Jesus." I wrapped my arms around myself as the doors closed and carried us upwards.

But by the time it stopped at our floor, I could hardly walk. Rhys moved in, grabbing my arm and holding me steady as we strode into the apartment. They checked the rooms, finding Evan's empty, then returned.

Shocked. Stunned. We looked at each other, unable to say a word as the winds howled outside the window. They had to find Kat...*they* had *to find her*. "She has to be here, right?" My words grew thick and hoarse as tears pricked my eyes. "She *has* to be."

"Hey." Rhys strode forward, grabbed my shoulders and pulled me close. "They'll find her, okay? They'll find her, and then, as soon as this fucking cyclone is gone, we're getting the hell off this island."

I nodded as one lone tear spilled free.

He pulled away after a while, strode to the kitchen, and hit the button for the coffee machine. We waited like that for what seemed like hours. The Commander's man answered his phone, turning away to mutter, "Yes, sir. She's here and safe. Yes, sir, I will...*I understand*."

Even from where I stood on the other side of the living room, I could hear Mateo's rage. The guard flinched, then swallowed hard before slowly lifting his gaze to me. I saw it then, saw it in his eyes, saw the moment he narrowed in on me.

"Everything okay?" Rhys asked as he carried a mug of steaming coffee toward me.

"Fine," the bodyguard answered carefully, never once shifting his gaze from me.

Dark clouds choked out any light outside, and as I drank two cups of coffee and paced a line in the tiles along the living room, desperately waiting for any news, I realized the afternoon was leaving us.

Night would come soon...

And Kat still hadn't been found.

"Is there any news?" I lifted my gaze to Rhys, who just stared out the window, his gun still in his hand.

"You asked me the same thing five minutes ago."

"I can't just do nothing." I shook my head, the need to do *something* howling inside me. "I need to..."

Beep.

I looked down.

Finley: Fuck standing around, we're searching buildings, you in?

"Fuck, yes," I barked, punched in a reply, and strode toward my room.

"Where the hell are you going?" Rhys demanded.

"*Searching buildings with the others,*" I snapped as I stepped into my closet and opened my safe. I yanked on my shoulder holsters, then drew out my two Barettas and slipped them into place.

"*Like hell you are,*" Rhys growled from the doorway.

I pushed past him. "Like hell I'm not. I'm not some fucking princess, Rhys. So you're either with me, or against me. Either way, this is happening."

"Xael...*for fuck's sake!*" he snarled behind me.

It wasn't the first time he'd said those words...and I doubted it would be the last. Still, I headed for the elevator and stopped before pressing the button to look over my shoulder. "Are you coming?"

His lips curled, then moved as he muttered, cursing me out. But Rhys was loyal to the core, so along with him and my new babysitter, I made my way to Kat's building.

There was a small crowd by the time we got there and night was closing in, making it hard to search. Lights flickered and danced above us as I stepped into the foyer and met Fin's gaze.

Anna was there, her cheeks shining with fresh tears. He had one arm around her, holding her close as the foyer filled with others from the island, guards and heirs, cooks and rich fucks who'd put everything else aside to find one of our own. Our determination and savage desperation howled like the cyclone bearing down on us.

I strode through the doors to Lazarus's building as he strode through the foyer headed my way. "Take buildings one through five, I'll take six through eleven."

"Laz, no," his bodyguard, Freddy, protested behind him. "This could be a fucking setup. You can't go on your own."

I strode forward, meeting Lazarus's gaze, and answered. "He won't be on his own."

Behind him, Mateo lifted his head, those savage, brooding eyes fixed on me. My breath caught as a charge of power tore through me and in that moment, I didn't know if I should be turned on or terrified...because I was a little of both.

"We search together," Bruno muttered as he followed me into the foyer. "That okay with you?"

"Yeah," I responded. Logan glanced at my holsters and his eyes glittered with stark appreciation. They'd forgotten who I was... maybe it was time to remind them.

"Okay then." I met Lazarus's glare and motioned toward the stairwell door. "When you're ready, sweetheart."

"I'll take the stairs," Lazarus commanded. "You take the elevator."

I shook my head...*men,* and headed for the stairwell door.

"I told you—" Lazarus started.

I stopped in an instant and glanced over my shoulder, my gaze finding Mateo's intense stare before I snapped at Lazarus. "Let's get one thing straight, Rossi. Be worried all you want, but don't be a dick, 'kay? We're not Freddy or Logan. We don't take orders from you."

With my heart in the back of my throat, I pushed past him and climbed the stairs. By the time I reached the top, I was frantic. *"Kat!"* I screamed. *"Kat, can you hear me?"*

She had to be here. Probably knocked out somewhere...somewhere they'd left her. All we had to do to find her was search every goddamn room and every goddamn building. We'd search until we found her, it was as simple as that. *"KAT!"* I screamed.

Bruno came with me and we strode to the far end of the empty apartment and started searching. I pulled out a gun and stepped into the darkness. But I left nothing to chance, flicking on every light as I searched bathrooms, closets, and living rooms before turning around to find Bruno.

"Let's go." He gave a jerk of his head. We had a lot of ground to cover, and it was almost dark. Lazarus and Logan searched the other apartment on that floor before yanking open the stairwell door.

I followed Bruno down to the next floor, with Rhys close behind, and searched all over again. Every room that came up empty made the desperation inside me grow.

"Kat!" I screamed her name. *"Katerina!"*

Lazarus growled at that name, until his cell vibrated. "Yeah?" he answered, then scowled. "I'm on my way."

I glanced over my shoulder, as did Bernardi.

"They think they found something," Lazarus said as he ended the call.

"Oh, thank fucking God," I moaned, relief flooding through me for a second before I realized Lazarus wasn't happy at the news.

"I'm heading to the command center." He hurried down the stairs.

"Wait." I surged forward. "I'm coming too."

I followed him, leaving his building behind. He wasn't excited...*why wasn't he excited?* That chill snuffed out the surge of excitement inside me as we hit the foyer floor and charged through the doors out into the night once more.

I holstered my weapon, knowing Rhys was right beside me, scanning the dark. "We have to find her." My words were snatched from my lips. Still I felt an ache, one that thrummed inside my chest.

They weren't the Commander's men...

The words resounded as we hurried across the grounds to the main building. If they weren't the Commander's men, then whose men were they? Logan lengthened his stride, slammed his card against the scanner outside the main doors, and waited for us to enter before he followed.

The thud of our boots mingled with the sound in my chest, that panicked thunder skipping and surging as we headed along the hallway to the command center. *The command center, where Damien worked...*

"Shit." I suddenly slowed, causing Rhys to plough into the back of me.

"What?" He jerked his gaze around, then met my gaze.

His gun was already rising at some threat he thought I saw. But the threat wasn't the one he thought of, and it wasn't out in the howling winds, ready to descend...

It was in there...the control room.

Rhys lifted his gaze, his scowl deepening as he glanced at the door where the others were headed. "I'll be at your side," he declared as though he finally understood.

I forced myself to keep moving, following the others as they stopped at the control room door, scanned a card against the lock, opened the door, and stepped in. I swallowed hard and followed them through the door into a darkened hallway.

The hum of electronic equipment danced over my skin. I could say that was the reason the hairs on my arms stood on end, but it wasn't...it was him. *Both of them...*

I stepped around the end of the hallway and into an expansive room. Banks of monitors sat against the walls with screens as big as TVs and just as bright. I swallowed and moved closer, drawn by the images racing backwards, then glanced at the man behind the desk...and flinched.

"I want the shoreline searched first," Mateo commanded, standing behind Damien. "Then once were certain she hasn't been taken, we can work our way back from there."

I stepped closer, catching the movement as Damien turned his gaze to me.

You'll be sorry...

His words resounded as he met my gaze.

All of a sudden time seemed to stand still.

Cold. That's how he looked at me. *Cold...detached.* He hated me after what I'd done to him...and he had every right. Mateo followed his gaze and my heart hammered at the movement. I couldn't feel more tortured with the two of them standing there, both pinning me with their gazes.

Until Damien turned his head and looked back at the screens.

But Mateo kept staring, his frown cutting deeper the longer he stared, until I was the one who looked away.

"There." Logan pointed at a screen. "Play that back."

Damien leaned closer, using the controls to rewind the footage, then pressed *play*. On the screen, two men hauled Kat's limp body down the beach and into a waiting dinghy that'd been beached.

"No..." Lazarus growled, and took a step forward.

His breaths were hard and fast, his hands fisted at his sides as the temperature in the room suddenly plunged. A moan tore from my lips as I watched them cast her body into the boat before jumping in and taking off.

She didn't even move...

Not one flinch.

Not one effort to fight.

"Track them!" Lazarus roared. *"Where the fuck did they go?"*

"I can't." Damien changed cameras and zoomed in, but each time he did, we still couldn't see any further out to sea.

"The mainland." Logan took a step backwards and glanced at Lazarus. "It's the only possible destination."

"I agree." Mateo glared at Logan. "I'll have men search the marina."

"That's *not good enough.*" Lazarus forced the words through clenched teeth before he added coldly. "I'm going."

"Have a man ready on the boat in five minutes," Logan ordered, stepping backwards as Lazarus lunged for the hallway. "We're going after her."

22

Mateo

Fuck!

This can't be happening. I yanked out my phone and pulled up the number of one of the cruiser's captains.

"Commander?" he answered.

"We have a problem. Get down to the boat and have it ready to go to the mainland in five minutes." I lifted my gaze, listening to the *boom* of the door as it slammed shut. "Someone's been kidnapped."

"*What?!* Jesus," he groaned. "I'm on my way."

I lifted my gaze to her as I ended the call. She just glanced at me nervously, then looked away...at the guard sitting in front of the monitors. But she didn't look at him the way she looked at me. She just flinched, swallowed hard, then turned, mumbling something under her breath before she walked away.

Oh, fucking no, she didn't.

The desperation returned, dragged from those moments when I'd thought she was in danger. I'd been fractured in those moments...shattered and no longer me. *I'd been the Komandant,*that same man who'd come for those who'd harmed mine.

I'd murder the world just to make sure she was safe.

And as I listened to the thud of her steps, that desperation rose inside me.

"Commander..." Damien called from behind the desk.

But I left him behind and went after her, striding along the hallway and yanking open the door. She was already hurrying, she and her damn bodyguard. *But she couldn't run forever.* I knew this was bad...knew this was the kind of moment there was no coming back from.

But I'd fucked up the first one...

I'd broken her damn heart, and mine, and I wasn't about to make that same mistake again. The swoosh of the automatic doors sounded. Xael was a blur through the windows, streaking through the night. I picked up my pace, hit the doors, and strode out of the foyer. *"Xael!"*

She shot a panicked look over her shoulder. That was all it took to trigger that hunger inside me...the one what screamed her name. I lunged, slamming my boots into the ground. A damn woman had been kidnapped, Katerina VanHalen of all people, and yet here I was, unable to think about anyone but Xael.

I had to have her...

"Xael, for fuck's sake," I roared, and clenched my fists.

Her bodyguard slowed and turned to me. He wanted a piece of me, wanted to keep me far away from her. He was smart. But I wasn't. I was beyond being smart now...beyond playing it safe. Because she wasn't...when she wasn't with me.

I lifted my hand and pierced him with a savage glare. "I'm not going to hurt her, so stay the fuck out of this."

I saw the moment he thought about making his move, and saw that he knew it'd be his last. I lifted my gaze to her as she ran. I wasn't going to hurt her...*I wasn't...*

Then her bodyguard stepped to the side and muttered something about he hoped she'd shoot me. Then I was lunging, driving my body through the winds as I ran after her. I caught her at the edge of her building. Fuck, she was fast...*faster than I'd expected.*

Her black hair lashed the air behind her, skimming my hand as I grabbed her shoulder. "Xael! *STOP!*"

She did, shoving her hand out as momentum and the heavy gusts caught her, sending her against the wall. Instinct took over, punching my hand out to cushion the impact of her shoulder against the wall...and all of a sudden, I was back in that moment when I'd lunged through the doorway of my apartment on the mainland and caught Xael waiting for me, barely clothed and looking defiant.

But it wasn't just defiance I saw as she spun and hit her back against the wall of the building. *"WHAT?"* she screamed, her eyes full of disgust and hate.

Was that for me?

Did she hate me...

Either way, I couldn't stop the words from tearing from that savage desperation inside me. *"Get to my fucking office, Xael...now."*

She froze for a second...*stunned.* "Why?" She lashed out, driving her fists against my shoulders. "So you can humiliate me some more?"

I grabbed her hand when she hit again, my fingers wrapping around her wrist as I shoved one hand against the wall beside her head. I wasn't as gentle as I wanted...this wasn't what she deserved. My phone vibrated in my pocket. Chaos was about to descend on this island...even more than the cyclonic winds could unleash. But I had to have her...I had to keep myself from unraveling.

I swallowed hard and stared into her eyes. She wasn't scared of me, she'd *never been scared of me.* Even as I stood there at that window at the gala and caught her as she helped herself to my single malt Laphroaig she didn't even flinch.

"You want to break my fucking heart all over again?" she growled, baring her teeth in a snarl.

Fuck...me....

My heartbeat was deafening in my ears. The phone was dancing against my thigh for the third fucking time. Everything was falling apart, *everything but her.* "Office...now." I forced the words through clenched teeth as my phone *beeped again.* "I'll be there in five minutes. You don't want to know what will happen to you if you're not there when I get there, Xael."

Then I shoved away from the building, turned, and walked away.

23

Xael

Get to his office?

I sucked in the rain filled air and tried to remember how to breathe as Mateo walked away, shoving his hand into his pocket and pulling out his phone.

Get...to his office?

Why, so he could berate me about Damien? He'd seen...he'd seen something, that I knew. He'd seen the moment Damien saw me...a man like Mateo missed nothing. But it wasn't rage I'd felt from him just now. It was something else.

Something darker.

Something far more dangerous.

"X...you okay?" Rhys glanced over his shoulder as Mateo disappeared into the night. "Did he...did he hurt you?"

I just shook my head and met his gaze. *Physically? He only meant physically...because the man who'd just walked away* from me had caused maximum damage to my heart, the kind no one else saw. "No," I answered. "No, he didn't."

"What the fuck did he want?" he pushed.

Boom...

Boom...

Boom...

My pulse was deafening, drowning out Rhys' words as he spoke to me. "What?" I shifted my focus to him.

"I said...*he's dangerous*," he repeated, scowling, then he stilled. "But I guess you already knew that."

Five minutes, Xael...you don't want to know what will happen to you if you're not there when I get there...

A shiver tore through me. That was the problem, wasn't it? That was that sickness inside me, because I did want to know what'd happen if I wasn't there.

I wanted to know very much.

But I wanted to know what'd happen if I was there even more.

I swallowed hard and pushed off the wall, taking a step.

"X, no..." Rhys shook his head. "I've watched you fucking tear yourself apart this last year, watched how you made stupid fucking decisions. You go after him, and it's going to be just another stupid decision, it's going to be the end of everything good you have going for yourself."

"You don't know that," I muttered as a flare of panic rippled through me.

But I did...I *knew* that.

"A man like Mateo won't stop until he consumes and destroys."

I flinched at the darkness of his tone, but it didn't matter what my mind was saying...not anymore. My soul was in the driver's seat now, and it knew what it wanted...*him.*

"I understand," I answered, but I was already walking.

Already leaving him behind as I made my way back across the grounds once more, I didn't feel the wind as I headed toward the main building. I didn't feel anything at all other than the thrumming in my veins and that desperate need be with him once more.

I hurried, tearing through the automatic doors. I could hear him, his deep growl coming from the open door in the conference room. And I wanted more than anything to push that door open and find him. But Kat was missing, and I wanted him to find her more than I wanted him to be with me.

I stepped past the open door, dragging my gaze to the end of the hallway. The distance his office door was cracked open, had he left it open for me? I knew the answer deep inside.

I'd never seen him that way, not so unraveled, not so desperate. I had a feeling it wasn't just the abduction that had him rattled like this. I made my way along the hallway and headed toward his office, but the moment I reached the doorway, another door opened further along. A woman stepped out, so focused on closing the door quietly she didn't notice my presence until she turned, and froze.

"Hi," she said carefully.

I glanced at the door that she'd come out of, then the door further along, which I knew was Mateo's personal quarters.

Panic ripped through me, what was she doing so close to his rooms?

"No, this *is* what it looks like," she murmured, taking a step toward me, then lifted her hand to press it against her side.

The way she walked, the way she held herself, slightly hunched over, her face pale... A face that felt somewhat familiar. "Do I know you?"

She licked her lips and glanced along the hallway to where Mateo's voice drifted out. "He trusts you, right?" She turned her head, meeting my gaze. "He left the office door open for you, told me you'd be coming. He told me you were safe."

"Safe?"

She took a step toward me and carefully reached out her hand, keeping her voice low. "My name is Evan Valachi. I guess I was meant to be your roommate. It's nice to finally meet you, Xael."

Evan Valachi? I shook my head as that knowing returned. "Wait, no...Evan is..."

"An imposter, worse than that..." She lifted the corner of her shirt, exposing a bandage taped to her side. "She's a fucking murderer, and of a dead woman at that."

The woman in front of me was fueled with rage, it sparkled in her eyes. She closed the distance between us, and for some reason, deep down inside me I knew she was right. The woman I had been sharing an apartment with wasn't one of us. I'd known the moment I met her, and that feeling had only grown in the days we'd shared our space. But this woman, this woman felt like power. She felt like determination. She felt like she belonged. I glanced at the wound on her side, then met her gaze. "She did that to you?"

She just gave a nod. "The bitch thinks I'm dead. I'm about to show her otherwise."

A tremor tore through me at the words. Yeah, she was definitely an heir. The sound of a door came from somewhere in the distance. She glanced my way. "Let's just keep this between us, okay?" She took a step away before turning.

"Of course..." I said as she took another step. "Evan, just be careful, okay, there is something really fucking wrong with her."

"Oh, don't I know it,"she answered, giving me a wink and a smile before hurrying down the hallway, leaving me behind.

The ˋEvan Valachi? Holy shit...

I should trust my instinct, it'd never let me down before. I glanced toward the open door of Mateo's office, maybe just this once. Still, I stepped inside, turning and closing the door behind me.

I waited, invading his space. It seemed this was my MO. I invaded, and touched what wasn't meant to be touched. I'd drunk from his well...and was sickened.

The heavy thud of fast steps drew my focus as the tiny *beep* of the lock came before the door was opened and Mateo stepped in. His breaths were savage and there was a strange look on his face, one that both scared and exhilarated me.

My pulse spiked as I swallowed. "You wanted me here...well, here I am."

He didn't move...just stared at me before he lunged.

24

Mateo

Papers. Pens...and my fucking lamp went flying as I hurled myself across the desk and grabbed her. Her guns in her shoulder holster pressed into my chest. The bite of that steel only seemed to incite the beast inside me. I gripped the back of her neck.

"Mateo..."

She started, until I swallowed the rest of her words. I kissed her, driving her backwards until she hit the wall. And she was mine once more. Familiar. Addictive...and I was losing my mind. I stepped back, grasped her throat, and slid my thumb along the line of her jaw. "You fucking broke me...no one's done that before."

Her dark eyes glinted. Her lips were red from my savage attack. Christ help me if I didn't want to ravish her...every fucking bit of her. I dropped my head and leaned in close, that savagery inside me howling with the need to have her.

I didn't need to draw my focus to the fact I was rock fucking hard. Every breath drew her deep inside me, and I was desperate to drown. "I can't be gentle," I growled. "I can't play it safe, not when it comes to you."

"Then don't..." she whispered. "If you don't fuck me, I'm going to go out of my mind."

I pulled back, seeing the truth in her eyes. She looked at me...*she fucking lo—*

I kissed her...*hard,* pushing her shirt and holster up to expose her bra. Fuck me, I'd missed her...like I'd miss my goddamn soul. I felt empty without her, half the man I was when I was with her. I reached up, cupped her breast over her black lace bra, and watched as she closed her eyes.

Her moan filled my ears as I gripped the cup of her bra and yanked. Her breast bounced free, pale against the black webbing of her holster, the dusky pink nipple tightening as I lowered my head. Fuck me, she was stunning, savage, and when she was pissed, utterly terrifying.

I took her nipple into my mouth and closed my eyes. My tongue danced around the tightening peak as I reached down, fumbled with the button on her jeans, and yanked them down.

"Turn the fuck around, Xael." I pulled my mouth away.

She did, shoving her jeans and panties down at the same time. I yanked my belt, unbuckling it before I tore open my pants. I couldn't wait for her...couldn't be the kind of man who was gentle, not when all that remained was a beast. I pulled her hips backwards and drove her shoulders forward until she was bent over the desk.

Her ass was warm and soft, fucking perfect under my hand as I slipped my finger along her crease. She dropped her head, moaning as I crested her pussy and danced around her clit. Fuck, she was wet...so goddamn wet. Warmth soaked to my knuckle as I sank into her and looked down at my fingers driving where I wanted my cock to be.

I pulled out, grabbed my shaft, and eased inside her...and felt my soul come back into my body.

Home.

She moaned, gripping the far side of the desk, and somewhere in the distance my phone started to ring again. Ten minutes... that's all I wanted with her. Ten goddamn minutes. I thrust inside again, and something dangerous rumbled in my chest.

"Harder," she moaned.

I clenched my ass, driving inside her, then leaned forward, braced my hands on each side of her, and rammed home.

"Fuck...*you*..." she moaned.

I fucked her...harder, driving my cock deep inside. She was all I wanted, all I craved, all I'd leave everything for. "No, Xael, *fuck you.*" I thrusted even harder, making her moan again.

Christ, I missed that sound.

Missed it more than anything. I leaned down, covered her back with my chest, and jutted my hips upwards, burying myself deep in her sweet heat. "I fucking love you." The words just slipped free.

"I...*fucking...love...you,*" she gasped around my thrusts.

My balls tightened with her words, as a chill raced through me. She drove her ass against me with every unmerciful thrust, driving me deeper inside her until she threw her head backwards, gripped the desk's edge, and moaned loudly.

My body tightened a second later as I came hard, jerking inside her, releasing all the desperation inside. She dropped her head back onto my desk, the sound of her hard breaths filling my ears. I wanted to stay like this for just a second and forget the world existed for a little longer...but my phone rang once again.

"Go," she murmured through a deep breath. "Do what you do best. Find her, Mateo...then come back to me."

"You're not going anywhere." I pulled free of her and instantly felt the loss. "Never again...you understand me?" I reached down, fumbled with the pocket of my pants around my knees, and grabbed my phone free.

"Yeah?"

"About goddamn time you answered," a low snarl echoed down the line.

I scowled. "Who is this?"

"This is Haelstrom Hale...Katerina VanHalen's fiance."

I stilled as those words registered, and slowly pulled away. "I wasn't aware Ms. VanHalen had a *fiance.*"

Xael slowly straightened, reached down to grab her jeans, and tugged them up as she cut me a look of concern. I didn't need to meet her gaze to know that was news to her, as well.

"Well, now you do," he answered. "I'm on board my jet now and have men in the area headed your way. I want no expense spared in bringing my...*fiancee*...home to me."

But it wasn't the word fiancee he'd wanted to say.

I knew what kind of man I spoke to now. The kind that owned, that controlled, that allowed her just enough chain to choke herself. Katerina VanHalen had contacted me a number of times to come to the island, and each time her father had shut it down...until that last call. Then he'd said yes. Now I knew why.

It was because of this man...this *Haelstrom Halle.*

"I understand," I answered. "Believe me when I say finding Ms. VanHalen is my upmost priority."

The sound of a jet's engines started in the background. "Good. Then I'll be seeing you soon, Commander, and when I do, I'll be taking Katerina home with me."

He hung up the call, leaving me stunned.

"Who was that?" Xael buttoned her jeans and yanked her shirt into place.

"That was Haelstrom Hale...reportedly Kat's soon-to-be husband."

She shook her head. "Bullshit, Kat doesn't run like that. She doesn't sleep around, and I'm pretty sure that after last night she's made her intentions known."

"Then someone needs to tell him that," I answered, my focus narrowing in on her.

She shouldn't be out here, she should be in her apartment...*no,* not her apartment, not the one she shared with the damn psycho. "I don't want you going back to your apartment, okay? Message your bodyguard, tell him to get your things and meet you here. You can stay in my quarters until this is all over."

"This have anything to do with Evan?" She took a step toward me, reaching up to wind her arms around my neck. I slid my hands along her arms, craving every touch like it was the most natural feeling in the world for me.

"You know about that?"

She just smiled, then jerked her head toward the door. "Let's just say I met a new friend tonight."

Fear coursed through me as I lowered my gaze to the guns strapped to her chest. "I forgot how incredible you were, how fucking fearless."

"Then it's about time I reminded you, Mateo," she said, reaching up with one hand and, without missing a goddamn beat, pulled a gun free to press it between my legs, the slide resting against my cock. "Break my heart again and that will be the last thing you ever do, you feel me?"

My lips curled into a smile as I nuzzled her neck. "I feel you... very fucking much. But you realize what that means, right? If we're together."

"Better than you can understand."

I met her gaze. What...just like that? She lowered the gun, holstered it, and jutted her chin in the air...and then it hit me. She knew...she'd always known. She understood that it meant we'd have to go against her father and the entire Commission.

And she was ready for it all.

25

Xael

I let Mateo walk me to his private residence and give me his spare card before he pulled me close and kissed me. "Stay inside until I come for you," he murmured, and stared into my eyes. "Send me your bodyguard's number. I want to make sure I know where you are."

"I thought you had cameras for that?"

There was a twitch at the corner of his mouth before he leaned close. "Not in here there aren't."

He took my mouth with savagery, leaving my lips pulsing when he pulled away. Was that an invitation? Or did he mean...*wait.* "Your office?"

His smile only grew wider as he turned and walked away without saying another word. "Sonofa..."

Beep.

I looked down at my phone as the front door to Mateo's apartment opened, then closed, leaving me alone to find Rhys' reply. *Got your things, I'm on my way.*

My pulse wouldn't slow as I lifted my gaze to the hallway and it had nothing to do with the attacks on the island and everything to do with him. *What the hell just happened?* My body still hummed with the sudden assault. I touched my lips, remembering every kiss and every savage thrust of his body.

None of this was real...

I pressed against the throb of my mouth and looked around his apartment. But it was...it was very real. A pang tore across my chest as I moved around his space, inhaling his scent, and tried to stop those memories of him ripping my heart out. Maybe it was a little *too* real.

A hard *thud* came at the door. I hurried forward, peering through the peephole to see Rhys, then opened the door and stepped back.

"What the fuck are you doing?" he snapped as he walked in carrying two suitcases.

I swallowed hard, flinching at the bite in his tone. I knew it was coming, I just didn't think he'd—

"How many times I gotta tell you, X?" He dropped our stuff on the floor and turned to me. "Don't just open the door, not like that. Not even for me, okay?" He exhaled long and slow, combing his fingers through his hair. "Anyone could've been waiting on the other side. Someone with a gun to my head, someone wanting you."

I swallowed, fear coursing through me as the image of that filled my head. A gun pressed to Rhys' head as he stood on the other side of that door, knocking, waiting for me to answer. "Then I'd open it."

"If you did, then you'd be dead. You're smarter than that, X," he growled, then glanced my way, finally meeting my gaze.

I came down from the high of Mateo in a rush as it all hit me. Baldeon...Kat...*everything.* A tremor tore through me, making me wrap my arms around my middle. Rhys flinched at the sight and strode to me, pulling me into his arms and against his chest.

He'd never made contact like that, never been so...*personal.*

"You need to be smarter, X." His voice echoed through his chest. "My job is to protect you, but you need to protect yourself too, and that means from me, as well."

I shook my head and pulled away, tears prickling my eyes. "You're not going to hurt me, Rhys."

"No, but someone else could hurt me to get to you." He stepped away, realizing how close he'd been. "So, no opening doors without making sure no one else is waiting, okay?"

I gave a nod.

"Okay." He glanced around the apartment. "Let's get you settled."

He bent, grabbed my suitcase, and headed for what looked like Mateo's bedroom. But his words stuck with me. They stayed with me all the way through the night as the building shuddered and shook from the wind. Rhys made a bed on the sofa in the living room, his gun beside him as he switched off the lights. My body slumped with exhaustion, but there was no way I could sleep, not knowing that Kat was somewhere out there, terrified if she was still alive.

God, please be alive.

I closed the door to Mateo's bedroom and pulled out some clothes that Rhys had packed for me as my phone flashed, the battery icon red and almost empty. But as I searched the suitcase, I realized he'd forgotten one critical thing, my phone charger. "Shit."

I moved closer to the door and cracked it open, listening to the deep, heavy breaths coming from Rhys on the sofa. He was tired, beyond exhausted, like the rest of us. But I needed him to be rested, and I could be quick, hurry to the building, grab my phone charger from next to the bed, and be back before he even knew I was gone.

The heavy snore that came from the living room made up my mind. I opened the door wider and slipped out, hurried across the apartment, and quietly slipped the card from the kitchen counter as I made for the front door. I barely made a sound as I eased open the door and stepped out, scanning the corridor of the building before I made my way along the hallway and headed for the automatic doors.

I couldn't see anyone, the place was eerily silent, and I didn't like it. A brutal gust of wind hit me as the doors shuddered and shook as they slowly opened, forcing me to lower my head and drive myself into the wind. Each step was a battle as I drove myself forward. By the time I got to the other side of the main building, my eyes were watering from the wind.

I pressed my card against the scanner then lunged for the doors as they barely slid open, and pushed inside. My breaths were just heavy gasps and my ears were roaring as I lifted my gaze to the elevator. I hurried, each beat of my heart like a ticking time bomb in my chest, and punched the button for the elevator, waiting for it to open before I stepped inside.

I shivered, chilled to the core as I rose. In my head, I was already snatching the charger from the nightstand, until the lights in the elevator flickered, sending a surge of panic through me. I jerked my gaze up, whispering a sigh of relief as I came to a stop and the doors opened.

Mumbled, erratic cries came from the other Evan's bedroom. I jerked my gaze toward the sound and stepped quietly as I moved toward bedroom. All I needed was a few minutes, then I'd be gone before she even knew I was here. But the moment I cut across the living room the lights flickered above me once more, then plunged into darkness.

A scream ripped through the apartment and for a second, I forgot how dangerous she was and lunged forward, tearing along the hallway to her room. "Evan!" I screamed and smashed my fist on her door.

But her screams continued in the dark, and on the other side of the door something terrifying was unleashed. I dropped my shoulder, and lunged, throwing myself against the door. I didn't care about the agony, or the danger. In that moment, all I thought about was Kat, she was somewhere out there, just as terrified. It was her screams I heard in my head, her terror I felt booming inside me as I slammed my body against the door once more. "Evan! It's me, Xael!"

One more hard shove and the door flew inward. The psychotic Evan spun, her eyes wide. Even in the dark, I saw her and I knew something was very wrong. She raked her nails down her face. "No...*no! You betrayed me...YOU BETRAYED ME!*"

I lunged, grabbed her hands, and dragged them down. *"Hey!"* I roared, shaking her.

Something hit the floor, white, plastic. The container bounced as a streak of lightning flared across the sky, illuminating the room. I bent and picked it up. It was a bottle of pills, and even though I knew what Mateo and the other woman who said she was the real Evan had said, still, deep down there was a part of me that hadn't understood or believed...

Until now. "Sophie Harrison?" I read from the label, then met her gaze. "Who the hell is that?"

"No one," she roared, lunging to snatch it from my hands. *"Don't touch things that don't belong to you!"*

It was true...everything they'd said...it was all true.

The thought took flight right before the neon glow of the lightning was gone...and she attacked.

I was hit hard, knocked sideways and slammed into the wall. She was gone in a blur of movement, tearing through the darkness to leave me floundering.

"What the fuck..." the words were a gasp as the *boom* of the stairwell door resounded through the apartment, making me jump.

My world swayed, blurring under the thunderous pounding of my heart. I hadn't wanted to believe them...hadn't wanted to think someone like this...*Sophie* could do something like that. Who the fuck would kill someone in cold blood and steal their identity?

Someone dangerous...

That's who.

I inched upright on the wall, then shoved away and left her room behind. I hurried to my room in the dark, grabbed my charger and cord, and waited. I couldn't take the elevator and the stairwell was fucking terrifying. Still, I clutched my charger and cord and crept closer, cracking open the stairwell door and listening before I stepped into the pitch-black gloom and reached out, groping for the railing and praying I didn't hit anything warm, waiting...and deadly.

26

Mateo

Lights sparkled, growing brighter as the boat neared, the engine roaring under the strain. I gripped the railing on the dock, steadying myself as the wind howled across the water and slammed against the island. But it was more than the cyclone bearing down on us that made my gut clench, and that savage need to lash out rise inside me, it was him... The man about to descend on the island.

In the hours since I'd spoken with Haelstrom Hale, I'd done some digging into who the man was, and I didn't like what I'd found. It seemed he and Sebastian VanHalen were quite the buddies, so much so that they'd decided to make the journey from the US to the island together.

They were the kind of friends who were a matter of convenience, sick, twisted convenience, and no doubt they were here to make sure that convenience continued...and I still had Damon Zakharov to contend with.

The sniveling, pathetic excuse for a man roared louder the closer his buddy, Hale, came to the island. I'd had just about enough of his ranting about how Hale would be the end of this island. I released my hold and straightened as the boat turned and nosed toward the dock, then glanced at the man standing next to the captain.

Rich or not...money does not make the man.

In my experience, it only hid who he truly was and I didn't need any fucking intel to tell me who Haelstrom Hale truly was, the one conversation over the phone had done that just fine. The engine roared, white smoke spewing out as the damn thing worked three times as hard to get him here. But then the sound eased as the boat turned sideways, letting the waves do the work and carry it toward the dock.

Two of my men were there, waiting to throw the rope and secure the boat before Hale climbed off. He steadied himself for a second before lifting his gaze to mine, then headed my way.

"I want a full briefing.," he snapped, "in five minutes. First, I need a goddamn drink, then an explanation as to how the *fuck* you allowed this to happen."

I clenched my jaw as the bastard met my gaze. He actually thought I answered to him...how fucking cute. "This way, Haelstrom."

"Hale," he snapped. "We are neither friends nor family, Mateo."

I turned on the bastard, taking a step in, closing the distance. "Then in that case, it's Commander, *to you*. You neither pay my wage nor deserve my goddamn *respect*."

He flinched, and that was all I needed as behind him, Sebastian VanHalen also flinched. No matter how much money Hale had, it couldn't shake me. He managed to hold my stare, until my men headed toward us, then he broke the gaze. "Some refreshments, at least," he muttered.

I lifted my hand, motioning toward the buildings. "By all means. This way, gentlemen."

He followed me, along with my men, as we headed up the rise toward the main building, and the moment we stepped inside, the deafening roar in my ears quieted. I strode along the corridor and motioned to the open door of the conference room. Hale stepped in, made his way to the drinks counter, and poured himself a glass of Scotch. I gave a nod to the communications officer as he worked on the link between us and the rest of the Commission.

"VanHalen," Hale muttered, turning the glass in his hand. "He's to be included in this conversation."

"The hell he is." Dominic Salvatore growled through the audio link, his face coming into focus with the connection of his camera. "You are on Commission ground and *we* are the *only* ones who decide who is included in private conversations, Haelstrom."

If Hale thought that he'd be able to come here and throw his weight around, then he was sadly mistaken. He had no idea who he was playing with.

"Get the fuck off me!" The snarl came from outside in the hallway. I looked toward the doorway as Lazarus and his bodyguards entered.

"Laz...*wait*," Rossi's bodyguard growled as he strode in after the kid.

Kid...

Lazarus might've been a kid once, but he wasn't anymore. Cold, cutting blue eyes scanned the room, stopped on mine for a second, then shifted to Haelstrom Hale. There was a twitch at the corner of his lips and his fingers clenched into fists, drawing my gaze to the blood smeared across his knuckles.

He'd been searching for Kat on the mainland, along with Finley Salvatore, who strode into the conference room right behind Rossi. The two of them even standing in the same room without killing each other, or at least throwing hands, was a fucking achievement...but to work together, to...depend on each other, now that was almost unheard of.

"Laz," Fin murmured carefully as he set sight on Hale.

Seemed like the slimy piece of shit was making friends all over the place. Did Lazarus know about the arranged marriage, I wondered?

"Let's get one thing straight." Lazarus stepped closer to the Armani-clad scum. "When this is over...when *I* find Kat, you will leave *without her*."

So, I was taking that as a yes on the information angle.

Tension crackled through the room like an oncoming storm, standing the hairs on the back of my damn neck.

"Fin." Dominic Salvatore's growl was warped and weird through the connection.

I tore my gaze from the pissing contest in the middle of the room and strode toward the computer. "Looks like the storm is getting closer, let's get this over with."

"Yes," Lazarus snarled. "So I can get back to finding her."

"We need a count of men." Orlando Rossi's voice came through the speaker, although we couldn't see him. "I have a team of ten special-forces-trained men on their way, they should be there within the next five hours."

Hale just chuckled and shook his head, stepping around Lazarus. "I'll have her located before then. My men are combing Mauritius as we speak." His phone gave a *beep* before he looked down. "Look at that...they already have contact with information."

A low, threatening sound came from Lazarus before Logan reached out and grabbed his arm.

"Easy," the bodyguard said, meeting the Stidda heir's gaze.

Beep.

My phone vibrated in my hand. I glanced down. It was a message...from Kurti. My pulse picked up the pace.

"Commander?"

I jerked my head up at the sound. "Yes?"

"Did you hear me?" Orlando Rossi asked.

I licked my lips, feeling the attention in the room shift to me. "Please, repeat the question."

"If we're distracting you..." Dominic Salvatore leaned forward until he filled the screen, those dark eyes piercing through the camera.

"No." I slid my phone back into my pocket and forced my attention to the room.

"I asked what provisions have you made to secure the rest of those on the island," Orlando Rossi repeated.

"The same ones I gave you an hour ago...*when you asked the last time,*" I snapped.

I didn't have time for this fucking bullshit. The cameras jerked and shuddered.

"Sorry..." Rossi's words were garbled as the connection flashed, jumbled, and dropped out.

No connection...

The words flashed on the screen.

"I don't think they heard you," Lazarus said carefully, then turned and met my gaze. "Lucky for that."

I sucked in hard breaths, listening to the wind howling outside the building, until the door opened and Damon Zakharov, with his busted-up face, strolled in. The bastard's father had forced me to let him free, on the provision he stayed the hell away from Kat...

But that was before.

Before it had all gone straight to Hell.

He glanced my way, feeling brave flanked by his bodyguards. Lazarus just watched him with a savage stare as the rapist pile of hyena shit strode through the room. Lazarus's lips curled, revealing teeth. I knew that kind of hatred, that viper coiled in your belly, waiting for the moment to strike.

Lazarus was more than a little unhinged when it came to Kat. He was a man possessed...a man who looked exactly like the one I saw in the mirror when it came to Xael. He shifted his gaze, watching Damon Zakharov as he strode toward Hale and they exchanged muffled words.

Damon flinched, then glanced over his shoulder at Lazarus before turning and heading to the door with his men.

"Nice teeth," Lazarus snarled.

The asshole was busted and broken. The cracked teeth that cut the inside of his cheeks with even the slightest twitch of his mouth were jagged and disgusting, leaving Zakharov nothing but to flip him the bird as he passed.

Hale and Sebastian VanHalen followed, taking their fucking stench with them.

"I fucking hate him." Lazarus stared at the doorway as they left. "*I hate all of them.*"

Logan cleared his throat. "They're her family."

"Not Hale," he spat. "No fucking way."

"Did you know about that?" Freddy took a step forward and nodded toward the doorway.

"Not from her, no," Lazarus answered, and cut a glare my way.

But I didn't flinch. I didn't move at all.

"So she didn't tell you anything about that Hale jerk?" Freddy muttered, and scowled. "Makes perfect fucking sense then."

I held myself still as Lazarus turned to his bodyguard. "What makes sense?"

But Freddy didn't want to spill. He just shook his head and turned away.

"*What* makes sense, *brother?*" Laz strode forward and grabbed his arm.

"Nothing." He tugged his arm free. "Forget I said anything."

But there was no forgetting a damn thing when it came to Laz and Katerina VanHalen. He stepped in front of his bodyguard. *"Tell me,* Freddy."

He licked his lips and cast a nervous glance at Logan, who just nodded, urging him on. "I don't know for sure, okay?"

"Just fucking spit it out," Lazarus snapped.

"She denied it, laughed it off like I was imagining things." Freddy looked away. "But I wasn't imagining things. Not things like that. I saw the way she moved when she forgot I was there, saw the way her hand cupped her belly, and saw the way her fingers traced the fluttering. It was the exact same way Connie did. She lied to me when I confronted her, but I know without a shadow of a doubt she's pregnant."

Lazarus stumbled backwards like the guy had just been shot in the chest. There was a tiny shake of his head as though he wanted to deny what he'd heard. But Freddy was already turning to him.

"What the fuck did you say?" The deep snarl came from the open doorway.

Hale took a step inside, his gaze fixed like a predator on Freddy. "*My* Katerina is pregnant?"

SHIT...

That flaming turd just smiled as he stepped further into the room, and Lazarus looked like all he wanted to do was throw up and commit murder, probably at the same time.

"Then congratulations are in order," Hale murmured, but there was no one wishing him anything but a quick, violent, and painful death. "It looks like I'm about to be a father."

"I came to tell you I'll be taking command." Hale seemed to grow larger by the second, swelling and consuming, eating the space around us with his presence as he glanced toward Logan. "I understand you have men on the ground on the mainland, and I want their details. You will report to me...and *only* to me. *Everything* involving Katerina is now mine."

Lazarus looked fucking gray. His lips curled, and that glint I'd seen so many times was now shining in his eyes. But Hale didn't seem to be aware of how close to death he actually was. If anything, the bastard met Laz's gaze when he gloated, before he turned and strode from the room.

I hadn't liked the rich scumbag before...I liked him a whole hell of a lot less now.

Lazarus took a step after him, hate seething in his eyes. *Not here.* I wanted to speak the words. *Not yet, at least.* Hell, when the time came to take that rapist slimeball down, I might even help.

"Laz," Freddy called from behind him and reached out, placing a hand on his arm.

"Laz, I'm sorry," Freddy murmured, pain flashing in his eyes.

"It's okay, Freddy." Lazarus stared at that empty doorway a moment longer, then left.

The moment he did, I breathed a sigh of relief, until I remembered the text on my cell...the one waiting for me from Kurti.

I yanked it free and stared at the message.

Kurti: Besnik home and quiet. It's not them, brother. Stay safe.

"It's not them?" I scowled and reread the message as my pulse thudded heavily in my chest. *It's not them...*

I lifted my gaze to the empty doorway as the communications asshole worked around me unraveling cords. "Commander," he called my name, forcing my attention back to the room.

"Blake?" I growled, and met the bastard's stare.

All I could see in that moment was his hand on Xael's arm back in the airport and his eyes on someone he shouldn't have been staring at.

"Are you finished with the equipment, or did you want me to leave it set up?"

I turned away. "Leave it," I answered, and headed for the door.

No doubt there were many more bullshit calls to contend with...unless the damn cyclone took us all out.

Twelve hours ago, that might've been appealing.

But not now...I turned my focus to Xael and turned for the doorway.

No, now I had one very good reason to live for...*and fight for, as well.*

27

Xael

I made it back to Mateo's apartment without being seen or killed. My panic was screaming in my head even louder than the wind as I slipped inside the building. As I made my way along the hallway and into the apartment, I could hear soft snores still coming from the sofa in the living room,

The moment I stepped into the kitchen, Rhys cracked open his eyes. "Where are you going?"

"The refrigerator," I lied, my voice shaking.

He just closed his eyes again, mumbling something about getting some sleep. I grabbed a bottle of water and closed the refrigerator door before retreating to Mateo's room. Once I eased the door closed behind me, I let out a hard breath. *Jesus...* I grabbed my charger and tossed it onto the bed, watching it bounce and come to rest on its side, and as it did, the memory of the wide, unhinged gaze of the woman I'd shared an apartment with returned. That wasn't the real Evan Valachi. If I'd been unsure before, I sure as hell wasn't now.

Sophie...

That's what the name on the bottle said.

I sat down on the side of the bed. First Baldeon, then Kat, and now Evan...and the damn cyclone. This island was a fucking death trap. I lifted my gaze to the closed door as a shudder of desperation ripped through me. "Please let us make it out of this alive."

The *thud* of the closing door made my heart leap. I moved to the doorway as Mateo's growl echoed out, then opened it and stepped into the living room.

He gripped the edge of the kitchen counter and bowed his head. I'd never seen him like that, never so *unraveled*. Rhys slowly pushed up from the sofa, the look of concern on his face saying he thought the same thing.

"It's not who I thought it was." Mateo lifted his gaze to mine.

His dark eyes shimmered with fear, which only made me more frightened.

"And who did you think it was?" Rhys asked as he slowly climbed to his feet.

Something moved behind Mateo's eyes, something that made me catch my breath. He was dangerous in that moment, cold, savage...not the man I saw when he was with me. No, this man was dangerous. Heat moved through me, and excitement followed. I should be terrified of that look in his eyes, but I wasn't...if anything, it made him fucking hot.

"Besnik," he answered, and straightened, realizing he'd spoken the word out loud...*to us*. "I thought it was the Besniks."

"I don't know them." Rhys moved toward the counter as Mateo grabbed two glasses, then glanced my way. I shook my head, leaving him to place them on the counter before pouring Scotch.

"You won't. No one really does, but I killed some of their best men years ago, and they didn't like it."

I swallowed at the chilling words. The way he said it was like it was no big deal, kill a few guys, they'd come back for revenge. Just a normal day kind of drama. Only it wasn't, was it?

"Sounds fair." Rhys grabbed a glass and drank.

The guy looked like hell, gaunt and wired, even after his nap on the sofa. He took another swallow.

"But it's not them." Mateo raised his glass to his lips before finishing. "So now I'm back to square one."

"Does it matter who it is?" Rhys asked carefully with a shrug. "The way I see it, it doesn't."

Mateo narrowed that dangerous stare on him. "Continue."

So formal.

So cold.

Continue...

Rhys never missed a second, just grabbed his glass and tuned. "This isn't like the real world. We're basically a world of our own. A world we need to protect, or escape from. Either way, it doesn't matter who the targets are." He glanced my way. "We're all in danger."

Mateo licked his lips, those dark eyes sparkling as he gave a slow nod, then finished his glass and looked at me. There was that formidable glint, that one that made my pulse race and that quiet voice in my head scream *be careful of him!*

He left his glass on the counter and came toward me. "Flee or protect," he murmured, coming closer until I took a step backwards into the bedroom.

Which is exactly what he wanted. He closed the door behind him carefully, never once shifting those dark eyes from mine. "Flee or protect," he said carefully. "Those are my options."

He glanced toward the bed and I knew what he wanted.

What we both wanted.

"So, what are you suggesting?" I murmured. "We run? In case you've forgotten, Mateo, we're on a damn island with a cyclone bearing down on us."

"I haven't forgotten." He moved closer and I moved backward, until the back of my legs hit the bed. "I haven't forgotten a damn thing. Especially the moment you left this apartment when I *specifically* told you not to."

A charge of excitement tore through me. He knew...*he knew.* "I..."

"I?" He edged nearer until the muscles in my back strained as I leaned away under him. "I what? I decided to put my own life at risk for a damn..." he glanced at the charger in the middle of the bed. "Charger?"

"My phone was almost dead," I answered carefully.

"The phone which required a basic charge that many of us have here." He stepped away, walked around to the other side of the bed, and bent down, lifting the same damn cable from the nightstand drawer. "Including me."

Shit...

Heat rushed to my face as he glared at me. "I didn't know," I protested.

"You didn't ask. If you had, I would've told you that what is mine, is yours," he answered carefully, striding back around the bed toward me. "As are you, Xael."

My breath caught and my eyes widened. He reached and grasped the back of my neck. I could taste the Scotch on his breath as I closed my eyes, taste it on his lips too as he kissed me. My heart hammered and my body melted, leaning against him.

I was lost in the moment stolen from the terrors of this place, until he broke the kiss. "I can't." He said, his brow furrowing as his phone gave a *beep*. "Not right now."

"I get it." I glanced at his phone as he stared at the message, then turned away, yanked open the door, and left without a word to me.

"Fuck!" he shouted beyond the bedroom door, picking up his pace.

His heavy steps boomed like thunder.

"What is it?" Rhys called, tracking the movement from the kitchen.

But Mateo was already gone, slamming open the apartment door and leaving his rage resounding in the air behind him.

28

Mateo

Goddamn bastards! I'll kill them...just wait till I get my hands on their scrawny goddamn necks.

"They're already leaving," Dom said as I strode out of the apartment and along the hall.

I jerked my gaze to his and snarled, *"Then fucking stop them!"*

He just flinched as we raced out the doors and across the grounds, heading for the hangar.

I couldn't hear the damn engine over the howling wind as I threw open the hangar door and lunged through...but I could see the rotors whirling as Vad, Leila, and Alexi Kilpatrick climbed onboard, closing the door behind them.

"No!" I screamed, hurling myself through the air as the jet pulled forward, then accelerated hard. They were gone before I had a chance to reach them, gone even before my roar was snatched away by the wind. My boots slapped hard against the

asphalt, shooting shockwaves into my ankles before I skidded to a stop, watching the jet's wheels lift at the end of the runway and my only hope of escape climb into the sky.

"FUCK!"

That was going to be our way off the island. Option goddamn B...now there were only the boats left. Boats that could be outrun by a bigger motor...boats that could be destroyed. Selfish goddamn assholes. Vad Kardinov I understood. The lowlife fucking scum was a damn weasel. But Alexi...and Leila, of all people. After all the things I'd done for him. When this was over...I'd kick his goddamn ass.

"Commander!" Dom called behind me.

But I couldn't face him, couldn't meet his gaze. I wanted to kill someone, and the bodyguard was far too close for comfort. *His comfort.* Instead, I turned away, until my phone vibrated in my pocket at the same time a crack came over the two-way.

"There's two men in black heading toward Building Five," the control room operator barked. "Three more coming from the east end of the island now!"

I jerked my gaze toward the eye of the cyclone out over the water, then lunged, reaching for my gun as my phone started to ring.

I yanked it up. *Caller ID Unknown* and I let out a curse before answering. "Not a good time, bro."

"Well, *bro.*" Edon gave a grunt before a *pop* sounded through the call.

A sound I knew only too well. But I didn't slow, just kept on running, charging around the open side of the hangar toward the water as something hissed past me and cracked into the side of the metal building.

"Shit!" Dom roared, and opened fire on a dark blur that ducked back at the edge of the building.

"Gotta go," I muttered. "Got a situation here."

"Mat—" he started as I ended the call and shoved the phone back into my pocket.

The gunman charged out from the corner of the building, raised his gun, and fired. The shot narrowly missed me, but hit Dom as he rushed forward, firing at another as he came from the water's edge.

He gave a grunt, stumbled to the side, and went down to the ground as blood bloomed through the dark material of his black khakis. In an instant, the island was invaded. Men dressed in black rushed toward me. Instinct kicked in, forcing me to track the movement with the muzzle of my gun before I squeezed the trigger.

Crack!

I hit one, but three more took his place and opened fire. I lunged, driving toward Dom as he struggled to stand. I grabbed the massive man, heaving him to his feet. *Xael...*

Her name slammed into me, forcing me to glance toward the building in the distance.

"Go!" Dom roared, shoving me away.

I left him behind, my heart hammering as bullets shot past, narrowly missing me. My phone rang...and rang, the vibration distracting me. All I wanted was her...to see her...to protect her. I kept driving my body forward until I was hit in the side.

The sting was instant, slamming me sideways until I fell. I raised my gun as the image of Xael's face filled my mind. *Get to her!*

But my damn hand shook as I took aim. Agony roared through my side as I squeezed the trigger...but the shot found its mark. The gunman went down, clutching his knee as he went. Darkness moved over me, sweeping in like a wraith...and as I lifted my head, I knew it was over.

The muzzle of the shotgun was aimed at me, point blank.

There was no escape from that, not from this end, and as I stared down the barrel, it wasn't the faded recollection of my parents I thought of...it was her, *Xael*. The one good thing I had in my life, and now I was about to lose her for good. I lifted my gaze to the cold empty eyes of the assassin. My lips curled and bared my teeth. "Do it," I snarled.

But he didn't have a chance to squeeze the trigger.

Crack!

The shot filled my ears, making me flinch.

The gunman flew backwards and hit the ground with a sickening *thud*. Blood trickled from a neat hole in the center of his forehead. That vacant stare was one I knew all too well. I jerked my focus over my shoulder, finding the man who'd saved my life. Edon lowered his sniper's rifle, his gaze fixed on mine before he strode toward me, his long, powerful legs closing the distance quickly.

"I tried to tell you," my brother growled. "But as usual, you didn't listen."

"Where the hell did you come from?" I glanced at the building behind him, but of course he was alone.

"You want to spend time discussing my arrival or kill those who mean you harm?"

He was just so matter of fact. A stone-cold killer...one born in the cells of Ispeli's prison.

I shoved up from the ground, my knees trying to buckle until he lunged forward, grabbed me around the waist, then looked down. "You've been hit."

"It's nothing." I forced my knees to lock and take my weight. "I need to get to her...she's in danger."

"If you haven't guessed already, brother, you're *all* in danger." My brother motioned his head toward the building. "Go, find her, then we leave."

I took a step toward the building, then stopped. "Why?"

He shook his head and glared at me with a look of exasperation. "Why can't you just once do what I ask!"

He lifted his rifle and squeezed off a shot over my shoulder. I glanced back as another gunman fell. "Go," the clipped tone of my brother grew impatient. "Find your female, then come. I'll be waiting."

My knees trembled as I took a step. But the protective crack of gunfire came and one by one men fell.

It was a different time and a different place. Still, echoes of the past rippled through my mind. I was back there, striding through the towering gates of that hellish prison with my brother's brutalized body in my arms.

Mine...

The word resounded.

It was more than blood...more than loyalty. I lifted my gun again, taking aim as I caught a blur of black rushing toward the automatic doors of my building. I squeezed the trigger as the doors opened, catching the bastard in the chest. But he'd been sloppy, no vest to protect him, and not even a spare magazine. He looked like a cheap hired asshole who was in way over his head. He went to his knees hard as I neared and ended him with a single shot.

I'd leave no one alive behind me, not when it came to war.

My knees grew steadier and the agony in my side faded away, leaving me to stride through the doors and across the foyer of my building like I'd never been hit at all. Gone was the man... the one Xael knew, at least. Now there was only the monster, the one I'd never wanted her to see.

Boom!

Outside, something exploded. I was guessing it was the boats. That's what I'd do if I wanted to wipe out an entire island of Mafia offspring, cut off any hope of escape and flood the island with as many gunmen as possible. They'd run like rats...which is exactly what we were doing.

The door to the spare apartment flew open and the real Evan Valachi stumbled out, her eyes wide and haunted as she lifted her gun toward me until she realized who I was. "What the hell is going on?"

"We're under attack," I snapped. "Get back into the apartment, Evan, and lay low, for Christ's sake. Do not come out until I give the all clear."

But she just looked toward the foyer. "Bruno."

"Forget him..." I strode past, yanked my card from my pocket, and slammed it against the scanner. "You need to think about yourself."

Guilt wrapped around me. They were just kids, just kids on a goddamn battlefield because of the blood they carried. There was nothing I could do for them, not with just the men I had. "Shoot to kill, Evan. That's the only way you're going to stay alive."

I shoved my way inside my apartment. "Xael!" My voice resounded. *"Xael!"*

I tore through the apartment, searching the bedroom and the bathroom. But the place was empty. *For fuck's sake...where the hell was she?*

I sucked in hard breaths and yanked my phone free, pulling up the list of cameras on the island.

No connection.

"What the fuck?" I closed the application and reopened the icon, waiting for the cameras to load.

No connection.

"Christ, I don't need this shit!" I roared, and strode toward the foyer. There was only one option. I needed to go to the command center and search for her there.

I yanked open the door to the apartment and took two steps before the hairs on my arms rose on end. Something was happening...something was...

BOOM!

I was lifted into the air and slammed backwards as the command center hallway exploded...destroying the entire communications base on the island.

29

Xael

"Hurry!" Rhys roared, his voice fighting the wind as we tore out from the corner of the building and raced for the dock. "We get on a boat and we're out of here."

BOOM!

Orange flames exploded into the air ahead of us. Black smoke followed, and the closer we came to the dock, I saw what it was...or what it had been. Our way out of here.

"Fuck!" Rhys yelled, racing forward to skid to a stop halfway between the buildings and the water. He stumbled under the brutal gust of the cyclonic wind.

Gunshots cracked out, fighting the roar in my ears. I jerked my gaze over my shoulder, finding a man dressed in black racing from the corner of the building and lifting his gaze to me, and then his gun.

I lifted mine, took aim, and squeezed the trigger, feeling the weapon kick in my grasp. But the winds were too strong and my shot missed its mark.

"Rhys!" I screamed as more of them came from everywhere. I squeezed off shot after shot, fighting the wind as Rhys rushed back toward me.

He began firing as they came from around the building in front of us. Their shots narrowly missed me, hitting the wall inches from my face.

"We have to take cover!" he roared.

Plumes of black smoke engulfed the island from the burning boats. I glanced around as the gunmen came toward me.

Hide, but where?

We were outnumbered by at least three to one. Rhys squeezed off a shot, hitting one of the gunmen. Screams fought the roar of the wind as he went down hard.

"Xael!"

I spun at the sound of my name, finding Damien. Confusion flared inside me as he stepped forward, lifting his gun as more shots cracked out.

"What the hell are you doing out here?" he roared, and glanced toward Rhys, then the burning mess of what was left of the boats on the water.

"They exploded before we could get to them." Rhys called.

Damien nodded, turning his gaze toward us. "Come on." He motioned us forward. "I have somewhere you can hide."

Hide? I looked to Rhys as he squeezed off a shot, taking down another one of the gunmen, watching as they scurried toward the corner of the building once more.

But I didn't want to hide...I wanted to find Mateo. I shook my head. "I can't!"

"What do you mean, you can't?" he barked, shaking his head.

"Move, Xael!" Rhys drove me forward.

I was running before I knew it, following Damien as he led us around the side of a building and raced through the towering palms of a garden before tearing out the other side.

"They've headed toward the other side of the island." Damien roared, and lifted his phone.

I remember the cameras, the same link Mateo had on his phone. I lifted my gaze, catching the CCTV camera above as I ducked under the palms and raced after him.

Where the hell are you, Mateo?

The icy grip of fear coursed through me. It was more than the attack, more than the boats. It was something else...an emptiness resounded inside me, one that whispered things I didn't want to know. I swallowed and glanced at the phone in Damien's hand. It was more than the need to survive that drove me forward to follow him.

If I could get his cell, then I'd be able to search the cameras myself. Glass shattered to my right. I ducked as Rhys whirled behind me and opened fired. We ran, cutting across the grounds, following Damien as he skidded and charged through an open door to what looked like one of the storerooms to the classroom buildings.

The door was ajar and darkness waited inside. Damien grabbed the door and shoved it open, then winced, grabbing his side. I glanced at him as I followed him inside.

"You're hurt." I tried to track him, blinking as my eyes adjusted to the murky gloom.

"It's fine," he answered.

I caught his motion in the darkness, then turned as Rhys charged through the door, shoving it closed behind him.

"Did they see you?" Damien asked.

But Rhys just bent over, braced his hands on his knees, and sucked in hard breaths.

"Did they...see you?" Damien asked again, stepping closer.

I caught the shake of Rhys' head as he straightened. "No."

"Good."

Boom!

The sound of the gunshot was deafening in the tiny space. I flinched and froze, unable to move as Rhys fell, crumpling to the floor. I just stared...unable to process what had happened. Stared as movement came from behind me...stared as I was grabbed and shoved forward...*what...what just happened?*

I jerked my gaze to Damien. "What's going on?"

He didn't answer, just shoved me through the room in the dark.

"Wait." I tried to wrench my arm from his hold, and lunge back there. "Rhys' is hurt!"

"He's DEAD!" Damien roared, jerking me against him.

I saw the motion coming as he grabbed me around the throat and shoved me backwards, driving me against the wall with a *thump.*

"Get off me!" I screamed, punching my fists against his shoulders.

I didn't understand what was happening. None of this made any sense. Through the blur of panic, I saw Rhys' still body. I shoved against Damien as the tears came. "Get off me...*get the hell off me!"*

He did, tearing my gun from my hand as he took a step backwards. I lunged, driving my body through the darkness and fell to the floor at Rhys' side.

"Hey!" I grabbed him, losing my hold as my hands came away slick. *"Rhys!"* I screamed, yanking him from the floor and into my arms. "Rhys! Don't leave me! *RHYS! DON'T YOU DARE FUCKING LEAVE ME!"*

Through the blur of tears, I saw his wide, open stare, then the way his skull sank inwards. I flinched at the sight, my fingers curling away from his body. "Rhys." His name was nothing more than a husky hiss. "Rhys..."

"We need to move." Damien stepped closer from behind me.

Tears slipped down my cheeks as I jerked my gaze over my shoulder. *"Why the fuck did you kill him?"*

He just stared at me, those dark eyes unflinching. He'd once looked at me with a glint of danger and excitement. He'd looked at me with lust. But there was no lust now...just the kind of savagery that chilled me to the bone.

I released my hold, leaving Rhys' body to slump to the floor in front of me, and slowly rose. "Who the fuck are you?"

He didn't flinch, didn't fucking answer, just...*smiled.* "You need to move, Xael." He motioned deeper into the dark. "Now."

"Fuck that." I stared into the nothing darkness while outside the door the *crack...crack...crack...*of gunfire continued. I looked at my gun in his hand...the phone was gone. I glanced at his pocket as the realization dawned. "This is because of you, isn't it?"

He stepped closer as those last words he'd said to me rang inside my head...*you'll be sorry.*

A tremor coursed through me. "This was all you."

That smile grew wider. "Surprise."

Panic filled me as I slowly put it all together. There was no *mistake* when he'd knocked into me at the terminal. No lonely nights to fill when he waited for me outside my building. This had been a set-up from the first fucking day...*and I'd fucked him.*

I flinched at the thought and took a slow step away from him.

I'd fucked him, and now he'd killed Rhys.

"Stay the hell away from me," I ordered, taking another step toward the door.

I'd risk getting shot out there, risk anything I had to in an attempt to get away from this crazy asshole. Mateo was out there...*somewhere.* I jerked my gaze to Rhys. Had Damien killed Mateo too? My steps stilled at the thought as agony ripped through me.

Did he…

Movement carved through the darkness as Damien strode forward and snatched my arm before dragging me with him. "No more fucking around, Xael. *Do what you're goddamn told!*"

Agony roared in my arm under his grip. I fought, jerking my arm free, and swung a fist toward his face. But he moved fast, dodging the blow, and unleashing one of his own. His fist caught me on the side of the head, knocking me sideways until my knee gave way. I went down, *hard.* But the fighter in me reared up. I flung my hand out punched against the floor, and shoved upwards before I lunged for the door.

My fingers skimmed the hard steel, catching around the door handle before I was wrenched backwards, my feet lifting from the floor.

"Stop it!" Damien roared in my ear. *"Stop fighting me!*

"Fuck you!" I screamed and thrashed, fighting with all I had. I would *not* let him take me, *not* let him hurt me like he had Rhys…*and Baldeon…but Kat…Oh, Jesus, Kat.*

I froze for a second at the thought of her, and he tossed me through the air until I hit the wall with a sickening *crack!* Agony ripped through my head. His face blurred before slowly sharpening. "Did you do it?" Fire lashed my throat with the words and tears slipped free. I couldn't stop them now, no matter how much I wanted to. "Did you kill Kat?"

His breaths scattered strands of my hair as he leaned close. "Yes, now do what you're told, or I'll do the same to you."

I'd never felt fear before today, not true fear, like the one that made you so small and pathetic. The kind of fear that took everything away from you, rendering you incapable of doing anything other than try to survive. I'd never understood those women who climbed into the car at knife point, or the ones who stayed in a loveless, violent marriage. I'd never understood what made a woman do exactly whatever their attacker said.

Now I did.

"You hear me?" He leaned closer, his breath hot on my cheek when I turned my head. He grabbed my jaw, fingers digging in deep as he forced my gaze to his. "Why don't you like to look at me, Xael? Do I have to remind you, you let me do a lot more than look at you?"

"Fuck you." I glared into his eyes. "You lying, betraying piece of shit."

He just smiled, easing away. "You should be nice to me if you want to make it out of here alive."

"With you, you mean? I'd rather take a fucking bullet," I barked.

His grip clenched until I moaned, and when he'd forced my gaze back to him, he snarled, *"That can be arranged."* Then he kissed me.

30

Xael

His lips were cruel and savage, crushing mine against my teeth until I groaned in agony. Only then did he pull away, leaving my jaw aching and my lips throbbing. "You should've picked me, Xael" he growled.

But when he pulled away, I caught the twitch of his body and the catch of his breath...as though he was hurt. I licked my pulsing lips as that thought hit me. He was hurt, and there were others who were dead...*Mateo.*

"What happened out there." I tried to temper the hate in my tone.

"Let's just call it a changing of the guard," he answered carefully, those dark eyes glinting.

I flinched. "What does that mean?"

His smile was chilling as he pulled away. "Start walking, Xael, or you'll personally find out what happens to the heirs of the

Commission when they cover up the murder of an entire family."

"An entire family?" I whispered.

My ears rang with the stabbing pain inside my head. Damien just turned his gaze toward the doorway. "We're in the eye of it now. The eye of the cyclone, and of my wrath."

The roar of the wind was gone, leaving a deathly, painful silence behind.

"Now move." He yanked me from the wall and shoved me forward.

I stumbled, unable to do a damn thing but obey him as my mind raced. Get him talking...get him saying anything. "Your family..." I started as I fumbled my way deeper into the gloom.

"The family yours killed."

I swallowed hard. "I don't know anything about that."

"Of course you don't. In there." He raised his gun and pointed to a doorway.

I reached out, my fingers shaking as I clawed the air, and felt nothing.

"You need to get closer, Xael." He pressed the gun to my back, the bite of the muzzle making me wince.

I stepped closer, swallowing the panic inside me, and tried again. My finger smacked a handle. I gripped it, turned it, and yanked the door open. Faint light hit me, enough to see it was a storeroom of some kind. Under the door at the end of the room, a little more light spilled in.

"Move," Damien commanded.

I moved between the racks filled with chemicals and cleaning equipment to the door at the end, yanked the handle, and stepped out into one of the lower floor hallways of the building. "What are we doing here, Damien?"

"You'll see."

I moved ahead, then stopped, waiting as he motioned me forward again. I watched him in the corner of my eye, stepping slowly as that panic raced through my head. "What are you going to do with me?"

"Less than you deserve," he muttered, and motioned me toward one of the classrooms at the end of the hall.

I knew this place, knew the classrooms, it's where we'd had weapons training. My pulse picked up at the thought as he gestured toward the end of the hall.

Boom!

The faint sound of an explosion resounded in the hallway, drawing his focus over his shoulder. The second was all I had...*so I took it.*

I lunged, hurling my body toward the end of the hall, slammed my hand against the wall, and shoved myself around the corner.

"Xael!" Damien shouted.

But I didn't stop, just willed my knees not to buckle as I ran for my life.

Crack! A gunshot exploded, hitting the wall behind me as I screamed.

Don't hit me...

Don't hit me...

Don't...

"I'll fucking kill you!" Damien roared.

But the hallway was ending and there was no way out to the foyer from here, a dead end...with only two classrooms to possibly save me. I lunged for the closest door, grabbed the handle, and yanked.

But it was locked. I tried again, straining as I twisted and pulled. Desperation screamed inside me as I tore toward the other door.

Crack! The shot hit the glass panel of the locked door, sending shards flying through the air to shower me. The stings were instant, making me cry out and stumble sideways before I rushed forward again, throwing myself toward the only other door at the end of the hallway.

Please...please...PLEASE. I grabbed the handle, twisted it, and pulled as Damien came charging toward me, roaring like a bull. The handle sank and the door opened outward. I was through in a blur, yanking the door closed behind me and hitting the lock.

Through the long panel of glass in the middle of the door, I watched as he punched the door from the other side. "Open the fucking door, Xael!"

His face was a mask of rage, making me stumble backwards. My breaths came hard and fast as I turned my head, scanning the room. It was a weapons room...with no goddamn weapons.

Open cases sat bare, apart from a few loaded clips. I stumbled toward them, yanking open the doors to the cabinets and searching the empty racks.

Boom!

I jerked my gaze to the door, my heat jumping into the back of my throat as Damien shot at the lock.

"I'm going to fucking *kill you!*" he bellowed.

Boom!

The door shuddered and the glass panel cracked before he reached through. I jerked my gaze back, frantically searching through the cabinets, and found a switchblade knife...it was better than nothing. I gripped the blade in my shaking hand and spun as he flicked the lock and shoved open the door.

"All you've done is piss me off, Xael." He stepped inside, his arm bleeding from the glass.

"You stay the fuck away from me." I gripped the knife and stepped backwards. "Don't make me hurt you."

"Hurt me?" He came closer, glancing at the knife in my hand, then lifted that savage stare to me. "I'm the only way you're going to make it out alive."

He kept on walking, as though he was *daring me to stab him.*

The need to protect myself battled with that part of me that knew killing another was wrong. But in that moment, survival was all I could think of.

"Put the knife down, Xael. We both know you won't hurt me," he said carefully, coming cIoser.

I flinched at his words, the knife slipping in my grasp. He reached out, his fingers splayed to capture my wrist, until that howling need to stay alive kicked inside me.

I swung, but not with the knife, with my fist instead. He wasn't ready for the blow, jerking his focus toward my fist as he automatically blocked. But I was already moving, driving the knife in my other hand through the air to impale his side.

He stiffened, jerked away from me, and looked down.

A trickle of blood seeped out from around the knife. He looked stunned, as though somehow, he hadn't fully expected me to do it. As though he fucking knew me.

But he didn't know me...

There was only one man who truly did.

Only one man I'd let inside the wall I'd built. I glanced at the phone in his hand, then lunged, tearing it from his grasp, and stumbled backwards. "I warned you," I gasped as I looked down at the screen and pressed the button.

But it was locked, the screen glaring, waiting. "The code."

"Fuck you." He pressed his hand against the blade and wince.

I lunged, that savagery tearing free from inside me as I smacked the knife hard, making him groan. "I *will* fucking kill you! *Now give me the goddamn code.*"

He lifted his gaze, his face paling as he smiled. "Five, five, six, nine, three."

My fingers trembled as I punched in the digits. I expected it to be a fucking lie, because everything else about him was...but the code wasn't. The screen unlocked with a *blink*. I punched the same icon I'd seen on Mateo's phone and waited as the screen from the CCTVs loaded.

But there was nothing, just a blank screen.

"It's gone," he said almost happily.

I jerked my gaze up, to find a smile creeping across his lips. 'What do you mean *gone?*"

"Press replay. It'll show you the last recording."

I didn't want to press the icon, didn't want to see what he was so eager to show me. But that panicked desperation forced my hand. I saw the movement of my hand, but I was unable to stop it from happening as I pressed the icon and watched the screen.

I knew instantly where it was. The camera angle caught the edge of Mateo's office, the same office where I'd waited for him...the same office where we'd come together. But as I watched the view now, I saw him rush forward, gun raised, with a look of desperation that made my heart stutter until, in a deafening flash, the image ended.

"Boom," Damien murmured, that sickening smile stretching wider.

I didn't understand what he meant...until I remembered that explosion...that had *rocked the air*. I jerked my gaze to the screen, then lifted it to him once more. I didn't feel myself in that moment, not my breaths, not my heartbeat. "No," I whispered and squeezed my eyes closed. *"No..."*

"Yes," The glee in his tone snapped me out of it.

I jerked my eyes open...*and lunged*. "You fucking *BASTARD!*"

I threw myself through the air to slam into him. My desperation was in control, forget everything else as I rained blows down on him. But this time he was ready and grasped me around the throat, then with a grunt, he drove me backward until I slammed against the wall with a *thud!*

Stars danced behind my eyes with the blow as his grip tightened.

No!

Fear bucked inside me, forcing me to move. I lashed out, driving my fist through the air toward him. I tried to focus on the knife in his side, but his grip clenched until there was no more air. Fire lashed my face as I tried to breathe, sucking in *nothing*.

My chest caved, my vision blurred.

Crack! The blow rocked my head, snapping it to the side.

"We could've been good together."

Crack!

"WE COULD'VE BEEN GOOD!

Crunch!

The room swayed, growing darker. I tried to hold on...tried to claw the darkness, tried to keep myself upright. But the world around me grayed, blending into darkness, until I couldn't hold on anymore.

31

Mateo

Get up...MATEO! GET THE FUCK UP!

I blinked and sucked in air that bit and clawed, trying to understand what happened.

"Are you good?" Edon's blurred face swam in my vision.

"Edon?" I whispered, my voice choked and hoarse.

"It's me, brother. You with me now?" He scanned my body, fear crowding those dark eyes.

I licked my lips. "Yeah." I shoved and sat up, trying to remember what the hell happened.

"You're goddamn lucky I was coming after you." My brother shook his head, the fear shifting to cold, hard rage as he looked behind him.

Boom! The deafening sound of the blast filled my head. No wonder my damn ears were ringing. I pushed against the floor and staggered upright, looking at what was left of the command center. There was nothing but rubble. Nothing but a hole, nothing but...*Xael.*

Fear punched through me as I scanned the ruin and turned. "Xael." I looked to my brother, who just scowled.

"You didn't find her?" His brow furrowed as if the same sick wave of dread washed through him, and he was never scared.

I shook my head, glancing toward my apartment. She wasn't there...she wasn't...

"I have to go," I muttered, and turned just as gunshots cracked out again.

Edon snapped his gaze toward the sound as it grew louder and then strode forward, lifting his rifle from his side. "Go, I'll take care of as many as I can."

I jerked my gaze toward the sound of gunfire as it exploded, then licked my lips as I took a step toward what was left of the hallway. Agony ripped through me as I moved. Something deep howled in my side, but I didn't look down...didn't focus on anything but her. "Stay safe, brother."

"Always," he answered, already lifting the muzzle and taking aim.

Crack!

The shot exploded as I left him behind. Blood called to blood inside me. That ache throbbing and snarling, demanding that I stay by his side. But there was a louder part of me that demanded obedience, the part that clenched and throbbed, that ached for another even more.

Xael occupied a space inside me that even blood couldn't touch. In the darkness...she was all that remained. I lifted my hand, drew my gun from my holster, and winced, striding toward the automatic doors as they opened. Well, at least we hadn't lost power.

I lowered my head as the cyclonic wind died away in an instant, leaving me stumbling until I caught my balance. Above me...there was blue sky once more. "What the fuck?"

Dark clouds swirled around the island in the distance. But right now...we were in the eye of the storm. The eye, that would pass much too soon, then the winds would return, even worse than before.

Crack!

Crack!

The sound of gunfire drove me forward. I ground my teeth and lengthened my stride, scanning the buildings. *Where the fuck are you, Xael?* Plumes of black smoke drifted over the buildings in the distance, coming from the water. I tried to think like she would...but it was the bodyguard whose image rose in my mind's eye.

He'd want her off the island, no matter who he left behind.

He didn't care about anyone else...which was exactly what a bodyguard should do. I strode toward that black smoke as the idea took hold. He couldn't fly the jet, and he wouldn't take the risk, but the boats...now those he'd use to get her away from here. I would.

I'd hoped to...until the goddamn attack.

Crack!

I smothered the urge to turn around, to open fire alongside my brother, and kept walking, raising my hand to the roaring agony in my side. *Get to her...that's all that matters. Just get to her.*

I strode forward, heading past the buildings and toward the water. The black smoke drifted through the still air, causing me to cough and gag. I slapped my hand over my mouth as I strode toward the water. But the closer I came, the less I could see through the smoke...but I could hear enough to know she wasn't here.

The burning hull of one of the cruisers bobbed in the water beside the dock, then slowly sank. I spun, searching the water and the island. Where the fuck was she?

I had nowhere else to go, nothing but to walk. I made my way back along the dock and climbed, that tearing in my side growing fangs with the effort, until I crested the side. *Where would they go? Where...*

I scanned along the buildings as instinct pulled me forward. Flashes of memories came rushing back to me, memories of when they'd called me *Komandant*...memories of when they'd feared me. I rounded the corner of a building as the past took hold.

In an instant, I was the soldier they'd sent in alone, the one they knew wouldn't hesitate...the one they'd feared. I lifted my weapon as I neared one of the buildings, then stopped. Something made me turn my head toward a building in the distance. Instinct drove me forward and I followed that dark whisper, cutting across the grounds as the sound of gunfire continued to crackle.

Darkness seeped out from under the external door on the far west side of Building Three. It was an access door, one that led to a storeroom and the inside of the building. A door that was supposed to be locked...

Through the gap at the bottom, an inky blackness seeped out, and the closer I came, the more I realized what it was...*blood.* The island was under attack, the heirs of the Commission being hunted, and I was sure more blood had been spilled this day than any in the history of the controlling Mafia families. But it was that blood that made me freeze, *that blood that made me take notice.*

I reached into my pocket and pulled out my card, praying like hell the security hadn't been damaged. The closer I got, the more the biting stench of the smoke gave way to something sweeter and metallic. I didn't need to reach down to know my instinct was right. Instead, I pressed the card against the scanner and yanked open the door.

Darkness gave way to smoke-hazed air. I blinked through the dimness, catching the wide-open stare of Xael's bodyguard. "No." I jerked my gaze up to scan the gloom before turning to him once more and knelt beside his body.

A single shot to the head, the exit wound...substantial. *Had Xael done that?*

The thought rose swiftly. If she had...then she'd had a reason.

I stepped across his body and headed further into the room, leaving the bodyguard without a second thought. He was no use to me now. Need burned inside me like the sting in my eyes as they watered. All I cared about was her...Finding her...*protecting her.*

Then getting her the hell off this island.

I made my way through the storeroom to the open door of the hallway.

"Stupid fucking bitch!" The male roar drew my focus.

Instinct snapped something inside me...and savagery followed. I headed toward that sound, drawn by the sick tremble of rage, and neared the broken-open door of one of the weapons rooms. But one of my guards stood at the other end of the room, bent over, screaming at someone on the floor.

Someone curled up.

Someone with their back to me.

A woman.

I stepped in as thunder boomed in my head, knowing, but not wanting to believe. The guard wrenched his boot backwards and then lashed out, driving the blow into her back.

Her...

Xael's hair splayed out behind her. I flinched as though slapped and silently moved deeper into the room.

"You think he's going to come for you...HE'S DEAD!" the guard screamed, then jerked his boot back once more.

The movement triggered the beast inside me.

I lunged, diving through the air, and unleashed a savage roar.

He whirled, his eyes wide as he saw me. *"No,"* he whispered the second before I hit him.

I drove him backwards, taking us both to the floor. Rage was all I felt...*Xael was all I saw.*

Unmoving.

Her hair fanned out on the floor.

The bastard roared and pushed upwards, swinging his fist, and that was when I recognized him, the guard from the command center. *"Blake?"*

He stilled, his clenched fist hovering in the air. His lips curled against his teeth.

No. Not Blake, even if he wore the name...

"Who the fuck are you?" The words slipped free before I realized.

The sneer shifted to a smile. Darkness glinted in his eyes. The kind of savagery I'd seen before, and all of a sudden, I was back in that house again. Only this time, the girl crouched in the corner was Xael, motionless on the floor.

"I'm going to kill you." I kept my gaze glued to him, aware of his every breath.

In a second, the world stilled...my pulse slowed. There was no more panic now. *Just a knowing.*

This was the end.

Of her.

Of us...

Of me.

"Mateo." A low moan came, forcing my gaze to her.

Movement followed, her fingers curling as her hand reached out, her hair shifting as she lifted her head. Those dark eyes were all I saw...and that surge of hunger roared through me. Not to survive...*but to protect her.*

I jerked my gaze back as Blake let out a roar and drove out his fist, catching me on my cheek. *Crack.* My head snapped sideways, but I turned right back to him.

I didn't care about any pain, only that roaring inside me that scanned the bastard, stopping for a moment on the knife sticking out of his side. I didn't have to ask what had happened. *That's my girl.*

He yanked his fist back, planning for blow number two. He didn't make it. Something roared inside me as I lunged. I unleashed a fast punch, smashing him in the nose and hearing the crunch as it broke. He fell back, his eyes widening, stunned.

I shoved upwards, desperation driving me. He wasn't expecting me to react...*because he didn't know me.*

I reached down, jerked him upright, and spun him, then wrapped my arms around his neck from behind , standing at his back as I tightened my hold. Xael lifted her head and carefully turned over on the floor, unable to take her gaze from mine

Here was the beast, the monster that lived inside me.

The Komandant.

I released one arm as the bastard gasped and struggled, swinging his fists but unable to do me any damage. He should've been more careful, as I grasped the knife in his side and yanked the blade free. "You shouldn't have touched her," I said. "Shouldn't have touched what's mine."

I held her gaze, thrusting the knife until the blade punctured his chest. He jerked and gasped, his muscles screaming as he tried to twist his body against me...*until I stabbed again.*

Thump.

Thump. Thump. Thump.

I plunged the blade in deep, only stopping when his arms fell to his sides. His sharp, hard gasps were punctuated with the spray of blood. Droplets flew through the air to splatter the floor. He stilled and his body slumped against mine. All I saw was her eyes fixed on the man dying in my arms, then they slowly moved to mine.

I expected shock...was prepared for disgust, especially when I released my hold around his throat and his body slid down to fall on the floor with a *thud*. But the bastard wasn't dead...*not yet*.

Xael shoved upwards, her arms trembling. She fell before trying again, then lunged for me. She hit me with a *thump, her* arms clinging around my neck. "Jesus...*Jesus,*" she cried. "I thought you were dead."

"Murdererd..." the slow hiss came from the piece of garbage at my feet. "My family."

I gripped hold of her, taking comfort in the warmth, in the feel...in her stare as she gazed into my eyes.

"*I* thought *you* were dead." My voice was husky and hoarse, my throat burning from the smoke.

"Fucking *whore.*"

She snapped her gaze to the bleeding asshole on the floor. But I caught the flinch in her eyes as she slowly turned her gaze to mine, waiting for my reaction. She thought I didn't know? Thought that anything she did before us made a goddamn difference to how I felt about us?

It didn't...and as I held her gaze, I let her see just how much I felt. "It doesn't matter," I declared. "Anything that happened between you was one hundred percent my fault."

"Still...*a fucking wh—*"

She stepped away from me, took two steps, and lifted her boot to unleash it straight at him. Her boot connected with his chin, cracking his head backwards with a sickening blow. "That's for Rhys, you sick piece of filth."

She wobbled, her knees trembling as she tried to remain upright. I tightened my grasp around her waist.

"Mateo!" Edon's roar came from the hallway and the heavy thud of steps followed a second before my brother burst into the room.

He took one look at Xael as she stood over Blake as he lay dying on the floor, then turned his icy stare my way. Xael moved in an instant, turning in front of me to face him as my brother murmured, "Came to save your sorry ass...but it looks like I was too late."

32

Xael

I froze, watching as a man stepped through the doorway. A man I didn't know. He glanced at the dying man at my feet, then met my gaze. Cold...*Jesus, he was cold.* That lethal stare lingered on me and for a second, I thought he was *one of them.* One of the men sent to kill us...

I turned in Mateo's arms, shielding him as best I could, drawing the man's deadly stare. "Came to save your sorry ass...but it looks like I was too late," he announced with what I thought might have been a twitch of his lip.

Save him? I stilled, sucked in a hard breath, then turned again, wincing with the movement as I found Mateo's gaze. Something familiar lingered, forcing my gaze back to the man who was crossing the room.

A soft moan came from Blake at my feet. The bastard was still alive, until the familiar looking stranger who was striding toward us almost casually lifted the rifle in his hand and squeezed the trigger.

Crack.

The shot echoed in the room as the bullet struck, hitting Blake between the eyes. He twitched for an instant, and then he stopped. There were no more foul fucking words from his lips, no more hate in his eyes...just the same empty stare he'd left behind in Rhys' gaze.

A pang tore through my chest at the memory of my bodyguard.

"Xael," Mateo murmured behind me. "I'd like you to meet my brother, Edon."

I looked at the man. "Brother?"

No wonder the man looked familiar. He held my stare as I searched his gaze. Echoes of Mateo were in his face, the same jaw line, same dark complexion, but his eyes...they were empty, with the kind of darkness that terrified me. They might be blood, but they weren't the same.

"The rest?" Mateo murmured.

"Dead...what was left. The other heirs of the Commission held their own. I just helped them even the playing field a little."

"And killed everyone in their path," Mateo finished.

Edon just held my stare. "It's what I'm good at."

I swallowed hard and glanced at the very dead Blake. I had no doubt about that. None at all.

"Who the fuck was this?" Edon asked.

"Him." I jerked my head toward my biggest fucking mistake in a long line of them. "He said he was the last of the sixth family. The one they told stories about."

"The sixth family?" Mateo repeated, and shook his head. "That's bullshit, there never was a sixth family."

I scowled and shook my head. "Yes, the stories—"

"Are nothing more than a fabrication. A tale someone made up to make the Commission seem even more dangerous."

I'd heard the stories, had even asked my father about it once, earning myself a slammed door in my face. I was sure...

"Ask them yourself." Mateo just shrugged, stepped closer and held out his hand. "Most of them will be here tomorrow."

I flinched, meeting his stare, and took his hand. "Tomorrow?"

"They were already on their way before the attack started," he said as we made our way out of the room, leaving the dead behind.

The thought of that weighed heavy in the pit of my stomach. My father hadn't wanted me to come here in the first place... and now...I glanced at Mateo. After this, I'd be controlled even more. I tried not to think about that as we walked through the foyer of the building and out as the winds started gusting once more.

"Looks like we're through the eye!" Mateo yelled in my ear.

I just nodded, unable to care anymore. Agony was a fist beating in the back of my head. My knees buckled as I stepped and I began to fall, until strong hands caught me.

"Easy now." Mateo lifted me carefully.

He clenched his jaw, agony roaring to life in his eyes. "Hold on to me, Xael. Let me take care of you."

It wasn't in me to be weak, not after all I'd been through. But as I wrapped my arms around his neck, it didn't feel like weakness. It felt like fate. I lowered my head to his chest as he carried me back toward the main building. As the doors opened and we started to step through, I realized we were alone.

"Your brother?"

"He'll be around." He carried me along the hallway, stopped outside the door to his apartment and reached for his card. "He's always there when I need him."

I wanted to ask him more about his brother, somehow I knew he was more than important...but very, very dangerous. But none of that mattered as Mateo opened the door to his apartment and carried me through. I let everything else fall away.

"Put me down, Mateo," I murmured. "I want to take care of you too."

He stilled, searching my gaze, then slowly lowered my feet to the floor. "If we do this, we need to make a pact."

I waited...

"No more secrets." He lifted his hand, brushing aside a strand of hair from my cheek. "No more hiding the truth from each other, no matter how ugly that truth is. No more..."

"Protecting me." I broke in. "And breaking my goddamn heart."

Sadness roared to the surface as he nodded, lowering his head to kiss me. "Deal."

But I pulled away. "One more thing." I held his stare. "But you won't like it."

"Try me."

"No more of this..." I glanced around the apartment.

"The apartment?"

"The island," I demanded.

He just smiled. "I'll do you one better. No more Commission."

My breath caught as it hit home. No more lies, no more danger. It was what I'd always wanted, to get away from my family and their bloody business. "For both of us."

"Deal?" he murmured.

My answer was a smile as I pulled him down until his lips met mine. *Deal.* I kissed him, for not nearly as long as I wanted, until I pulled away. "Okay, now how do we do this?" I lowered my gaze to the bloodstain on his side.

He grabbed my hand and guided me into his bathroom. "You first," he murmured, searching my eyes. "Always."

He tugged the bottom of my shirt, lifting it until he looked down. I raised my arms, letting him slowly undress me. The moment wasn't about sex, but still that burn of desire moved between us as he lowered his head. His hands skimmed my body, gently finding the swollen, painful parts.

"Turn around, Xael."

I did as he said, lowering my head and gripping the edge of the sink as I stood naked in front of him. His fingers were sure and careful, moving my hair aside as he probed the base of my skull, until agony was a sledgehammer blow that ripped through my skull.

A low snarl followed, but he didn't stop, just moved even more carefully until he'd searched every part of my skull, then moved back to the painful area. "Here? Is this where it hurts the most?"

I nodded, swaying as darkness bled into my mind.

He strode to the cupboard and pulled out a first aid kit, then unzipped it to grab a small flashlight. "Follow the light." He shone it into my eyes as I tracked the movement. "No concussion and nothing is broken, looks like it's a nasty contusion. Christ, you were lucky, it could've been worse...a lot worse. I have you." He pulled me against him. "Can you manage the shower?"

I nodded, letting him bend and start the spray. Steam filled the space, the mist warm, white, reminding me of the black smoke from the boats...and then Rhys.

A moan tore free from that wounded part in my chest. Mateo jerked his gaze toward me and stepped closer. "What is it?"

I carefully shook my head. I couldn't answer, because no words would ever ease the pain. Tears slipped down my cheeks. I couldn't have stopped them even if I'd wanted to...and right then, I didn't want to.

"Hey." Mateo wrapped his arms around me. But he didn't offer any words of comfort.

Somehow, he knew that wouldn't help me at all. He just did the one thing I needed, the one thing no one else ever had for me...*he just let me cry*. Holding me against him, he eased me under the shower spray.

Warmth hit my back, washing away the bitter stench from my skin. If only I could wash the last few weeks away from my mind just as easily. But I couldn't. Mateo stepped away, made sure I was steady, then dragged his shirt off and unbuckled his pants. I glanced at his gun on the vanity and realized in an instant who he was. He was a killer...a dangerous, merciless killer. The memory of him rose in my mind, his arm wrapped around Damien's throat as he ripped the knife from his side. *Then thwack. Thwack. Thwack.*

He'd stabbed him without flinching, without wrestling with the darkness inside him, almost like he knew the darkness...almost like he...

"Xael?"

I flinched and jerked my gaze to his.

Darkness glinted in his eyes. But it wasn't a savage glint. No...it was one filled with fear, as though somehow he knew exactly what I'd been thinking, *or remembering*. But that darkness in him didn't frighten me.

"I'd never hurt you," he whispered, brushing my hair back. "Not physically...and I'm going to try my fucking best not to hurt you emotionally, either. But I'm a monster, Xael. There's nothing soft inside me, nothing *kind*. I've never needed to be." He stared into my eyes. "Until now. For you I want to try. For you, I'll do my damnedest."

He didn't realize...he was exactly the man I wanted.

The same man who'd stood in the shadows of his study and watched a reckless woman drink his expensive Scotch and dare him to make a move. He'd made a move alright. "I know you will," I whispered. "And I'll do my damnedest to keep you on your toes."

He stilled, then slowly smiled. "I wouldn't want it any other way."

I let him kiss me, slowly and carefully, then pulled away to grab the washcloth and gently run it over my body, a body he'd touched before. But this time it felt different. This time he touched me with care and compassion, searing his touch like a brand across my skin.

"I've never cared before," he murmured, lowering his lips to my shoulder.

I closed my eyes with the sensation and leaned my head back into the warm water, letting it course against the throb at the base of my skull.

"I never wanted to," he continued. "But I care about you, Xael… so much it fucking terrifies me."

I kept my head back, letting him murmur his confession into my skin, until I slowly met his gaze. Thunder echoed inside me, the kind of thunder I'd never heard before, but one I knew instantly. This was it…he *was it*. My home.

"I love you," I whispered the words I hated, the words I'd sworn I'd never whisper again. The words that had almost broken me last time, and yet here I was…saying them all over again.

"You love me?" Mateo lifted his head to gaze into my eyes.

I was tired of lying, especially to myself. "I do. I fucking love you. But I swear to God, Mateo. You fucking ruin me like you did before, and I'll kill you."

"Not before I killed myself," he whispered, grazing his fingers along my spine. "I thought I was protecting you. Thought… thought I was saving you from me."

"Don't you get it by now?" I met his gaze. "That's the last thing I wanted saving from."

He gripped my chin, tilted my head up, and kissed me.

I let him take care of me, let him steady me from the shower and help me dress. I let him do what he wanted, laying me down on the bed and curling his body around mine. When his phone rang, he switched it off, shutting out the world.

We lay like that, taking comfort in the feel of each other, and slowly that brutal throb in the back of my head subsided, letting me close my eyes. It was Mateo who lingered when darkness came. Mateo who held my gaze as he stabbed a man to death.

I slept, but woke when Mateo called my name, dragging me from the depths. The doctor came, checking my injuries and then his. But I was thankful for the thud of the front door closing, and when Mateo came back and slid under the sheets beside me, I knew in my heart that this was right.

WHEN I NEXT CRACKED OPEN MY eyes, I felt like I'd been hit by a truck. For a second, I didn't know what had happened, slowly licking my lips as the memories slipped in like an assassin. The attack, the boats exploding, Rhys... then Damien.

"Morning."

I blinked, rolled, and instantly regretted it. Agony roared through my head as I turned to find Mateo sitting beside me, dressed in his usual suit. All of a sudden, the memories that'd been kept at bay rushed in. Him, his brother...and us.

"How long was I asleep?"

"A good fourteen hours. You needed it, but I'm glad you're awake. I was sure you wanted to be up when they arrived."

"They?"

"Yes," he answered. "Your father will be here within the hour."

"My father?" Panic tore through me.

"As well as a few other members of the Commission."

The way he said it made me freeze. There was a hardness in his tone, and it scared me. I carefully pushed up from the bed, meeting his gaze. "You're worried."

"And you're not?"

Only a fool would stand against the Commission and not be afraid of the outcome, and Mateo was anything but a fool. "Then I'll shower and get dressed."

A nod of his head, and I pushed the sheets aside, catching my breath as that cruel throb came to life again. But I swallowed the moan and headed for the bathroom. I needed to be strong now, stronger than I'd ever been before.

It wasn't just my father we were up against...

It was *everyone*.

33

Mateo

By the time the boats carrying the members of the Commission came, the island was almost empty. The cyclone had gone, leaving blue skies and the dead behind. A steady stream of helicopters had shuttled the remaining guests to the mainland. My men, Xael, and I had stayed behind.

While she'd slept, I'd seen to those desperate to leave, sending Bruno Bernardi and Evan Valachi, as well as Annalise Eden off the island, and then everyone else. We searched the buildings for the murderer, Sophie Harrison, who'd come to the island under the guise of Evan, but after endless hours, the search had been called off. All of that had happened while Xael slept.

I hadn't had the heart to wake her.

The truth was, I wanted her here when I faced them...her father and the Commission.

I'd sent the reports outlining what'd happened in the wake of the attack, along with all the information I had on Damien

Blake. After the attack, it'd been found he'd been just a disillusioned idiot with a hefty trust fund to his name.

He'd grown up in and out of mental institutions, until his father killed himself, leaving behind a stack of letters. Letters that told him they were meant to sit alongside the members of the Commission. A full-blown investigation was underway as to who he and his father really were.

But so far, they were saying nothing if they'd found anything.

The sixth family was all a lie...*wasn't it?*

The sound of the boats' engines drifted on the breeze. Sunlight glinted on the windows, catching my eye as I stood on the embankment. Fingers captured mine. I glanced at Xael, standing beside me. She was worried, but then again, she wasn't naive, knowing exactly the kind of force I was up against.

No one left the Commission, not alive, at least, and if you'd asked me a week ago if I cared about that, I would've said no. I'd had nothing worth living for. I clenched my grip around hers, taking solace in her touch, and faced them as the two luxury cruisers sidled up to the dock and the deckhands threw ropes to my men waiting for them.

But they weren't my men anymore.

They belonged to the men stepping from the boats.

They weren't all here, but there were enough.

Dominic Salvatore was the first to step onto the dock, heaving his body up with the hands of two of his security. I'd seen him in a video conference barely a week ago, but it might as well have been a lifetime. He'd aged in the days since I'd seen him... but hadn't we all?

Benjamin Rossi was next, stepping onto the dock and striding forward, dressed in black as though he was attending a funeral. The idea of that weighed heavily. Adrian Bernardi followed, then the man I was dreading, Taran Davies, Xael's father.

She stiffened beside me as he strode toward us, his gaze fixed on her.

"Commander," Dominic muttered, and looked around the island.

I waited, watching his reaction without seeming to watch them at all. I didn't know what they'd do, if they'd blame me for the entire attack and come guns blazing from the team of mercenaries that stepped off the second boat and came behind them, or what.

A nod from Dominic Salvatore and most of the men dispersed, invading my island. *The island...not* my *island, not anymore.* But a number of them stayed behind, flanking out to the sides, just as I would've commanded.

"Xael." Her father motioned her forward. "Come."

She stiffened beside me as I fixed my stare on him. I didn't like him...not one bit. He was a pig of a man, using his kin like pawns. I'd watched him over the years as he became not just a vile human being, but a cruel one, especially where his daughter was concerned. He didn't care about her, only about what embarrassment she'd bring him. No wonder she'd acted out.

I wasn't scared of him...I wasn't scared of any one of them. I had stayed under the idea that they'd protect Edon, that they were seen by Besnik to be the bigger threat. But I could see now that I'd been wrong.

They wouldn't protect us...not unless they could use us. Just like Taran had used his daughter.

"Xael," he growled. "Come *now.*"

"Yeah, I'm gonna take a pass on that," she answered.

I fought the twitch in the corner of my lips and added, "As will I. You can consider this my formal resignation. I'm out...and I'm taking Xael with me."

Dominic Salvatore nailed me to the spot with a dangerous stare. There was a glint in his eyes, one I'd seen many times before. Dominic Salvatore was a very dangerous man...one most people underestimated. Luckily, I wasn't most men.

The hairs on the back of my neck rose as we stood out in the open, unarmed, while his soldiers lifted their weapons, flanking our sides. Was he really going to do this? Was he really prepared to have them open fire, killing me...while Xael stood at my side?

The thought of that burned in my gut. Ruthless, low-life piece of shit.

"You know as well as any man that no one walks," Dominic Salvatore started.

A tiny red light danced in the middle of his chest. His head security officer jerked his gaze toward the thing and scowled. "Uh, sir," he murmured, then glanced toward the buildings in the distance.

"Unless they make a better offer," I finished.

I didn't like this offer...fucking loathed it if I was honest. But Edon had spent a good six hours trying to convince me this was the only way out. Made no difference to him, he said. A kill was a kill, regardless who paid.

Unless the kill was for family.

Which Dominic Salvatore was finding out.

The Commission leader didn't bother to look down at the sniper's mark dancing in the center of his chest. It was as though he'd known the moment he'd stepped off the boat how this would play out.

The corners of his lips twitched. "You were saying?"

"It seems my brother is in need of employment, on a contract basis, of course."

He just gave a nod. "Of course."

"In exchange for me...and Xael."

"What the fuck?" Taran jerked his gaze to Dominic.

But the head of the Salvatore line just held my gaze. He knew... he knew everything. The man hadn't missed a beat when I'd spoken to him on the phone yesterday after the attack. He'd just told me to prepare for their arrival. So this was me, being prepared.

"I take it this...leave of absence is nonnegotiable?" he asked.

"Very."

"You understand what that means?"

Taran just snarled. "No fucking way, Dominic, this is my goddamn daughter you're talking about."

"No." I glanced his way. "I'm talking about my future wife."

Xael jerked her gaze to me. "You are?"

I met her surprise. "I am."

In a second, the Commission and their army faded away, leaving her behind. I wasn't a man of words...only of action. I'd walked into that prison and carried out my brother...now I was carrying out my wife.

If she'd have me...

"Yes," she answered, as though she heard the tremor of fear in my head. "Fuck, yes."

"Then that solves that." Dominic nodded. "She's a member of the Commission, and as head of the Commission, I grant you two permission to marry and start a family."

"What...*now?*" Xael barked, her eyes widening.

I couldn't hold it back. The deep chuckle rumbled in my chest. "No, Xael. Not right now. When we're ready."

"Of course," Dominic agreed.

Taran Davies was deadly quiet. I didn't need to meet his gaze to know he didn't like this one bit. The sound of rotor blades grew louder. "Looks like our ride is here." I announced.

Dominic just glanced down at the red dot hovering on his chest. "I take it you'll be taking your brother with you."

I just shook my head and turned to leave, my smile lingering. "Nope...he's all yours."

I heard the confused mutter behind me as the leader of the Commission tried to work out if that was a good or bad thing. I was sure they'd work it out...*eventually.*

34

Mateo

Some time later...

"MR. RISTANI," the clerk nodded, his thick Australian accent strange to my ears as I strode through the doors to the hotel, leaving the heat of the island behind, and stepped into the cool air-conditioning.

Mr. Ristani.

That's how they knew me here.

Not Commander.

Not *The Commander.*

And not Komandant.

I lifted my gaze to the sprawling resort grounds. Green palm trees swayed in the summer breeze. It was the same cool ocean breeze, the same roar of the ocean, but everything else was different.

Crystal blue water shimmered clearer in the heat of the Whit-sundays. The beaches were whiter, the sand fine under my bare feet. I gripped the bottle in my hand and clutched the bag in my other, lifting it to clutch the access card in my fingers as I pressed it against the glass door, then stepped out, heading to our private villa at the far end of the resort.

I glanced down at the bottle of champagne in my hand and wondered if any of this was real—if *I* was real. Heavy steps echoed as I lengthened my stride. Movement. Warmth. The same tone in my voice. The same body...but everything else in me was changed.

I wasn't the same as I'd been before.

And it was all because of her.

I lifted my gaze, stepped up to the door, and pressed the card to the scanner. The lock clicked open and I pushed the door open, leaving it to close behind me with a *thud*.

But there was only silence.

"Xael?"

"Out here," she called.

I stepped through the cool air of the sprawling private rooms and headed to the doors to the outside...*and there she was.*

My gaze went to the long line of her neck and a surge of desire coursed through me as I stepped out the door onto the sprawling patio.

She'd wound her hair up, but a few long, midnight strands had rebelled, like the woman herself. They fell down, brushing the bare skin of her shoulders. Christ, she made me hard.

"Did you get them?" She lifted her gaze as I rounded her chaise lounge, flourishing the bag.

"Fresh off the trawler, didn't even make land."

She smiled at that, those dark eyes twinkling as her lips curled. Her gaze drifted, finding the open collar of my white shirt. "Delicious."

"Which?"

She met my gaze. "Both."

I placed the champagne and the bag of fresh oysters onto the table and turned. Against the backdrop of the fire, the ocean waited. Crashing, surging, blue with splashes of pink against the dimming sun.

We'd been here for a month. Long enough to forget who we were and where we'd come from...for a while at least. She lifted her bare foot, her skin beautiful and tanned, and ran it up the inside of my leg, crested the bend of my knee, and reached higher. "Always with the suits, Mateo," she teased, those perfect eyes twinkling.

I stepped closer, reached out to grasp the half-full glass from her hand, and placed it on the table beside the sprawling outdoor chaise. "Is that a complaint?"

Her head tilted, following my movement. "Not at all."

"Good," I smiled, and captured the thin strap of her dress with a finger, dragging it down those stunning goddamn shoulders. "Because while you care about what I'm wearing, I'm only caring about the fact you're wearing anything at all."

"Is that so?" A devious look surged to the surface. "Well..." she said slowly, never once taking her eyes from mine. "On that note..."

In an instant, she surged from the chaise, barreling into me as she lunged, racing for salvation.

She should know better...

She made it to the edge of the white pebbles, far enough to feel the grass under her bare feet before I captured her, winding one arm around her waist and lifting her off her feet.

"Woman," I growled as I heaved her into my arms.

But she kicked and bucked in my arms. Playing the part even as she fought to laugh.

I carried her like that, trapped by my arm as she flailed and snarled...*well, tried to, at least.*

She didn't put up much of a fight as I carried her toward the door of our apartment and strode through it, heading for the bedroom.

She fucking consumed me, this woman.

Made me forget who I was...

When I was around her, I wasn't *him*...that man born from necessity in a world filled with violence and death. I tossed her gently onto the bed, watching as she shoved, rolled, and sprang to her feet like a wildcat. Her dress moved with her, the thigh-high split giving me a glimpse of what I wanted.

And in an instant, that same hunger that had driven me most of my entire life came roaring back to the surface.

"You want some of this, Mateo?" She clenched her fists, her eyes as mesmerizing as the sky here on the other side of the world. Her smile was radiant, her lips curled with delight.

My body's reaction to her was instant, hardening, thumping. My heart was like a goddamn thunderstorm in my chest. I looked to her fists, clenched and thrust out into the air as I stalked her around the king-sized bed. "Some?" I met her gaze. "Woman...I'll be taking all of you."

I moved faster than she could track, lunging around the end of the bed toward her. She let out a tiny squeal as I grabbed her, pulled her with me to the bed, and rolled, trapping her underneath. I slipped my legs between hers, then spread them, driving hers apart until her dress strained and could go no more...but it was enough.

There was barely any fight in her as I grabbed her wrists and pinned them above her head with one hand. No fight at all when I reached down and cupped my hand against her sex. "And when I say all...*I mean all.*"

I teased her, rubbing the outside of her sheer black panties.

The woman was insatiable...and warm.

I slipped my finger under the edge of her elastic, finding her slick and ready. I lowered my head to whisper against her ear. "You're wet?"

Her hips surged upwards. "Always when I'm with you."

With a growl, I shoved her panties down, bending far enough until I could tear them free, then reached for the zipper of my pants.

"Always with the suits, Mateo," she repeated as I pulled my zipper down and surged between her legs.

Heat closed around me as I sank into her, driving all the way inside. She let out a moan and closed her eyes. "Yes..." the word was a hiss.

I gripped her hip with one hand, and clasped her hand in my other. My fingers slipped against the band on her finger. I lifted my gaze, finding the gold. "Mine," I growled, and drove my body into her, staring at the wedding band on her finger.

A month...

A month to become not just a man...

But a husband.

I lowered my gaze to hers. She was all I thought about, all I wanted.

She drove the darkness from my mind and let in the light.

"Yours," she moaned, clenching her other hand around my ass cheek. "Now, fuck me harder. We've got a baby to make."

I grinned at the words from her perfect potty mouth, and did exactly as she demanded...

After all...she was my wife.

35

Xael

"Shit."

I stared at the two faint lines in front of me. They were barely there. I squinted, peering closer. Maybe they were too faint to be anything. I glanced at the stopwatch on my wrist, watching the numbers race. Too faint to be real. Too faint to be...

But as the seconds passed, those two red lines grew bolder. So bold, they were unmistakable.

I sat back. *"Fuck."*

What was I going to say to him? Now of all times. It wasn't the right moment. Not for a conversation like this. *Ah, hey. You know a few weeks ago when you railed me all damn night in the middle of your quiet, moody, withdrawn moment. Well...surprise!*

"No." I whispered, grabbing the test and tossing it in the bin beside me. "Not a time for that conversation at all."

I rose, buttoned up my jeans, met my stare in the mirror before I flushed the toilet, washed my hands and walked out. He was sitting in the study, his legs crossed and his focus on the laptop positioned on his knees. Christ, when he was like that, he looked so...

Old.

Too old to want to be a father.

"Everything okay?" He never once looked up. Still, he was as in tune to me as though I were under a microscope.

"Yeah."

"Then why are you hovering?"

"I'm not...*hovering.*"

"Well, you're *something.*" He lifted his gaze from the screen, then closed the computer. "Talk to me."

I almost said it. The words were there, caught in my throat, desperate to come out. But as I opened my mouth to speak, I saw the sadness in his eyes and the dark circles he tried to hide by not looking at me.

The last few weeks, he'd been getting up in the middle of the night. He tried to be quiet, his bare feet barely making a sound on the tiled floor. But I sensed him, cracking open my eyes the moment he left our bedroom.

He was a caged lion.

At first, I wanted to blame it on the aftereffects of that island and the terror we'd endured. God knows, I still had nightmares of that place. I still dreamed of *him...the sick fuck who'd tried to end us all.*

But it wasn't that place.

It was something else.

Maybe it was me?

I searched those brown eyes, then lowered my gaze to the laptop on his knees. "Working on something?"

"A little consulting work, nothing major."

"Consulting." I made for the sofa and sank down onto the black velvet cushion next to him. "You didn't tell me you were doing consulting work."

He gave a scowl, then turned toward me. "I didn't think it'd be an issue."

"It isn't." I gave a shrug. God, I sounded like I was nagging. "Just wish I'd known is all."

I wish you'd let me in.

That was the issue. He'd shut me out and this...*consultation work* was just one more thing. I gave a sigh and rose. "Are you hungry? I'll make us some dinner."

"Sure. Let me help."

He did, seasoning the steaks. I winced at the smell of the meat and turned away, resisting the urge to gag. *Jesus...what the fuck was wrong with me?* Those two red lines rose to slap me in the face. *Oh, that's right.*

"Xael?"

I turned back, pasted a smile on my face. "Just feeling a little off."

That perpetual scowl deepened as he turned instantly, washing his hands at the sink before coming my way. He pressed the back of his hand against my forehead. "Are you sick?"

I smiled and shook my head. "No. Maybe I'm just a little fatigued. Someone has been getting up every night in the middle of the night. Don't know who that is, do you?"

My pulse was racing as he winced and lowered his hand, taking the bait. "I thought I was quiet."

"Not quiet enough."

"Apparently."

"Want to tell me what's going on with you?"

He gave a deep sigh. "I wish to hell I knew." He rubbed the back of his neck, then turned to the meat. I clenched my fists, stilling the shakes. That was close. Too damn close, and I had no idea why I was so scared to tell him.

"I just feel restless. Have been like this for a while now. I think it's...I think it's—"

"Go on."

*Say it...*the words rose. *Say what's really keeping you up. You want out, don't you? You want out of this life and back into the Commission. You were made for that life. Not this one...not the one where you're a—*

"I think I just need to find a hobby or something to occupy my time."

I turned away. "A hobby like the Commission, you mean?"

"What? No, not the Commission. Why the hell would you think that?"

I turned back, facing the real issue head on. "Because a man like you was made for violence, Mateo. A man like you was made for more than...*this.*" I gestured with my hand and looked around.

Our house was immaculate.

Expensive.

Very fucking expensive.

And yet...

"I just want you." He came closer and wrapped his arms around me. "I want this. I do. I just wish that fucking feeling would go away."

I bowed my head and slid my hands along his arms. I wanted this too. I just wished I believed him. We hugged, then ate, but I mostly pushed my food around on my plate. Normally, by now I would've demolished the steak and salad. But not tonight.

Tonight, I was restless...and a mess. Still, I forced a smile when Mateo lifted his head, chewed, and swallowed, watching me with that careful stare. He missed nothing, this man, not my pretense that everything was fine, or the fact I was feeling queasy.

"Not hungry?" He asked, motioning to my plate.

"I ate earlier." I lied. "I guess it's still sitting heavy."

One slow nod and he finished, wiped the corners of his mouth, and rose, taking my plate as he made his way to the kitchen and cleaned up. I watched him, taking in the precise way he moved.

Everything about him was careful.

But there was a time I'd made the mighty Commander come undone.

My mind slipped into the past.

Yes, there was a time when I'd made this stoic male desperate and demanding. When the man they called 'Commander' was a desperate mess. He'd driven me to follow him halfway around the world, only to shatter my heart when he was forced to align with the Commission...

Look how well that'd worked out.

After the night of the attack when we were forced to kill or be killed...he'd forced Dominic Salvatore into a position the head of the five main Mafia families didn't want to be in. Mateo had given him a choice, let him walk...*with me.*

But what he hadn't planned on was the ruthless Salvatore taking his brother Edon as a replacement...and using the hitman for all his dirty work. Mateo still wrestled with that, the guilt weighing him down.

It had been me...

Or his brother.

He rinsed the plates and stacked them into the dishwasher before rinsing the cloth. Fuck, the man was sexy. I rose from my seat and made my way over, rounding the kitchen counter to pull the cloth from his hand. He met my gaze, that crease between his brows furrowing.

I might feel queasy enough not to want to eat, but that lack of hunger made itself known in other ways.

"Xael?" He murmured.

"Mateo." I answered, tossing the cloth into the sink and pulling him with me toward the bedroom.

He didn't require much convincing.

That need still burned between us, smoldering and seething, like a battleground of desire. We made our way through the house to the bedroom. The sound of the ocean crashed outside, filling our room with that thunderous, rhythmic sound. I let go of his hand and moved to the buttons of my blouse. But I needn't have worried.

He strode forward, gently pulling my hands down to replace them with his own. The buttons were released before he pushed my blouse over my shoulders, letting it fall to the floor. Then he grabbed me around my waist, lifting my feet from the floor.

I slid my fingers through his thick, dark hair, finding a few more grays at the edges. It only made him look more handsome...and unfathomable. That's exactly what Mateo was...the darkest, deepest depths of desire. I held his gaze, then lowered my head and kissed him.

Hard lips gave way under mine.

Movement blurred before he lowered me to the bed.

He broke away, watching me as he slowly unbuttoned my jeans, then moved to my boots and tugged them off.

"You won't tell me what's going on with you tonight."

Bang.

My boot hit the floor.

"So maybe I can fuck it out of you, instead."

Bang.

My other boot landed.

I dragged one strap of my bra down. "You can give it your best goddamn shot. How about that?"

The curl of his lips sent my heart fluttering. "Challenge accepted."

He peeled my jeans from my body, then my panties were next as I reached around and unhooked my bra, pulling it free. He was still dressed. Still wearing those perfectly tailored slacks and white shirt with the sleeves rolled up against his muscular forearms.

Fuck, he turned me on when he dressed like that...and as he straightened, rising above me like a glorious and murderous god, I knew he knew how he affected me. I saw it all in the mischievous glint in his eyes. He looked down at me, taking in every inch.

One knee lifted to the edge of the bed before he climbed on, then leaned down to lick my nipple. "I might just start here."

I closed my eyes and leaned my head back. "That's a *very* good place to start."

"Then move here." He kissed the underside of my breast and moved lower, skimming the ridges of my ribs until he kissed the curve of my hip.

My pulse raced as he moved across to my abdomen, kissing me gently before he moved lower. I pressed my hand against the back of his head. If I told him now, then what...he'd push that empty feeling aside, that's what.

Until when?

A tiny voice whispered. He moved lower, dragged his fingers up my thigh, and pushed in. I shoved the doubt and the fear aside, pulling myself back to the feel of his hands and lips and tongue as he pressed against the tip of my slit and licked deeper.

I lost myself in that, letting him carry me away the only way he knew how. He , hooked his arm underneath my knee, lifted, and sucked my core before pushing his fingers further in.

Tell him.

A moan tore free.

I almost mouthed the words, almost spilled it all, but that delicious wave of desire flooded me, driving me upwards. I gripped his jaw, pulled his mouth to mine, and kissed him. He tasted like me, salty and sweet at the same time.

I reached for his belt and yanked it free. In a frenzy, he pulled his shirt over his head and fought the button of his slacks. One shove and he pushed them down, along with his boxers. He was settled between my legs in an instant and pushed in.

Desire glistened on his lips as they curled as he surged in deep.

"Fuck...*I...love...you.*" He grunted.

All I felt was him.

His cock, punishing.

His need, consuming.

His child...growing.

My core clenched, stroked by the length of him rubbing that spot inside. I spread my legs further apart and clenched my ass. "I...*love you too.*" I cried as my orgasm hit me,.

Sparks detonated behind my eyes.

I dropped my legs, my muscles quivering, as I gave into the release. Still, my husband...my *Mateo*, thrust once, twice, then lunged forward to brace his body above me and thrust one last time before he groaned low and guttural as he filled me with warmth.

I sucked in a hard breath as I reached up to caress his face. We'd made love hundreds of times, in every position and every second we could. Especially in those days following the attack. Still, it wasn't enough. It wasn't anywhere near enough.

It never would be.

He collapsed beside me, sucking in gulps of air until he managed. "You okay?"

I waited for a second, then met his stare. "Yes."

He rolled onto his side and rested his head on his hand. "Ready to talk now?"

I smiled, that delicious feeling stealing the fight right out of me. "I'm ready to sleep."

"Figures." He muttered, giving me a smile and reaching around my waist to drag me closer. "You just don't have the stamina you used to."

"Listen here, old man."

"Old, huh?" He thrust his softened cock against my thigh. "Do I need to fuck you again to curb that tongue?"

I closed my eyes as a wave of exhaustion swamped the euphoria and dragged me slowly into darkness. "If you do...just don't wake me."

My words were a mumble. That exhaustion was undeniable as it reached out, spread its wings around me, and swallowed me down. I slept, curled against his body, safe and protected, like I always felt when I was with him.

There was no fighting.

No guns.

No men coming for me.

Just nothingness.

Just…

BEEP.

I surfaced.

Beep.

Darkness waited when I cracked open my eyes. Deep snores ceased beside me.

Beep.

The bed dipped as he rolled to reach for his phone. I felt the movement and turned to see the muted backlight of his phone.

"Mateo?"

He pushed upwards, staring at the screen…not saying a thing. That worried me more than anything. I rose as fear pushed the darkness away. "Talk to me."

He lifted the phone, listening. But I knew something was wrong. There was no recording, no sound that came through the speaker, no voice on the other end of the line.

"He's in trouble."

That's all he said.

"Who?"

He rose from the bed and walked to the bathroom. "My brother."

36

Mateo

"He said that?" she asked.

I shook my head. "No."

"What was the message?"

My gut clenched as I flicked on the bathroom light. "Nothing."

"Nothing?"

"Nothing," I repeated and opened the cupboard, grabbing my shaving kit.

"Then how do you know it's him?"

I lifted my gaze to the mirror, to those dark, empty eyes. Ones that looked like my brother's. "I just know. He's in trouble. I have to go."

"Fine."

I stiffened, then turned. "What do you mean *'fine'*?"

She disappeared into the walk-in closet beside the bathroom. She wasn't fighting. *Xael has never not fought.* I strode out to watch her from the doorway as she grabbed jeans, a shirt, and a thick jacket, then reached for a heavy bag stowed away in the back.

"I mean what I said, Mateo. *Fine.*"

I scowled as she walked past me and dumped the bag and clothes on the bed. "I'm coming with you."

"Like hell you are."

She turned to me. Only then did I see the fire, the one she'd kept from her tone. It blazed to the surface now, alive and consuming, like it didn't just live inside her...like it *was* her.

"Oh, yeah?" She growled. That tone was as dangerous as I'd ever heard...from anyone.

I steadied myself. There was no way she was coming. No fucking way I'd take her if there was even the slightest risk. "Yeah."

She took a step. Even naked, she was powerful and glorious as she stopped in front of me and lifted her gaze. "Try and leave me. See what happens."

I shook my head. "Don't be stubborn."

"Oh, this is not me being stubborn, Mateo. I haven't even *begun* to be stubborn. This is me...*your wife,* going wherever you are."

I moved closer, reaching out to grab her shoulders. "I have no idea where I'm going. I have *no idea* what this is. I just know its's him. This is that feeling I spoke about, that nagging feeling that something isn't right."

"Then we work it out together, Mateo. This...marriage isn't one where you get to charge off into the sunset and leave me behind. If you wanted a wife who was going to be content with sitting here waiting for you, then you married the wrong woman."

I flinched, shaking my head.

"Did you marry the wrong woman, Mateo?"

"No." My answer was instant. "That's the only thing I've ever done right in my life."

She gave a slow nod, stepped out of my grasp, and moved to the bathroom door before stopping. "Do I have time for a shower?"

I stared at her, reeling...then slowly nodded.

"Good, I'll be ready in fifteen minutes." She answered, then stepped into the shower and started the spray.

I watched her for a second before I lifted my phone. The woman made me feel off center, always pushing me beyond my boundaries. If I said settling down with her like this came easily, I'd be lying. I was made for war, but I was also made for her...which is where the battle lay.

I pressed the numbers on my phone and listened to my brother's phone ring until it went to voicemail.

I didn't leave a message.

Because I already knew.

He wasn't going to answer.

I strode to my closet, grabbed a bag, and started packing. The fact she'd had a bag already packed nagged at me. The woman knew me better than I knew my own damn self. I walked to the bed and tossed my clothes inside, then went back, grabbed my weapons, and dressed as the shower spray switched off.

She was out before I knew it, toweling her hair with one hand as she dumped her bathroom supplies onto the bed beside her bag, then started dressing, pulling on black jeans, a black t-shirt, and heavy boots.

"You knew."

She laced her boots and straightened. "Of course I knew. I knew the man I married. I have no intentions of changing him… just like I'm sure you have no intentions of changing me."

She floored me.

Every. Single. Time.

"I'll make the calls," I murmured. "Find his last location. We can start there."

She stood, then bent down and lifted her bag. "That sounds perfect."

By the time I'd made a couple of quick calls, grabbed my bag, and headed out, she was right behind me. One call later and I found Edon had landed in Colorado two weeks ago. Since then, his handler hadn't heard from him. While Xael listened, she texted our pilot, instructing him to get our jet ready.

An hour after my brother called, we were driving to the airport. Darkness waited as I pushed the Lexus harder, listening to the engine respond as I left our coastal oasis behind and headed for the city, the private airstrip, and the sleek jet we owned.

I worked the gears while my thoughts drifted.

I didn't like this, not her silent and purposeful beside me.

Not her here at all.

My pulse raced as I narrowed in on that feeling. I'd known something was wrong, just like I'd known he was in trouble in Ispeli Prison in our home country all those years ago. It was a heaviness...a scream trapped in the back of my mind.

I felt that now more than ever. Our headlights swept through the endless dark landscape. There were very few lights out here, just a vast emptiness we both craved. Silence. Peace. *Each other.*

I glanced at my wife, who stared straight ahead.

She shouldn't be doing this.

Did you marry the wrong woman, Mateo?

Fuck, that question hurt. More than I expected.

The faint sparks of city lights glinted in the distance. I focused on the road, turned toward the airstrip on the outskirts of the city, and braked outside the towering ten-foot fence. The lights were on in the hangar. As I rolled down the window and leaned out, punching in the code for the gate, I caught a glimpse of the tail end of the jet.

We'd be in the air before I knew it...

Still, it wasn't fast enough.

I drove the car through the gate, parked in the extra bay of the hangar, and climbed out. Xael hadn't said a word, not for the entire drive. She climbed out too, pulled our bags out of the trunk, and headed for the waiting plane.

"Xael, Mateo." Our pilot greeted us at the foot of the boarding stairs.

"Warren." My wife answered with a smile. "Thank you for being on stand-by."

He should be, we paid him enough. I gave him a nod. "You have the details?"

"Flight plan has already been confirmed. We're ready for wheels up when you are."

"Good." I answered as I followed Xael up the stairs and into the plane.

She had the bags stowed away and was in her seat before I even got there. I scowled. This silence between us was turning awkward.

I sat near the window, sinking into the plush leather seat. "Are we going to talk about this?"

She lifted her gaze to the pilot as he disappeared into the cockpit. "Sure, talk."

I clenched my jaw. "You're being unreasonable."

She swiveled in her seat instantly. "Am I?" That anger seethed in her stare. "It's unreasonable that a wife wants to be there to protect her husband? It's *unreasonable* that you could let *anyone* fully into your life? Are you in this or are you just testing the waters, Mateo?"

"Testing the waters?" I repeated. "Where the hell did that come from?"

She turned back as the engine noise grew louder. "From the same place I've been this entire time. It's you that takes one step forward and one step back. Make your mind up, Mateo. The whiplash is making me dizzy."

She closed her eyes with that, shifting her ass to slide further down in the seat.

Make your mind up?

I lowered my gaze to the wedding ring on her finger. I thought I *had* made up my goddamn mind?

Anger flared. I opened my mouth to say exactly that...

But the words didn't come.

Instead, I looked at her closed lids, finding the dark circles under her eyes.

She needed sleep.

We *both* needed sleep.

The engine noise grew to a crescendo as we surged forward, rolling slowly at first until, with a roar, we picked up speed, tore down the runway, and finally lifted.

The weightlessness consumed me. I eased back into the seat and stared straight ahead, before I followed my wife's example and closed my eyes. But sleep didn't come. Instead, all I heard was Xael's voice inside my head. *It's you that takes one step forward and one step back.*

A twitch came at the corner of my eye. She was right. She was fucking right, and I knew it.

37

Xael

I jerked open my eyes as the jet jolted when the wheels touched down, the tires squealing as they connected with the runway. I lifted my head and found myself curled on one side, my head resting on Mateo's shoulder. He met my stare as I swallowed a yawn and tried to remember what the hell was going on...

Then it all came rushing back to me. The call. The fight...*the baby*.

"Bab—" I started, then my eyes widened as I caught myself, aware he was watching me.

"Babe." He murmured carefully. "Well, at least that's a better greeting than I was expecting."

Heart rushed to my cheeks, making that line between his brows deepen. He didn't buy it, not when I pulled away from him and turned away to hide the truth in my stare. I gripped the armrest as we raced along the runway. But one look out of the window, and confusion set in. "This isn't Colorado."

"No." Mateo answered as the jet braked hard and came to a stop at the front of the hanger. "It isn't."

I turned around. "Where are we?"

"Constance city."

"Constance?" I pressed the seatbelt clasp and rose. "What are we doing here?"

Mateo stood up, popped open the overhead compartments, and pulled out the luggage I'd stowed away. "Meeting Edon's handler."

"His handler?" What was he, some kind of greyhound?

I said nothing, just followed him out of the plane. The sun peeked out over the horizon, drawing my focus. Mateo spoke to the pilot, I assumed giving him instructions to where we were finally headed.

"Ready?" My husband called, glancing my way.

He nodded toward a car waiting for us through the open doors of the hangar. I followed him as he carried our bags toward the car, opened the trunk, and stowed them away. I climbed into the passenger seat. Sleep had slowly faded, but now I was fine, until I clasped the seatbelt and felt a pang low in my bladder, reminding me of the one glaring secret I hid from the one person I'd vowed to give my all.

Every inch of my darkness.

Every ray of my light.

Yet, here I was. *Thud.* The driver's door closed.

"You okay?"

I gave a nod, then met his gaze. "Do you know where we're heading?"

He pressed the button to start the engine. "I was able to get an address while you slept."

"Oh." I glanced his way, seeing the circles under his eyes once more.

It didn't look like he had had any rest. Worry deepened the creases in the corners of his eyes. I reached out and rested my hand on his as he headed for the city. It'd been a long time since I'd been to Constance and as I looked out, finding everything new, I grew worried.

What would we find when we tracked Edon down? Would we be walking back into the middle of a gun battle...*or worse?* I didn't know. All I knew was that we'd face it together.

That nagging ache in my bladder resurfaced, making me release a low moan.

"What is it?" He urged.

"Need a rest stop when you can." I winced, pressing my fist into my bladder.

"You should've gone on the plane." He growled.

Tears sprang to my eyes. Christ, that's all I needed, him angry with me. "Forget about it then." I tried to snap but my voice was thick and choked.

"Xael."

I swallowed and swallowed again, trying my best to force down the lump in my throat.

"Xael."

I jerked my gaze to his. "What?"

He stared at me, concerned. "Talk to me." He hit the turning signal, aiming the car for an all-night gas station. "Tell me what's going on."

I stabbed the seatbelt release as he pulled the car up outside the service center. I climbed out, desperate for a second. I was coming undone here, falling apart right in front of him. I strode toward the restrooms and pushed open the door, going to the nearest stall.

I needed to keep it together. Crying whenever Mateo said something wasn't going to do that. I shoved my jeans down and sat, closing my eyes as the relief hit me. That ache in the back of my throat resurfaced.

You have to tell him. You get that, right?

"Yeah," I murmured as I grabbed paper and wiped. "I know."

I flushed and made my way to the sink, using the time to get myself together. I could blame my emotions on the past resurfacing, but I doubted Mateo would be convinced. My husband knew me. Besides, I was the one who'd fought to be here, wasn't I? There was no way he'd believe I wasn't one hundred percent here for this, no matter what war we walked into.

So I *had* to keep it together.

I had to put this all aside.

For now.

I splashed cold water on my face, smoothed my hair, then headed out and climbed into the car once more.

"Better?" he asked as I snapped my seatbelt in place.

"Much."

We drove out, following the GPS as we headed into the city and made our way to a smaller residential suburb. I glanced at the dark houses as we passed, then turned instead to a more commercial area. Mateo glanced at the GPS, then pulled up outside what looked like a warehouse.

"I'll be back in a second." He murmured, putting the car into park.

But he didn't need to as we watched the towering gate roll open, leaving us to drive through.

"On second thought." He added.

We both climbed out after we parked. Hinges squealed as the gate closed, drawing my focus as I closed the door behind me.

"This way." Mateo headed for a set of stairs.

I followed and climbed. Before we reached the top, the door gave a *click*. Mateo glanced at me as he opened the door and pushed in. I followed him, trusting he knew who this guy was. Memories rushed back to me as I stepped into the gloomy darkness of a hall.

"Close the door behind you, please." Came a voice from nowhere.

It seemed like nowhere, at least. Still, I closed it behind me. The pungent scene of coffee filled the air, making my belly clench just like it had last night with the steaks.

"No, you don't." I whispered, driving down the nearly overwhelming nausea.

"Mateo." A male called as I followed Mateo into a faintly lit room and saw rows and rows of monitors fixed against the wall.

And in an instant, that security room on the island came rushing back to me.

We were back there.

Fighting for our lives.

Knowing deep down we weren't going to make it.

"Hayden. I appreciate you seeing us."

The guy in front of the monitor swiveled around, finally meeting our gazes. "So…"

"So." Mateo repeated.

"You're Edon's brother?"

"I am."

"The one they call *Komendant*."

Mateo didn't answer. He didn't like that part of his life surfacing. Not with strangers, not even with me. I knew nothing about his life before he came to the US. Nothing about his childhood, or the origin of his title 'Commander', but sitting here now, hearing the way this…stranger called him Komendant.

I knew it wasn't good.

The temperature in the room grew colder as Mateo stared the guy down. Goosebumps raced along my arms. For a second, I thought he was going to pull his gun and put a bullet through the guy's skull.

"He said you were a hardass." The schmuck murmured. "I can see now, he wasn't lying. So, *Mateo,* let's find your damn brother."

Mateo glared at the guy, even when he turned around and pounded the keyboard, bring up details on the screen. He was testing Mateo, pushing his buttons, seeing how he was going to react. I knew without looking at my husband that he was seconds away from ending the guy's life.

"The last contact I had with Edon was in Colorado."

"For the Salvatores."

"No." The guy disagreed. "No, not the Salvatores."

Mateo shook his head and stepped forward. "What do you mean, *no?*"

"I mean no." He repeated, pulling up a map and stabbed a red dot with his finger. "That right there, that's where he met his contact, and there." He pressed play. On the screen that red dot flashed once, twice...and then died. "And that right there is where he switched off his tracker. Not in all the years I've been working with E has he ever done that. In fact, none of my contacts have. It's the rule we had when we started working together, an *unbreakable rule.*"

I stared at the empty screen as he pushed back and turned once more, meeting Mateo's gaze. "I received one text from him. He said this wasn't a job, that it was personal."

"Personal?" Mateo scowled. "That's what he said. This is 'personal'?"

"That's what he said."

Mateo said nothing, but I knew he didn't like it.

Edon had nothing personal, not that anyone knew. Mateo was the only person in Edon's life, the only person outside of his contracts. The thought of anything else made Mateo shake his head and turn away. "Can you send me all the information you have?"

"Of course. Encrypted."

My husband stopped as he headed for the door. "Of course."

He left then. I glanced at Hayden, then turned and followed Mateo as he left. He said nothing as he made his way down the stairs and climbed back into the car. But I could see how this affected him.

I opened the door and climbed in as he started the engine.

"You want to talk to me about this?" I asked.

But Mateo was already unlocking his phone and making a call. I might as well have been invisible in that moment as the tiny sound of a number ringing on the other side of the world filled the car before it was answered.

"Ya? *Komendant,*" came a thick accent through the speaker.

Mateo started talking as he turned the wheel and drove out of the compound and I snapped my seatbelt into place. For the first time since I'd known him, I watched my husband become a stranger, a person I didn't know, one that spoke in a thick Albanian accent.

He spoke in a rushed, biting tone, one that made me wince. As we left the compound behind and headed for the highway that'd take us out of the city, I realized that this side of Mateo being an unknown, was as much as my fault as it was his.

I'd never asked.

Maybe it was me not wanting to pressure him into talking to me about things he didn't want to talk about. I knew he was close to Edon. But I knew nothing else, not about his parents, or any other siblings he might have.

I didn't ask, and he hadn't let me in.

That thought stayed with me as I listened to my husband talk in a language I didn't know.

It was just one more reason that shored up the decision to keep the baby a secret from him.

One more reason to guard my heart.

He wasn't fully in *this marriage…*

That same fear surfaced.

Maybe this whole thing with Edon would be the reason he returned to the Commission…

And left us behind.

38

Mateo

I pressed the button, ending the call. My focus split from the highway as it blurred in front of me. But really, I was back there, in my past...a place where I didn't want to be. My mind was racing, trying to find out who had taken out a contract on my brother.

It was the only thing that made sense. It had to be...but Kurti, my contact back home in Albania, assured me there'd been no whispers of retribution aimed at me or Edon.

It didn't make sense.

None of it.

Albania was the only 'personal' thing my brother had. So there had to be something I was missing. The white lines blurred as I kept pushing, taking us far from Constance as we headed for Colorado. The sun rose, shining brightly as I pushed the car harder, until I realized Xael hadn't spoken in hours.

I glanced her way, finding her staring out the window, lost in her own thoughts.

She was pulling away from me.

I'd felt it before.

But it was even more noticeable now.

I should never have brought her with me.

Should've never let her get on that goddamn plane.

She could be hurt.

She could be...I clenched my jaw and strangled the wheel, turning back to the road ahead. I could be handing her and her entire family on a platter to the goddamn Salvatores and there wasn't a fucking thing I could do about it. If I left her behind, then I'd damage what we had.

Maybe to the point it was irreparable.

I glanced at the GPS and signaled then pulled the car over into a diner parking lot. Xael glanced at me, but said nothing as I braked to a stop. We climbed out, stretching, before we headed inside. She disappeared toward the restroom while I ordered then headed to the restroom myself.

By the time I came back out, she still hadn't returned.

I sat down as the waitress approached, carrying a tray with plates of burgers, fries, and cokes, and set them down. I was so focused on the bathroom I didn't even say a word. When Xael came back out, I could tell she'd been crying...again.

Xael never cried.

She was a tower of strength, even in the most brutal of conditions.

To see her now, her eyes red-rimmed and her face blotchy, was like a bullet to my fucking chest.

I watched her slide into her seat, her focus on the food in front of us.

"I figured you'd be hungry."

She gave a nod as she poured some ketchup, then plucked a fry from the plate and dipped it before eating. I watched her for a second before picking up my burger and taking a bite. We ate in silence, just like we'd done everything in silence since last night.

I didn't like it.

Not one bit.

"How's your burger?" I asked, nodding to the food she hadn't touched.

"Fine." She answered, grabbing another fry and eating.

Until, with a heavy sigh, she pulled the plate closer and attacked the food with savage ferocity. I stared, mesmerized as she bit, chewed, and swallowed. She was hungry and no doubt exhausted. I finished my food and wiped my mouth as I watched her

There was something going on with her, something she wasn't telling me about.

Something that was eating her up inside.

Maybe it was me?

I swallowed hard as an ache bloomed in the center of my chest and I tried to catch her gaze. Xael was a woman who would be exactly where she wanted to be, and if that wasn't here, with me in this marriage, then I guess I'd find out soon, one way or another.

I turned my head and stared out at the harsh sunlight and the cars that sped past. The thought of losing her was almost as brutal as the thought of making her stay. She finished her meal and drank her coke, then rose.

I followed and paid the bill before we headed out and climbed back into the car.

I drove while she stared out the window.

I drove while she slept.

And as the road blurred and we passed city after city and town after town, I grew weary. Cars passed us in a blur until finally, the sun slowly went down. Oncoming headlights flared, making me wince.

"Mateo."

I flinched and turned my head, finding her staring at me. "Yeah?"

"I said you need to pull over."

"No." I shook my head. "I'm fine, I..."

"Stop being so goddamn stubborn for once." She snapped. "Let me in. Let me...help you."

There was pain in her voice. Deep, cutting pain.

I nodded, giving in. "Yeah, that's a good idea."

I hit the turn signal and pulled into a rest stop on the edge of the road. Pebbles kicked up as I braked and came to a stop. She said nothing, just climbed out of the car and walked around as I did the same. Then she slid behind the wheel, leaving me staring at her.

The driver's door closed.

My throat ached as I pulled the seatbelt across me and she drove out, accelerating hard once we hit the pavement. I didn't have to tell her how desperate I felt to find my brother. She just knew, pushing the Audi hard, then glanced at me, her gaze saying enough.

Sleep.

You need it.

I closed my eyes, just for her. But I knew I wouldn't sleep. I knew I wouldn't—

▭

I JOLTED, surfacing slowly. Then I came to with a rush and cracked open my eyes. Light flickered, glinting between the trees. I looked around at the brightening view. "How long was I out?"

"About six hours."

I jerked my gaze to hers. "Six hours?"

"I was just about to wake you." She gave a nod toward a sign that barrelled toward us.

Welcome to Colorado.

A surge of adrenaline coursed through me. I looked at Xael and was slammed with a wash of emotions. Gratitude and love made my heart thud louder, so loud it was hard to speak. Still, I swallowed and managed. "We're not far away."

She glanced at the GPS, then back to the road. "About an hour by the looks of the map."

Lights of a service center in the distance drew my gaze. "Maybe we should pull over there. Refuel, hit the restroom, grab a bite, and check out where we're headed."

"Do you really think he's there?"

I focused on those lights. It was the same question I'd been asking myself from the moment I saw that red light extinguish on the monitor. Was Edon still there? What exactly was I walking into? The fact he'd said this was personal sent an icy chill racing along my spine. "I don't know." I answered. "I wish I did."

I turned to her as she slowed the car and pulled over into the service center.

I might have little idea about what we were about to walk into, but I knew one thing.

The one thing that was hitting me with blinding clarity.

That I couldn't have a better partner by my side.

She might not be a highly trained mercenary. But she was exactly who I needed.

39

Mateo

I got out of the car, walked around, opened the driver's door for her, and held out my hand. She took it, too tired to do anything but give me a sad smile. Together, we headed inside. The last twenty-four hours had been a goddamn blur. In my head, I was still at home, still trying to work out why my wife was acting strange.

Not here, across the damn country and about to walk into a war zone. I followed Xael into the store and headed for the restroom as she disappeared. But the moment I found myself alone, my thoughts were all about her. I just couldn't shake that nagging feeling that there was something bigger happening here, something I couldn't quite put my finger on.

I used the facilities and washed my hands, staring at my dark eyes in the mirror, eyes that looked so much like my brother's. "Where the fuck are you, Edon?"

The words haunted me as I walked out, finding Xael waiting for me. We ordered food, Xael taking a fruit smoothie instead of a meal, and headed out to the car. The morning sun glinted off the windows of the diner as I ate, leaning against the car and enjoying straightening my legs. But Xael tried to not look at me. Instead, she stood away, focusing on the road that led into the next town.

"So, what's the plan?" She drank and glanced my way.

I gave a shrug. "We drive past his last location, then I'll go back."

She shook her head. "Uh-uh. *We'll* go back."

"Xael.

"If you *think* for one moment, I'm letting my husband walk into whatever this is alone, then you're mistaken, Mateo. We have no idea what we're walking into."

"Exactly." I stared at her. "That's exactly my point."

"So we face whatever it is together. I can shoot as well as anyone. You alone should know that, you've been the one training me for the last year."

"I know you can. You're one of the finest marksmen I know."

She took a step closer. "Then what's the problem?"

I wiped my mouth, scrunched up the rest of the sandwich, tossed it in the nearby trash barrel, and stepped closer, grabbing her by the shoulders. "You are my wife, my fucking heart, my *everything*. I should be the one protecting you, not the other way around."

"We are a team, Mateo. If we're nothing else, then we are that. We were a team before, and we'll be one now."

We were...and I'd almost lost her then.

I sure as hell wasn't losing her now.

So I had no choice. I had to be the man I'd tried to leave behind.

I had to be ruthless...dangerous.

I had to be the one in first to take out the threat and make sure that threat never reached her.

I gave her a nod. "On one condition: I go in first. You are backup."

"I'm backup."

"I mean it, Xael. So help me God..."

"I know. I promise." She nodded, and I saw the truth in her eyes. "I promise, Mateo."

I believed her.

"Good. Okay, we refuel, then take a drive past." I turned around and popped the trunk release of the Audi before going back and reaching inside for my bag. "I only have two weapons." I started. "So we're going to need to be careful."

"No need." She tossed her empty cup into the garbage and moved close, reaching over to grab her own pack. "I brought my own."

I looked her way as she unzipped the bag and opened it to reveal a lightweight protection vest. She pulled her sweater over her head and slipped the vest on, securing the sides with Velcro.

"The fuck..." I whispered, staring.

"You think I wasn't prepared for this day?" She laughed, and pulled her sweater on once more. Then she reached back in, grabbed not one but two Sigs from inside, and reached around to slip them inside the waistband of her jeans.

She astounded me.

To the point of speechlessness.

I wanted to pull her close, to feel her warmth and her love...for just a moment. But I didn't. I couldn't move, couldn't give into that softness. Not here...and not now.

Instead, I watched Xael close the trunk of the car and turn to me. "Are we going?"

I gave a nod and climbed in behind the wheel once more. The truth was...I was scared, scared of what we'd find, scared of how we'd survive. I was more scared now than I'd ever been in my entire life. It was all because of her.

Because she gave me something to be fearful about.

The thought of losing her.

I started the car and pulled out, following the GPS directions as I headed toward the town. I didn't know why he was here. There were no cities near the town, no reason for him to be here at all. I glanced at the marker as still closed shops appeared to line the streets.

We were headed for the outskirts of the town, what looked like an industrial area. Cars were parked outside a local cafe. I glanced inside as we passed, then turned my focus to the quiet street as we drove through the town and out the other side.

By the time we turned into the street we needed, I was prepared for the worst. This place wasn't one someone like Edon lived in, it was a place you were taken to be tortured...and die.

It was the only thing that made sense.

My brother had been captured and brought here to be broken by whoever wanted the kind of information someone who was a hitman for the Salvatores had.

Which was a lot.

"That's it, right?"

I glanced at Xael, then the GPS, as a storage yard came into view. Towering fences enclosed metal shipping containers. I slowed the car and crept past, searching the yard for any sign of life...

But there was none.

No cars.

No men.

No Edon.

I drove past and braked, turning at the end of the street. Xael turned to look behind us. "There's a street running behind it. Maybe we can park there and double back on foot?"

I turned along the street, slowed, then came to a stop at the rear of the compound. "I go in first." I reminded her.

"You go in first."

I parked the car and got out, scanning the fence in the distance before I opened the trunk and reached inside. The rolled-up tools stowed away in the back of the space gave me everything I needed. I grabbed the wire cutters and closed the lid before heading for the fence line.

If there were men waiting, then they were hidden amongst the shipping containers stowed away in the yard. I needed to be there first.

Snap.

Snap.

Snap.

I worked fast, severing enough strands to push through before holding it open for Xael. One glance in her eyes and she lifted the gun in her hand. But I was already turning, habit kicking in as I strode forward, the muzzle of my weapon aimed forward.

My boots crunched on dirt and rocks as I pushed in. Xael was right behind me, timing her steps with mine. Anyone who was waiting would think there was just one of us...and they'd be wrong.

I scanned the first container, then quickly moved through three more, pushing my way sideways through the compound. One after another were unlocked...until one wasn't.

The sun glinted off the thick shackle of the padlock attached to the largest of the containers.

I glanced around, searching for movement, then stepped closer.

Nothing short of a damn diamond-disc grinder would get through that. I glanced around, then lowered my weapon. There was no one here. I met Xael's gaze, then turned back to the lock. The one damn secured container in the entire lot. That had to mean something.

But as I looked, I realized it was a combination lock.

I knelt, my mind racing. If this was Edon's, then I had a good chance. I tried his date of birth, the lock stayed secure. I tried mine, with no luck. The date we'd arrived in the US, no luck either. I was about to give up until it hit me. My mind raced, trying to remember the one date that would be more important to my brother than any other...

Then my fingers worked.

The lock snapped open. I stared at the thing, dumbfounded, then met Xael's stare. Her eyes were wide, riveted as I worked the lock free, then opened the door. The metal hinges squealed as the heavy door swung open.

I expected blood...

I expected the body of my brother.

But I hadn't expected *this*.

It wasn't a container designed for torture. It was only designed for a base.

Stacked boxes filled to the brim were at the rear.

And a cot, shoved to one side, with what looked like his bags of clothes.

I stepped inside and moved to his belongings. The moment I opened the first bag, I knew it was his. "It's all his things. He was here alright...and by the looks of this, recently too."

"Then where the hell is he?"

I zipped up my brother's bag and rose. "That's a very good question."

I made my way out, securing the container behind me, and stared at the empty yard. "What the fuck are we doing here?"

I had no idea. But what I did know was that we both needed some place to shower, get some rest, and try to figure this out. "Come on." I murmured. "Let's find some place to stay."

"Thank God." She gave a sigh. "If I have to smell myself another damn second, I think I'm going to puke."

I couldn't help but smile at that and nodded toward the cut fence line. We made our way out, heading back to the car. Where we were going to find a place, I had no idea. But I'd find somewhere.

It took us almost an hour before I pulled into the fifth motel and strode into the office. The place wasn't the Four Seasons, that's for sure. But it looked clean and neat...and available.

I slid my credit card across the counter, watching as they charged me for the room. "If you were new to the town and wanted a place to hang out, where would you go?"

"Vetura's." The guy nodded. "It's a cafe-slash-bar. Nice and big, good food, too. Including breakfasts."

I gave a nod as I collected my card and the key. "Thanks."

I left the office, striding out to find Xael waiting outside the car with a look of agony on her face.

"You okay?"

"Key." She shoved out her hand. "*Now.*"

I held it out and watched as she snatched it free and all but ran for the room. I collected the bags from the car and followed, stepping inside as the sound of the toilet flushing filled the cramped space. The door opened as I dumped the bags onto the queen-sized bed and pulled out clean clothes. "There's a cafe-slash-bar that serves decent food."

She shook her head and winced. "No food for me."

"No food?" I turned to her, seeing how dark the circles were under her eyes, and how gray her pallor was. "Are you sick?" I strode closer, tilting her face to mine.

But she pulled away, shaking her head. "Just the stress. Once I shower and rest, I'll feel better."

"Are you sure?"

She gave me a weak smile. One that was as fake as the lie she'd tried to feed me.

But I let her go, watching the bathroom door close before the heavy hiss of the shower started. First my brother and now my wife. What the fuck was happening?

I needed to figure it out.

Fix one problem at a time.

By the time Xael stepped out looking somewhat refreshed, I'd found the location of the cafe. I made use of the cramped bathroom, showering and drying before I went into the bedroom and dressed.

We got back into the car and headed into town. The roads were busier this time of the morning, more people out as the stores opened. I pulled up outside and climbed out before rounding the car to open my wife's door.

My belly rumbled and the acid burned. I was in desperate need of food, drink, and time to think, and it seemed like this place was as good as any. I stepped inside, scanning the large room. It was busy, several tables were full with the breakfast crowd. I searched for a spot and found a booth toward the back, not far from the back door.

"Over here." I reached out, grabbed her hand, and led her to the booth. "Coffee?" I asked as she slid along the seat.

"Juice...please." She murmured. "Something cold and sweet. Nothing dairy or...strong."

Nothing *strong?*

Was this the same woman I'd married?

One who consumed coffee like it was air.

"Nothing strong." I repeated. "Got it."

We sat down just before a waitress walked over, handing us a menu. I ordered a full breakfast for myself and fruit for my wife as well as a smoothy. "Nothing strong." I murmured, paying before I glanced Xael's way.

She looked even worse when I slid into the seat.

I opened my mouth to ask her what was going on, but then I closed it. She didn't want to tell me. In fact, she didn't want to tell me a goddamn thing.

"So, what do we do?"

Her eyes were closed, head tilted back. But I knew she was focused.

"I don't know." I glanced at the kitchen as shadows cut through the light. "Go back to the container, search through his shit."

Voices filled the space.

The low drone nagged at me.

I tried to focus on Xael, on the grayish tinge of her face, as the waitress headed our way and smiled before sliding a plate of bacon, eggs, and toast in front of me. "Full breakfast and fruit." She smiled.

Xael opened her eyes as the door opened behind me. She froze and her eyes widened. "Edon?"

I stiffened, then whipped my head around, to wind up staring straight at my baby brother.

"Mateo?" He whispered, his eyes widening as he glanced from me to Xael. "What the fuck are you doing here?"

I shoved upwards, sliding out of my seat.

"What the fuck am *I* doing here?" I growled. "What the fuck are *you* doing here?"

"You shouldn't be here." His eyes slitted as he glanced toward the front of the cafe. "You need to go...you need to go *now*."

40

Xael

"What the fuck are you talking about?" Mateo grabbed his brother's arm.

But Edon shook his arm off and turned around, walking back out the door. "Go back home, Mateo."

"Go back home?"

I had no choice but to slide out of the booth and go after them.

"Edon...*Edon!*" Mateo barked as his brother strode into the alley.

It was just like them to walk through the streets and the cafes like they belonged. But they didn't belong. None of us belonged, not in this place, not anywhere.

But they kept walking. Edon tried his best to stride away, but Mateo wouldn't let him.

"Edon...*stop. EDON!*" My husband's accent came roaring through when he yelled.

Edon stopped walking, staring straight ahead.

"What the fuck is going on here?" Mateo pleaded.

He never pleaded.

The squeak of a door hinge came behind me. But Mateo didn't hear it as he took a step forward. "You called me."

Edon shook his head, but he didn't turn around, just muttered. "I didn't call you."

"The fuck you didn't."

Edon shook his head, before he slowly turned around. "I didn't call—" He stopped, frozen, staring over my shoulder.

"I did." The frail male voice came from behind me.

I spun around, watching as an old man stepped toward us. He was older, stoop-shouldered, with dark eyes which were fixed not on Edon...but on my husband. I scowled, my heart pounding.

From the corner of my eye, I watched Mateo slowly turn...

His gaze narrowed at first, as though he stared at a stranger... until he froze.

"You shouldn't have come." Edon murmured. "You should've stayed away."

"*Mateo.*" The way the old man spoke my husband's name sent chills along my spine.

"No." My husband shook his head. "*No.*"

"Please." The old man murmured.

"Please...PLEASE?" Mateo roared. *"WHO THE FUCK ARE YOU?"*

"Ma*teo.*"

"No...*no!*" My husband shook his head.

I'd never heard him angry like this, never seen him so...*unhinged.*

This wasn't the Mateo I knew. This wasn't even the Commander.

This was...

"Son." The old man stepped closer.

Son?!

Son...

I was frozen, unable to look away.

"I—I don't know you." Mateo's voice broke, and my heart shattered for him. "I don't...know...*you.*"

"You do." The old man stepped past me, never once meeting my gaze. All he saw was Mateo. "I'm your father."

"No." Mateo shook his head. "My father is dead."

The old man shook his head, anguish filling his gaze. "I wanted to be...I wished I was. It was...another life."

"No, it was *our* life." Mateo stared right through the old man. "The life you chose to leave behind, as well as your children."

"Your mother—"

Mateo shook his head, stopping the sentence. "No. That was you and her. You both left us."

"Mate—"

"YOU BOTH LEFT US!"

I flinched at the roar, watching my husband transform before my eyes. It wasn't the man I saw now. It was the boy, the frightened, abandoned boy...and my heart broke.

"You left us. You left us in that house. We had no idea what happened to you. You and Momma left for work, and you never came home. We were kids. We were kids with no food, no money, no family. Just us. Did you even care about that? Did you even care that Edon almost...he almost. He almost *died*."

"Of course I cared." The old man shook his head. "More than you know."

Mateo strode forward, grabbed the old man by his shirt and wrenched him close. My heart leaped at the sight of him towering over the frail old man. I fought the desperate need to step between them. It wasn't for the old man, either. It was for him...*my husband.*

Agony filled his eyes as he snarled. "You aren't my father. I have *no* father."

"Mateo."

It was Edon who spoke this time. Edon who strode forward, grabbing his brother's arm. "Let him go."

But Mateo was full of pain and rage. The kind that made my belly clench and drew my focus down...to the life that was growing inside me. The life I wasn't sure Mateo wanted and now I knew why.

Because of this...

Because of *him*.

It all made sense now.

"Brother!" Edon barked, yanking his arm away.

I shook my head, taking a step closer...and drew Mateo's gaze. That desperation was so real now, roaring to the surface as he stared at me. He sucked in hard breaths, never once looking away as he spoke to his father. "I'd kill you myself if I thought it'd change anything."

Those words were a punch to my gut.

My throat thickened.

Tears slowly filled my eyes.

Here it was.

The cold, hard truth of it.

This was the reason I hadn't told him.

The *real* reason.

He didn't want to be a father. In fact, I could see now that it was the last thing on earth he wanted to think about. His own father had ruined that for him.

I stopped moving, my hand dropping to my stomach in reflex, as though I wanted to protect the little thing inside myself. Even if I was protecting it from my husband.

"Baby." The word slipped free.

All heads turned toward me.

Edon scowled.

Mateo shook his head and took a step toward me.

Even his father finally looked at me.

"What did you say?" Edon murmured.

"She said babe." Mateo answered. "She called me babe."

"No." His father murmured in his thick Albanian accent. "I heard her, she said baby."

I was frozen under their gazes, those dark, piercing stares pinning me to the spot.

Inside, I was unraveling. My breaths raced and my pulse fluttered until the dark alley seemed to grow bright. So bright that it was blinding...and in an instant...it changed, plunging into darkness.

And took me with it.

41

Mateo

Xael blinked, staring at me for a second before her knees gave way and she crumpled toward the ground.

"Xael!" I roared and lunged, dropping hard to my knees to catch her before she collided with the asphalt.

"She said baby." The old man behind me muttered. "I heard her. She said—"

"Shut up!" I snapped. *"Just…shut the fuck up."*

"Mateo." Edon called my name as I pulled her onto my lap. *"Mateo."*

"WHAT!" I barked, glaring at my brother. Those dark eyes were wide and filled with panic.

But I didn't have time for him now. I didn't have time for *this.* Instead, I turned back to my wife as I cradled her head against me and gently touched her face. "Baby, I'm right here. Xael, Xael can you hear me?"

"Is she sick?" My brother asked.

I shook my head. "I don't know, I—"

It's just all the stress...

I closed my eyes as those words resounded. My heart was thundering, filling my head with a booming sound.

"We need to get her to a hospital." Edon urged. "Mateo..."

I nodded. "I know. I know. I—"

I needed to protect her. Needed to save her. Just like she'd saved me.

I slid one arm under her shoulders and the other under her knees before I lifted her. I was walking before I knew it.

"We're coming with you." Edon muttered.

I didn't have the strength to argue, just headed along the alley to the front of the cafe and made for the car. "Where's the goddamn hospital?' I barked, struggling to hold her and shove my hand into my pocket.

But my brother was there, spearing his fingers in and yanking my keys out. "You hold her in the back seat. I'll drive. I know the way."

I didn't say a goddamn thing, just pulled her against my chest as my brother opened the door. Xael let out a moan as I ducked down and slid in, carrying her with me. Car doors opened and closed. I didn't look at the old man in the passenger seat of the Audi. Didn't look at a damn thing, other than her.

Her eyes fluttered open, finding me.

She looked gray...

Real fucking gray.

"I've got you." I murmured as the car started and we reversed.

"Mateo." She whispered, sweat beading along her top lip.

"Shhh." I whispered. "It's okay. I'm here."

That seething anger I'd had moments ago turned to fear as my brother punched the accelerator, hurtling us through the streets of this town in the middle of nowhere. A town we'd come to thinking my brother had been attacked...or worse.

I glanced at my father in the front passenger seat. Never in my wildest dreams had I thought I'd see a ghost. One who wasn't welcome. But I couldn't think about that now. I turned back to Xael, peeling off her bullet-proof vest and removing her weapons. The last thing we needed was the hospital staff freaking out. My brother took the corner hard, and in the distance, the hospital rose.

"Mateo," Xael murmured. "What's going on?"

"You fainted, baby," I murmured as Edon pulled up in front of the Emergency entrance. "We're just going to get a doctor to take a look at you. That's all."

Her eyes widened as I shoved open the door.

"No," She tried to push upwards. "I'm okay. Mateo, I'm—"

Anger flared, more panic than anything. "You'll be seen by a damn doctor," I growled, climbing out of the car before I leaned back in and slid my arms around her once more. "Don't fight me on this."

"Mateo..." she whispered, shaking her head.

Only I wasn't listening. I was trapped in my head, reliving the moment her knees gave way and I watched my wife collapse to the ground. I carried her inside, sucking in the cold bitter tang, before I bellowed. "I need a damn doctor. My wife...my wife..."

Door opened before they wheeled a bed toward me.

I didn't want to let her go, not with how she looked.

"Sir." The nurse urged. "Let us take care of her."

She shook her head, tears filling her eyes as I lay her down. But she looked away from me at the last second and that hurt more than any goddamn punch to the chest.

"Brother." Edon urged behind me as they wheeled her away through the doors and disappeared. "Let her go...they'll take care of her."

The doors closed, and she was gone.

For some reason, that was too much to bear. "The fuck she is." I surged forward, pushing through the doors as they wheeled her into a bay and yanked the curtains around the bed.

"Pregnant." I heard her say it, and it stopped me cold.

"Please." She murmured. "My husband...he doesn't want—"

The...FUCK?

My body wasn't my own as I stepped forward and shoved the curtain aside. Xael snapped her gaze toward me, her eyes filled with tears.

"Mateo." She whispered, shaking her head.

"Is that what you think?" I asked as the doctor and nurses swarmed around me.

"Name, date of birth, and any known allergies." They asked as they hooked her up to monitors.

She shook her head, but her gaze stayed riveted to me as she gave them what they needed.

"You're pregnant, is that correct?" The steely-eyed doctor asked.

At first, she didn't answer, just nodded carefully, leaving the doctor to lift his head from writing on the tablet in his hand. He followed her gaze, narrowing on me. "And you are?"

"I'm starting to wonder about that myself," I answered. "I thought, doctor, I was her damn husband."

She swallowed hard and looked away.

"One who loves his wife more than anything," I continued, drawing her gaze once more. There was fear in her eyes as the doctor moved closer and listened to her heart.

"Any bleeding?"

She shook her head.

"And you're how far along now?"

She licked her lips. "Eight weeks, I think. I missed my period. It's never been regular, so I didn't really think...and then last night I...I took a test."

Last night?

Then it hit me. That's why she was upset. That's why she was angry when I wanted to come here myself. "You thought I didn't want you..." I lowered my gaze to her jeans as the nurse reached over and unbuttoned the clasp. "Cold gel now, honey, let's take a look, shall we?"

She was scared, so fucking scared.

Her hand went to the metal railing, her knuckles white.

I moved instantly, striding around the side to peel her hand from the cold metal. "I'm right here." I gripped her hand as they squeezed gel on her abdomen and pressed some kind of sonic wand against her skin before pushing it down gently.

I saw it all.

Every crease of her brow.

Every panicked flinch.

I gripped her hand as the sweat slowly trickled along her brow.

"So you said you fainted for no reason?" The doctor took the wand.

"Yes." She answered.

We were both riveted to that blurred black-and-white image on the screen. The one where tiny blobs shifted slowly. I had no idea what I was looking at, let alone try to work out what was wrong. The doctor stilled, leaning carefully over her belly before he gave a "*Hmm.*"

"Hmm? What do you mean, '*hmm?*'?" I muttered, jerking my gaze between his and the screen.

But he never answered, just pressed and moved...then pressed again before stopping. "Well, there you have your reason."

"What reason?" I barked, jerking my focus to the screen.

I'd killed men with my bare hands.

I'd been knocked out.

Taken prisoner.

I'd even been ambushed and held at gunpoint.

But I'd never felt this powerless.

"You're pregnant." The doctor answered. "With twins."

"What?" Xael whispered.

But I was frozen, staring at two little bean-shaped things. Two little things that moved and floated.

The doctor leaned over and pressed a button on the screen, taking a snapshot before he eased the wand off my wife's stomach.

"T—" I started. "Did you say...t—"

"Twins." He murmured, pressing the button and the monitor spat out the printed image. He grabbed the photo, then turned around and handed it to me. "You're having twins."

I swallowed hard, staring at the image in my hand. "Twins."

"Twins." He repeated. "Congratulations, Dad."

"Da...dad..." The word caught around the lump in my throat.

The world kept moving. The earth spun. The sun shone. But I stood still. Unable to think, unable to breathe. Unable to do a damn thing but stare at the image in my hand. The photo blurred. I blinked, desperate to keep staring at those little white spots against the darkness.

"You're crying," Xael whispered.

I lifted my gaze to hers, then in a rush, I leaned over and pulled her into my arms. "I love you," I croaked, burying my face into her neck. "I fucking love you so much."

"I didn't think you'd want this," She cried. "I didn't think you'd want this."

I pulled away, staring into her eyes through the tears. "Of course I want this." I lifted the image in my hand. "I've always wanted this. I've always wanted us."

"Your father." She whispered.

"He's the reason I want this. I want our son...or daughter... daughters to have what I never had."

"You wanted a project."

"I wanted *this*." I leaned down and kissed her. "I wanted this."

"I wanted this, too," she murmured against my lips.

I held her, kissing her, barely hearing the *beep...beep...beep...*of the monitor, until the doctor cleared his throat. "Maybe what she needs is some food, some fluids, and lots and lots of rest."

I nodded, gently laid her back down, and pulled away.

I'd brought her here to follow me into a goddamn battle.

She would've followed me, too.

All the while carrying my child...

No.

My children.

I leaned backwards. "Finish your tests, doc. I'm ready to take my wife home."

42

Xael

"Eat, drink, rest." The doctor murmured, carefully removing the leads to the monitor. "In that order, are we clear?"

But it wasn't me he looked at when he spoke. It was Mateo.

Through the thick tears, I watched as my husband nodded, then looked my way. My throat was throbbing, still thick with the lump I tried hard to swallow. One I couldn't seem to get down.

So many emotions flooded me.

Anger.

Relief.

Desperation.

Most important...*love.*

Mateo grabbed my hand as I slid my feet from the hospital bed and stood, my knees wobbling a little before I sat in the wheel-chair waiting for me.

"Easy." He slid his arm around my waist, pulling me against him.

This time I let him, leaning on him instead as we were wheeled out of the Emergency Room with Mateo clutching an image of our babies...*babies*...I was still trying to wrap my head around that as Mateo walked me to the front desk and proceeded to hand over the details of our insurance.

His brother and his father waited, standing as Mateo finished and turned around. My gaze went to the frail old man that looked so much like the two, dangerous men standing in front of me.

"Mateo," Edon murmured, glancing my way. "Is everything..."

"Twins," Mateo muttered, his voice still unsteady. "It's twins."

"Twins?" Edon looked at me in shock as his brother turned around and faced him and his father.

"Yeah," Mateo murmured, his gaze fixed on his father. "It's twins."

"Holy shit." Edon's brow rose. He dragged his fingers through his hair, then did something I'd never thought Edon could do...

He smiled.

Like really smiled, showing the whites of his teeth. "I'm going to be an uncle." He grinned. "I'm going to be a goddamn *uncle.*"

He moved fast, striding forward to slap his brother on the shoulder. Mateo took the hit. But I saw that tiny tremble at the corner of his mouth, the quirk of a smile before he glanced my way, then that smile died away. My knees trembled. I felt shaky as hell and he saw that.

"We need to get out of here. Xael needs to eat and drink...and rest."

Both men nodded, following us as we headed out of the door and to the car parked in the lot. No one said anything as we all climbed in. Mateo sat in the back with me, leaving his brother to drive once more.

It felt like mere minutes since Mateo had carried me through the doors. But it wasn't...it had been hours.

Hours while I'd lay there thinking my world was about to fall apart.

Hours as the world grayed and then brightened. Hours as I came to realize that I wasn't just pregnant with one baby...but two. I glanced at Mateo as we pulled out and headed for the town. He held my gaze, squeezing my hand.

He really wanted this.

I saw that now.

Saw the fear, as well.

One that stemmed from his own past.

I glanced at the stranger in the passenger seat.

Mateo stiffened as he followed my gaze. He wanted nothing to do with him. I saw that. But I also saw a wound that had never healed, one that would only split open time and time again. He'd always bleed. He'd always hurt. I turned to my husband, watching that deep-seated pain rise now.

"I'm right here," I whispered. "You can't get rid of me."

His brow pinched as he searched my eyes. We drove through the streets, pulling up outside the cafe we'd left. We climbed out. I held onto the car as Edon handed Mateo the keys, then glanced across the car.

They weren't speaking.

Mateo just scowled, refusing to look at his father.

I sucked in a hard breath. "Mateo, maybe we can just all go inside and have a drink. No pressure. No anything. I just need..." I splayed my hand against the car. "I think I just need a drink."

His gaze jerked to mine, panic flaring as my leaning registered. "Yeah. Yeah, okay."

He never looked at them, just took my hand instead and led me back inside.

At least the place wasn't as busy now. I searched the room and pointed to a large, quiet booth toward the back. "Maybe over there."

He nodded, his hand steady at my waist as we headed over. "Food and juice for you." He glared. "No arguing."

I had no choice but to nod.

"I'll follow." Edon murmured, leaving his father to slide into the seat opposite.

Like this wasn't awkward. Still, they left me, needing their own space to talk and headed for the counter.

"You are carrying my grandchildren." He spoke softly in his thick accent.

I met his stare. "I am."

Then he reached across the table and took my hand in his soft, wrinkled one. "Thank you. From the bottom of my heart, thank you. Please call me Francois. I would like to very much get to know you."

I didn't know what to say. Just stared as he held my hand. "You're ...you're very welcome."

"You are good for him." He glanced at where Mateo and Edon stood at the counter.

I followed his gaze to my husband as he finished ordering and headed our way. His father pulled away as Mateo stood over us, placing a large glass of juice in front of me. "You start off with toast and eggs, nothing too heavy."

I nodded. He was uncomfortable, that I could see, shifting his gaze from me to his father.

"Please." Edon came up behind him. "Just sit. Just listen. That's all I'm asking."

But Mateo didn't move. I knew he wouldn't. Not until I lifted my hand for his. Only then did I see that steely determination soften. He took it, sliding along the seat next to me.

The waitress soon followed, sliding a plate of eggs and toast my way and coffee for the others. I drank, draining my glass, and picked up a piece of toast as Edon started.

"Tell him." He urged his father. "Tell him what happened."

I stopped chewing, earning a glare from Mateo. "Eat, Xael."

Then I chewed, knowing this was probably the only thing keeping him here. I nodded, took a bite, and stabbed my fork into fluffy scrambled eggs.

"You are right." His father urged, holding Mateo's gaze. "I abandoned you. There is no excuse for that."

"You got that right." Mateo muttered.

"That day we left to go to work, we were attacked by a group of rebels. I tried to protect your mother, tried to fight them so she could get away. But there were too many. They knocked me out cold. When I woke, I saw her. Your mother was lying face down. They killed her while I lay there still breathing. I didn't know what to do."

Those wrinkled hands curled into fists.

There was real torment in his voice that still trembled as he recounted what had happened all those years ago. "They shot her and just left her beside the road. I was...not myself. Consumed with vengeance, I went after them."

Only then did Mateo stiffen.

"I tracked them down, one by one." His father's voice hardened, those small fists shaking with rage.

Now I saw my husband in the eyes of this old man. It was Mateo's rage that spilled from his lips as he told us how he hunted those men down and killed them. Some were husbands. Some were fathers. Some were vile pieces of shit. "They all deserved what they got." He murmured, meeting Mateo's gaze. "But by the time I tracked down the last of them, I realized what I'd left behind."

"And what, you didn't think to come and find us?" Mateo snapped.

His father seemed to shrink even smaller. His shoulders curled, as though his spine gave way under all the weight he carried. "I wanted to...but I felt ashamed. Shame I couldn't save your mother and shame I hadn't come to you."

Mateo shook his head and turned away.

I reached out by reflex, grabbing his hand and holding it. He met my stare. "We all do things we regret." I said, remembering the time this man had shattered my heart by walking away. "We all leave those we love behind, even if it's only until we realize what a mistake that was."

The realization hit him hard.

He swallowed, then turned back to him.

"We needed you."

"I know." He glanced at me. "But I'm here now."

"Why?" Mateo shook his head. "Why now?"

His father grew quiet.

"He's dying." Edon spoke for him. "Prostate cancer. Dad has six months left."

Mateo flinched as though he'd been slapped.

My heart broke for him. I could see it all in his eyes. He didn't want to care, didn't want to open himself up only to be ripped apart again.

"Francois." I turned to him. "If you have nowhere else to go, it would be an absolute pleasure to have you at our home for as long as you would like to be."

Those shoulders curled even harder, trembling, until a brutal sob tore from him.

I flinched at the sound. From the corner of my eye, Mateo turned to me.

"Xael...the babies." He shook his head.

"Are perfectly fine where they are," I answered, lowering my hand to my stomach. "Besides, we will employ a team of nurses to take care of your father around the clock. I'll just be there."

"No," he disagreed. *"We'll* be there."

My heart fluttered as I grasped his hand. "Yes. We will."

Silence grew around the table. I reached out, taking Mateo's father's hand as he wept silently, and my other grasped his son. If this was as close as they could get, then this was what I'd do.

I'd be the tether between them.

If that's what it took.

I'd be anything Mateo needed me to be.

I turned to him. Because that's what you did for love.

"I love you," he whispered.

I smiled. "I love you too."

We finished our breakfast, then left, heading back to the motel where we had booked a room. Edon couldn't leave, not now. This place was his base, and he was following a lead for Dominic Salvatore.

Some Assistant District Attorney had a hard-on to nail the Salvatores to the wall.

It didn't matter. He would come when he could, to spend days and weeks with Mateo and his father.

Until the end.

Then we would survive...together.

Because that's what family did.

And above all...that's what we were.

Coming soon

Every Underworld leader knows his name.

The mere mention makes them quake in fear.

To them he's known as *The Albanian.*

A young, *hungry* hitman who's finding his feet in a savage, bloodthirsty world.

But I know him as the painful stranger stranded in the same airport
I am.

One who just won't take '*go away*' for an answer.

In the middle of a snowstorm he hauls my files into the back of a
rental.

Files I need to nail a savage Criminal Underworld leader to the wall.
I'm one case away from exposing the biggest Mafia ring in the city.
One conviction that will be the highlight of my career.

Until this...*until him.*

Our chemistry is electric.

The lust undeniable, even if he is younger than me...*by a lot.*

When we find ourselves stranded and forced to take shelter in an
abandoned farmhouse that spark between us turns into something
bolder...*something hotter.*

Something that could set my world ablaze, and everything I love
with it.

As darkness bleeds from his world to mine I find myself forced into a
corner.

One where loyalties are no longer black and white...but more
splatters of red against the grey.

But was this a set-up?

Or some cruel twist of fate?

All I know is...I might never survive this.

And if I do...*it can never happen again.*